Tatiana

Duane, Tena, and Soys—

Thank-You for being my
second family and making
me feel accepted here.

God bless you as we will
be apart.

Love,
Maddy Brock

TATIANA

BOOK ONE
UPWARD WAY CHRONICLES

Madeline Brock

Rosway Press
WEST UNITY, OHIO

Rosway Press
11067 County Road 27 1
West Unity, Ohio 43570

Publisher's Note: This is a work of fiction. Names, characters, places, and incidents are a product of the author's imagination. Locales and public names are sometimes used for atmospheric purposes. Any resemblance to actual people, living or dead, or to businesses, companies, events, institutions, or locales is completely coincidental.

Cover Design by Cover Shot Creations
Edited by Pat Bray
Scriptures taken from the Holy Bible, King James Version

Book Layout ©2013 BookDesignTemplates.com

Ordering Information:
Quantity sales. Special discounts are available on quantity purchases by corporations, associations, and others. For details, contact the "Special Sales Department" at the address above.

Tatiana/ Madeline Brock. -- 1st ed.
ISBN 978-0-9905966-3-9

*"I'm pressing on the upward way,
New heights I'm gaining every day;
Still praying as I'm onward bound,
Lord, plant my feet on higher ground."*

— Johnson Oatman, Jr.

Acknowledgements

For years I have dreamed of publishing a book, and I want to thank the following individuals for all their help making this possible.

First, I praise the Lord for giving me the gift of writing, for washing my heart clean, and for making me His. God is gracious beyond measure.

Second, I would like to thank Marvin Lorenz from Rosway Press for his vision for this project and for all the hours he poured into making this possible.

I am also very grateful to Pat Bray, my editor, for her professional help, insight, and excellent work.

I want to thank Ryan Priest and Heather Lorenz for advising, encouraging, and inspiring me throughout the writing of this book. They helped me think of so many brilliant ideas.

And I can't possibly forget my wonderful, zany family. Always supporting me in my writing, they have been my greatest fans and my severest critics. They have never left my side and have been a great blessing.

Lastly, I am grateful to Jana Hunkapiller, Grace Meyers, and Lydia Brock for their guidance and input.

God bless you all!

CHAPTER ONE

The Fascinating Stranger

The early fog lifted as the sun rose above the green hills of Pennsylvania and warmed the dew-covered ground. Sleepy-eyed cattle swished their tails and plodded out into the gray morning. All over town mothers threw open the night shutters and shook their children awake. There was no mother to do this in the Bergman house, so the task fell to Gretchen.

Gretchen Bergman was a good-natured girl of fifteen. She had a pleasant but plain face, paired with a caring, diligent temperament that made her easy to love.

The second daughter, Rose, was not yet thirteen and was as lovely as her namesake. She was so quiet and un-assuming that her fair beauty was overlooked by most people.

The last young maiden of the Bergman household had been born ten years earlier, in 1831, and was spoiled from infancy by her doting family members. Tatiana was named for a fairy queen and could be just as demanding as a privileged little monarch. In contrast to her fair sisters, Tatiana had sleek black hair. Her complexion was pale; her lips were ruby red. Her vivid features made her stand out from her family members, and her attitude en-hanced the distinction.

Tatiana was imprudent, unthinking, rash, and utterly foolhardy. She would do anything that popped into her silly mind without taking the slightest caution, and she would blurt out the most heretical sayings regardless of time, place, or propriety. When her sisters weren't blush-ing with embarrassment over her words and deeds, they were sending up prayers on her behalf.

In fact, her older sister had quite ardently interceded for her that very morning. Gretchen prayed that Tatiana would not make a scene in church, because she frequently did.

"I do wish you wouldn't kick your legs in the air so, Tatty," Gretchen scolded. "It's not at all ladylike."

The three Bergman daughters were in the bedroom they shared. Tatiana was lying on her bed on her back, wildly circling her limbs in the air. She brought them down with a thump. "But it's fun! Besides, I'm not a lady yet. I'm still a little girl."

"And you'll never become a lady if you don't learn to be discreet," Gretchen said patiently, smoothing Tatiana's nightdress down over her knees. "You should be getting dressed."

Tatiana rose and trailed droopily over to the ward-robe. Rose was struggling to button the back of her dress, but Tatiana brushed wordlessly past her and left the task to Gretchen.

"I don't like going to church!" Tatiana complained. "The benches are too high and my legs get so sore from dangling. And Reverend Matthew always talks about the dullest of topics. I don't know why he has to be such a great windbag!"

"Tatty!" Rose gasped, and Gretchen turned from the mirror where she was brushing out her amber hair.

"May the good Lord have mercy on your prating tongue, Little Sister. James wrote that '... the tongue is a little member, and boasteth great things. Behold, how great a matter a little fire kindleth!' And your tongue, Tatiana, has certainly kindled fires beyond measure."

Tatiana wasn't listening to her sister—she never did when Gretchen quoted Scripture. She busied herself in choosing a dress to wear for church. When she had settled on one, she presented herself to Rose. "Button my dress, Rose. And hurry! I think I hear Father stirring the coals in the hearth." As soon as her dress was buttoned, she scampered over to Gretchen and demanded to have her hair done. Then she waited, quivering with impatience, while Gretchen combed out the tangles and plaited Tatiana's black tresses in two braids.

As soon as Gretchen finished tying red ribbons onto her sister's braids, Tatiana was off like a shot. She nearly flew down the stairs, taking the last four steps in one great leap and landing with a crash at the foot of the stairs. She blundered down the hall and through the kitchen door, saying "Good morning, Father!"

Hans Bergman looked up from breakfast preparations and beamed at Tatty. He adored his youngest daughter, despite her many flaws—and he did little to discipline her when she erred. Even when her sisters' faces turned scarlet with mortification at Tatiana's antics, Hans would laugh indulgently. Although he was scarcely thirty-eight years old, the loss of his wife and other hardships had aged him prematurely. His dark hair was salted with gray at his temples, and his face was creased with worry lines, but seeing Tatiana revitalized him.

The two older girls—especially Gretchen—reminded him so much of his dear wife that at times just being near them made his heart ache. Hans doted on his little daughter and strove to supply her with the very best of everything. However, he deprived Tatiana of the very thing that she most desperately needed—a firm hand to correct her when she did wrong.

When breakfast was over and everyone was washed, combed, pressed, and readied, the family went to church in their carriage. Once Hans had stabled the horse, they all walked up the church steps and shook hands with Reverend Matthew.

Tatiana very much disliked shaking hands with the minister because it brought her too close to his eyes. They shone from beneath the middle-aged minister's bushy gray eyebrows like glittering emeralds. They seemed to possess a light of their own, and Tatiana was certain that he could aim them straight into the depths of her soul. Perhaps he could even see that she had called him a 'great windbag' that morning!

The Bergmans sat in their usual place in the sanctuary. While the rest of her family gazed serenely toward the front of the church, Tatiana twisted around so she could watch the people entering the sanctuary. Hanging over the back of the pew, she scrutinized everyone who passed by in frank, goggle-eyed fascination. She resumed her seat when the organist played the first notes that opened the service.

Tatiana fervently sang along with the rest of the congregation. This was one thing Tatiana could do well. She had a beautiful, throaty singing voice that sounded surprisingly mature. So that her talent would not be polluted by pride, her sisters had never told her that she sang well, and her father didn't know enough about music to recognize her ability.

As she was singing, a movement caught her eye. She turned to look. A young couple, Mr. and Mrs. Smith, had arrived late. What captured Tatiana's attention was the tall lad who followed close behind them. "Rose! Rose!" Tatiana hissed, joggling her sister's elbow enough to rattle her teeth. "Is that boy an Indian?"

Rose held a finger to her lips, signaling Tatiana to be quiet. However, Tatiana was not so easily silenced. "You didn't even look at him, Rosie! He looks like a real Indian."

Poor Rose dared to take a tiny peek at the stranger and then dropped her eyes back to the hymnbook.

Tatiana was now prodding her sister's ribcage with her pointy index finger. "Well? Did you see him? Do you think he's an Indian?"

Gretchen leaned over to touch Tatiana's leg while shooting her a stern look.

With a toss of her braids, Tatiana said to Rose, "Well, I'm going to go sit next to him and ask if he's an Indian since you won't tell me."

Rose was so horrified that she nearly dropped her hymnbook. Her blue eyes flew wide open and she bent to whisper in Tatiana's ear. It was a fluttery little whisper, barely audible above the music. "Oh, but you mustn't, Tatty! Stay here and leave the boy alone."

Tatiana stole a look at her father. He was singing lustily, totally oblivious to the conflict among his daughters. "You can't keep me here," Tatiana sang saucily to her virtuous sister. Then Tatiana, brazen little savage that she was, flounced across the aisle to the Smiths' pew. With a smug smile she planted herself directly beside the intriguing stranger.

For a moment every eye in the church was on her. Though the singing continued, shock swept over the congregation. Tatiana was unaware of this because she was so pleased with herself. She gazed expectantly at the tall, dark lad. When he did not acknowledge her presence, she edged even closer.

Slowly, the boy turned his head to look down at her. Who was this outlandish little person who was so unabashedly crowding him? Tatiana flashed him a bright smile and sat up taller so she could bring her mouth closer to his ear. "Are you an Indian?"

His eyes registered surprise at her question and he quickly looked away. Imperturbable, Tatiana tapped his shoulder and repeated the question. The boy's face remained inscrutable. As the hymn was ending, he abruptly got to his feet. In one quick movement, he brushed past Tatiana and made his escape. The church door slammed behind him.

Tatiana slumped down on the bench as Mr. and Mrs. Smith eyed her suspiciously. Mr. Smith rose and slipped past her in pursuit of his charge, but he soon returned, shrugging and giving his wife a puzzled look. The little girl swung her feet in frustration. Never before had anyone rejected Tatiana and her curiosity in such a blunt manner.

Whatever is the matter with that boy? She blinked a few times to stop her tears. *Doesn't he like me? How could he be so unkind as to leave me like that?* The injustice of the whole situation infuriated the stubborn little girl so much that she stewed for the rest of the service. She didn't hear a word of Reverend Matthew's long-winded sermon. That was a pity, because he was speaking passionately about the need for self-control in one's life.

As soon as church was dismissed, she threaded her way outside and looked around for the elusive Indian boy. She thought for a moment about where he was most likely to be and then headed directly to the stables, where she found him sprawled across the back of a chestnut-colored quarter horse.

As she studied him for a moment, he was content to ignore her. He had a unique appearance: dark hair, high cheekbones, caramel skin, and eyes of the lightest shade of brown Tatiana had ever seen. They were so light that they were almost golden in color. As she considered him, she noticed that he had black freckles sprinkled across his cheeks.

Finally, wearying of being ignored, Tatiana cleared her throat and spoke. "You know you'll soil your shirt, lying on that horse like that."

The boy shrugged listlessly.

The girl tried again. "Why did you leave church so suddenly?" The tawny eyes only stared dully at her and Tatiana began to wonder if this creature was even able to speak. "Do you have a name?" she asked warily.

"Jonny Creek," the boy blurted. Tatiana jumped.

Straightening her spine, she replied, "My name is Tatiana Bergman, but my sisters call me Tatty. And you may also if you think Tatiana is too long." She did not usually make this offer, but it seemed obvious that speaking did not come easily to Jonny, and she wanted to make it as easy for him as possible. "So are you an Indian?"

The boy didn't answer or look at her, focusing instead on braiding the horse's mane.

Frustrated, Tatiana stamped her delicate little foot on the stable floor. "Why won't you answer my question?"

Jonny slid down from his perch on the horse and faced Tatiana. He was about a head taller than her. "Has anyone ever told you that you are very rude?" he asked simply. Then, without waiting for an answer, he spun on his heel and walked out.

Well, in truth, no one had ever told the Fairy Queen so clearly and in so few words that she was rude. Hearing Jonny say it ruffled her feathers. With a miffed little huff, she followed in hot pursuit to defend her wounded ego.

Even once she had caught up to the tall young man, she still had to jog to keep pace with his long stride. "I am not rude! You're the one who's rude: not answering me when I have straightly asked you a question several times!"

"What if it's none of your business?" Jonny asked coolly, heading across the town commons.

"I was only curious," replied Tatiana, "I should think that you should have no problem at all answering my question, unless you have something to hide!"

"You're a very skeptical little thing, aren't you?"

Tatiana took a gulping breath. Being angry and at the same time jogging to keep up with Jonny was quite an exertion. "For your information, I am not a 'little thing!' I told you my name and I would prefer that you call me by it."

"Well then, Tina, I will try. But in comparison to me you are quite little."

"Tina! My name is not Tina!" Tatiana squawked, and if she had been paying attention she would have seen the tiny smile that flickered across Jonny's face. "And I'm not little either. I'm ten years old."

"I'm twelve," Jonny announced casually. "Two years your elder."

"Two years? That's not an awful lot," Tatiana said dismissively, while thinking that it seemed like a decade.

"Perhaps not, but I'm almost grown up, and you're still a baby."

Oh, but that was hurtful! Tatiana wanted to cry, but that would only reinforce Jonny's latest jab. "I'm not a baby! How dare you call me that!"

"Have you lost all your baby teeth yet?"

Tatiana's brow furrowed. "N-no."

"Then you're still a baby."

Thoroughly flustered, Tatiana cried out, "You are the most uncouth, ungentlemanly, ill-mannered boy I have ever met! You don't even deserve to be in my company!"

"It's you who's following me, not the other way around," Jonny pointed out, and Tatiana felt foolish. They had come to the lovely little stream that babbled over rocks and collected in pools along the east side of the commons. It was surrounded on both sides by thick, swaying willows.

Jonny sat down on the roots of one of the trees and began to unlace his boots. "Well, I'm going for a swim," he announced.

Tatiana realized that his plan all along had been to bring her here and then leave her with no option but to stop bothering him. She eyed him distrustfully. Maybe he was just going to act like he was going to swim to chase her off and then not really do it. But no, he was removing his jacket and starting to undo the buttons on his shirt.

Scandalized, Tatiana whirled about and started away at a brisk march. "Wait, Tiffany!" He'd gotten her name wrong again, but she stopped in her tracks.

Jonny didn't say anything else, so she asked, "What?"

"I'm half Cherokee."

She stood still for a moment as the long awaited answer to her question echoed in her ears. Then a tiny smile came to her face and she picked up her skirt enough to skip across the field. Perhaps Jonny was not all bad.

CHAPTER TWO

Wolves and Guiding Spirits

Five and a half days out of the week, Hans Bergman worked as an overseer in a large textile factory. This left his three motherless girls home alone much of the time. Thankfully, Gretchen was so industrious and clever that she always kept the household running seamlessly. And of course Rose was always ready to help her with her domestic duties. The sisters' hardest task was keeping Tatiana out of mischief.

That very day she had already spilled a pot of soup on the floor, knocked the broom into the fire, and made a general ruckus about the house. Gretchen was at her wit's end and thought she might just go mad if she couldn't find something for Tatiana to do.

"Tatty!" she called, "I want you to take this list of groceries and run down to Weller's General Store for me." Gretchen would have loved to carry out this errand herself; she would have relished the fresh air, and perhaps she would have had the chance to chat with Mrs. Weller, but the relief of having Tatiana out from underfoot was more rewarding.

Tatiana, delighted to go on an errand, skipped out immediately. She felt very grown-up to be given so much responsibility, and so she quickly slowed her step and walked properly along the street. It was a beautiful day, and Tatiana felt beautiful in it. She sang along with every bird and cheerily greeted every person that she passed.

Katarina Siegfried, affectionately known as Kitty, lived only a few houses away from Tatiana and was the girl's only friend. Kitty's perseverance and patience allowed that friendship; she tolerantly bore every cruel word and action thrown her way by telling herself that was just how Tatiana was. Tatiana profited greatly by Kitty's long-suffering ability to not take her friend's bad behavior personally.

As luck would have it, Kitty was sitting outside in her garden. Tatiana spotted her and called out: "Good morning, Kitty! I'm going on an errand to Weller's. Ask your mother if you can come!"

"All right," Kitty agreed pleasantly. "It will only take a moment." True to her words, Kitty reappeared quickly, tying her bonnet strings under her chin. "I can come," she reported, slipping out the gate and threading her warm fingers through Tatiana's. "No bonnet, Tatty?"

Tatiana laughed. "No, I dashed out the door before Gretchen could think of it. Wasn't that clever?"

"Not if you get sunburnt," Kitty pointed out. "You are ever so pale."

Tatiana tilted her face sunward. "Well, I hope I get as brown as an Indian!" This made her think instantly of Jonny and she frowned. "Kitty, how do you think someone could be half Indian?"

Kitty mused over this for a while before replying: "I suppose if one of his parents is white and the other is Indian."

"Is that a bad thing?" Tatiana wondered.

Kitty sighed. "Some people would call it so. Indians often have all sorts of savage ways." She stole a glance at her friend. "Are you thinking of the boy Mr. and Mrs. Smith have taken in?"

"Yes," Tatiana admitted. "I'm ever so curious about him. I think I could ask him a hundred questions—and he would probably only answer one."

"Did you talk to him on Sunday?"

"Yes, I ..." Tatiana trailed off because the subject of their conversation was coming toward them. He had a stick and was running it along the picket fence, making a rattling noise. He stopped when he reached the girls. Then, in his own quirky manner, he stood silently and just looked at them. Kitty's grip tightened on Tatiana's hand. Tatiana stood taller. "Good morning, Jonny. How are you?"

The insolent boy raised one dark eyebrow. He was hatless and wore a plaid shirt, dusty trousers, and boots with the flaps hanging down about his ankles. "Want to see something?" he asked, ignoring Tatiana's greeting. When she looked unsure, he added, "I'm sure you'll like it, Teresa." Without waiting for a reply, he turned and began to trot off.

Tatiana turned instantly to her poor, confused friend. "Oh, let's go! I want to see what it is!"

"But ... but what about the groceries?" Kitty spluttered.

"Oh, they can wait," responded Tatiana, yanking Kitty along.

"W-why did he call you Teresa? He scares me!"

"Oh, he does that," Tatiana assured her. "Hurry, Kitty! We don't want to lose him."

"Don't we?" Kitty murmured unhappily.

The two girls followed the lithe boy down a side road and out to the edge of town. He ducked under a fence and started across a field. Tatiana started to follow, but Kitty caught her arm. "I'm not going in there. This is Mr. Grable's land; we oughtn't to be trespassing."

"You can stay here if you like," Tatiana said flippantly. "But I want to see what Jonny's so excited about." Kitty stayed behind; Tatiana, feeling daring, continued on. The tall, dewy grass rapidly soaked her skirt, but she pressed on. After passing through a patch of trees, she spotted Jonny leaning against a fence that surrounded a lean-to stable. She joined him and caught her breath.

"There," Jonny said, pointing into the stable. "Isn't she beautiful?" A darling little foal huddled close to a mare in the stable. The black foal had a white star in the center of her forehead; her glossy coat shone in the morning sun that lit the stable.

"She's lovely," Tatiana whispered.

"I call her Beauty."

"Hmm, I think you should have named her Midnight or Star."

Jonny looked offended. "Beauty is a much better name. It tells what she is, not just what she looks like. Papa always said I inherited the Cherokee wisdom for naming things."

Normally Tatiana would have contested such a claim, but she was fast learning that it did little good to debate with Jonny. "I see," she said quietly.

Jonny rested his chin on his arm, never taking his eyes from the foal. "I'm going to buy her."

"Do you have enough money?"

"No," he admitted. "But I'm going to work until I do. Mr. Grable said he could keep her for me until I get the money."

"How long will that take?"

He shrugged as if it was of no consequence. "A few months. Or maybe a year."

"That's an awfully long time," Tatiana said.

"Not really." He plucked a long grass and blew on it to make it shriek. "Some things are so important, you could spend years waiting for them, and it would still be worth it. And for Beauty, it won't even seem like a sacrifice." He gazed at the foal in open admiration.

Tatiana watched him, wondering how he could seem so dull-witted at times and so insightful at others. At the moment Jonny seemed only half aware of Tatiana's presence because he was so intently focused on the foal. She was accustomed to being the center of attention and didn't like being ignored. She spotted the corner of a white handkerchief peeping from Jonny's pocket. With one quick jerk, she pulled it out and scampered away from him, laughing.

Jonny immediately gave chase, and his longer legs allowed him to catch up quickly, but she darted and danced around him, waving the handkerchief just out of reach and pivoting away each time he reached for the kerchief. "Stop, Tatiana! Give it here!" he demanded. Fuming in frustration, he finally stuck his foot out and tripped her.

She hit the ground with a thump and rolled a little way. Her cornflower blue eyes stared up at him accusingly. "It isn't nice to trip a girl, Jonny."

He tugged his handkerchief from her hands. "It isn't nice to steal people's handkerchiefs either."

"I was going to give it back."

"You didn't tell me that."

Tatiana put on her most pitiful expression. "You shouldn't be so mean to me. I don't even have a mother!"

Jonny put his hands on his hips. "Well, I don't have a mother **or** a father. Figure that!"

They glared at each other for a moment, matched in their willfulness. Jonny's golden eyes bore down on an equally stubborn pair of blue. "What's that in your other hand?" Jonny questioned.

"A grocery list," Tatiana replied. Suddenly she gasped as she remembered her errand. "The groceries! I forgot about the groceries! Oh, Gretchen will be spitting mad! I must go at once." She picked herself up and vainly tried to brush the dust from her white dress. "Goodbye, Jonny!"

Jonny said nothing. He stuffed his handkerchief back into his pocket and raised his hand in farewell, but she was already dashing away.

Jonny was diligently splitting lumber for Mr. Weller, with Tatiana seated on a nearby log doing little but flapping her tongue. The boy had contemplated chasing her off, but she had brought him two licorice ropes, which he had enjoyed immensely, and now he felt obligated to listen to her for a short spell. "That ax looks so heavy. Don't you get tired of lifting it?" she asked.

"Yes, sometimes," Jonny answered shortly. Then he took advantage of this rare cessation in her stream of words and quickly said, "You'll never guess ..." Jonny paused his sentence to catch his breath, "what I'm doing tomorrow night." He rested the head of the ax on the ground between his feet. His shirt collar lay open, and sweat beaded his forehead.

"What?"

"I am going out into the forest to find my guiding spirit."

Tatiana ceased toying with her braid. "Did you ... lose your guiding spirit?" she asked uncertainly.

"No. I haven't gotten one yet. Once one of our people becomes a man, he must go and find a spirit that will guide him through life. It is time for me to find mine." He gazed down at the girl for a moment and added, "But don't tell the Smiths. They think it's a heathen practice."

This sounded strange to Tatiana. "Well, **is** it a heathen practice?"

Jonny scowled. "It's the way of my people."

Tatiana bounced to her feet. "May I go with you, Jonny? Please?"

Jonny looked at the girl in complete consternation. The very idea was absurd! "No, you cannot come with me! I must be alone."

"But it's no fun to go somewhere all by yourself," Tatiana argued.

Jonny hefted the ax again. "You are such a child! You are a foolish, spoiled little girl."

Tatiana's eyes flashed with indignation. "How dare you say that? I think I may just tell the Smiths what you're planning to do."

"You won't," Jonny said, fixing her with a belligerent look, "because if you do I won't ever talk to you again."

Tatiana tossed her head indifferently. "Fine!" she cried, but it wasn't fine. She knew deep inside that she couldn't afford to lose the odd little alliance that she and Jonny had formed. With a swish of her skirts she flounced off, calling over her shoulder. "I hope your guiding spirit turns out to be old and crotchety!"

Jonny kept his back turned and continued chopping, but a tiny chuckle escaped from his lips. Old and crotchety, indeed! The girl's naiveté never ceased to amuse him.

"Blast! My thread is tangled again! Fix it, Gretchen," Tatiana demanded, thrusting her embroidery hoop into her older sister's capable hands.

"You forgot to say please. Ask it the way you've been taught," Gretchen told her, but her fingers, seemingly of their own volition, were already teasing out the tangles.

Tatiana slumped lower in a green armchair, her dark head lolling against one of the chair's wings. "Blah, blah-blah, blah-blah. I don't feel like it," she answered insolently. Gretchen frowned at her.

"Must you always be so wicked, Tatty?" Rose asked in her ever-gentle voice. "I think Mother would be very displeased if she saw how you've been acting today."

"She would roll over in her grave, I'm sure!" Gretchen added with an emphatic jerk of Tatty's embroidery hoop. "I mean no disrespect, of course, but I'm thankful that she can't see the activities of her poor, motherless daughters. My child-raising abilities would be found much lacking when compared with our sweet mother's."

"Don't despair, Sister! You can't be perfect," Rose piped up. Gretchen turned to glance at her, thinking how absolutely angelic Rose looked, in counterpoint to her devilish younger sibling. The firelight danced on Rose's face and shone in her hopeful young eyes, making them shine like sapphires. *Thank goodness only one sister is rebellious,* Gretchen thought.

She shot a glance at Tatty, now drooping over the arm of the chair in a bored fashion and impatiently kicking her legs. "Surely, no one can be perfect," Gretchen said. "However, some people could most assuredly try a little harder to put a safe distance between themselves and complete failure!" She looked pointedly at Tatiana.

Rose giggled as Gretchen handed Tatiana's repaired sampler back to her. "Goodness, that took forever!" Tatiana complained loudly.

"Hush, Tatty, you'll wake your father."

"But I'm bored!" Tatiana's lower lip stuck out in a most unattractive way, and her ungrateful expression could have curdled milk. "I want to do something fun—not just sit here and listen to Father's snoring. Besides, spending the evening with two old maids like you is absolutely dull."

"Tatty!" Gretchen scolded, and Rose, who was now in a rather giggly mood, burst out laughing.

"Mercy, Tat, we're hardly old maids. You're such a sour little puss, aren't you?"

Tatiana stuck out a defiant pink tongue. Gretchen's frown deepened. "Tatty! Whatever is the matter with you tonight? Must you be so disagreeable?"

Pounding her fist against the chair, Tatiana cried, "Tatty this and Tatty that! Both of you are always so bossy. I get so sick of your telling me what to do. I'm tired of being good all the time!" With these words she tossed her embroidery hoop into the blazing fire. The flames caught it immediately, licking up the delicate fabric and burning suddenly brighter.

"Tatiana Grace!" Gretchen exclaimed, looking appalled. "That was our finest embroidery hoop! How could you be so beastly? Go to your room this instant!"

"I'd rather go there than stay here!" Tatiana sneered, storming toward the stairs, but she paused when she heard Rose pose a question to Gretchen, "Did she say she was 'tired of being good all the time'? That child is a wonder!"

Gretchen passed a hand over her forehead, smoothing away the anxious lines. "What am I doing wrong, Rose? She's a monster."

"Well, next time she ..."

Tatiana didn't wait to hear the rest; she stomped up the stairs. Their criticism seemed to burn its way into Tatiana's ears, and she was quite livid by the time she reached her room. How dare they speak of her in such a way? Everyone treated her as if she were no more than an infant!

Flopping down across her lacy coverlet, she stared moodily out her window. Gazing out into the darkness, she was reminded of Jonny Creek and his late-night undertaking. She could go find Jonny! That's what she would do! He might pretend to be angry with her, but she knew he would be glad to see her. And fie on Gretchen and Rose for sending her to her room! That wouldn't stop Tatiana Grace!

She pulled on her hooded cape of royal blue wool and carefully climbed out of her bedroom window. She shimmied down the large maple tree outside the window like a limber little monkey. She stood at the base of the tree for a moment to think of where to look for Jonny in all the nearby forests. Jonny would choose only his favorite spot for tonight. Pulling her hood up snugly over her ears, Tatiana started off toward the wooded area behind the parsonage.

Tatiana was not an outdoors person and had never been by herself in the woods at night. She hadn't gone far when she became frightened. She kept tripping on dead branches and jumping at each fearsome noise. The chilly wind whipping through the trees seemed like a living creature; its cold fingers tugged at her hood and pinched her chapped cheeks. It made dreadful howling and whistling noises in the girl's ears. Her eyes darted here and there; she expected danger to come rushing toward her at any moment. Tatiana was making up terrible stories in her head about spirit guides. . Her biggest worry was that Jonny's guiding spirit might find her instead of Jonny, and she didn't think she was ready to meet one—especially on a night as dark as this one.

The farther she walked, the more anxious Tatiana became. Worse still, she was beginning to sense that she was being followed. She trembled each time she heard the rustle of leaves or the crack of a twig, thinking it was some malicious creature trailing her through this formidable forest.

She stopped and looked back. She didn't see anything, but she distinctly heard a low growl. The girl began to run, fear thumping in her chest. "Jonny!" she screamed. "Jonny, where are you?"

She scrambled madly through the underbrush, tripping and recovering repeatedly. Suddenly she felt something grab her arm. Her voice rose into an earsplitting, terrorized howl.

"Hush, Tabitha, it's me."

"J-Jonny?" Tatiana whimpered, wiping her eyes with the back of her hand. "Did you find your guiding spirit?"

Jonny sighed. "I'm quite sure you've scared him away by now."

"Oh. I'm sorry," Tatiana apologized, although she hoped he was right.

"I thought I told you that I wanted to be alone," Jonny said sternly. He couldn't admit that he was grateful for the company. He had sat quietly in the forest for hours, waiting for his spirit guide to be revealed ... and absolutely

nothing had happened. He was losing faith in the existence of spirit guides, and his aloneness in the cold darkness had brought on a shivery uneasiness.

"I know you did, but I just thought..."

Jonny cut her off by abruptly snatching her hand.
"Tatty! Did you hear that? I could have sworn I heard
something growl." He scanned the shadowy trees and
then broke off a hefty dead branch. "We should keep
moving."

"Maybe it's your spirit guide," Tatiana suggested.

"Hmm, maybe," Jonny said in a noncommittal tone.

Tatiana caught the inflection. "Do you even believe in
spirit guides? I'm starting to think they're just made up.
The only spirit I know of is the Holy Spirit."

Jonny, lost in thought, said nothing. They came to an
open meadow brightened by moonlight. Jonny stopped
and looked around. Then his hand suddenly tightened on
Tatiana's and he pointed off to the right. Tatiana gasped.
A wolf in slinking silhouette came over a low hill. Whirling about, the horrified children saw several more loping
figures closing in from different directions.

Tatiana began to cry. "Your spirit guide is a wolf! Oh,
Jonny, we'll be killed!"

"Come on," he said, tugging her into a run. "Come on,
Tatiana!" The two of them began a mad dash across the
open ground. With fear pushing them, they ran their
fastest race, almost flying across the meadow. Tatiana's
heart was pounding so hard she thought it might fly right
out of her chest. "Lord Jesus, help us!" she cried. "Save us
from these wolves!"

The first tree they came to was a spiky pine. Jonny
lifted Tatiana and shoved her into the lowest branches.
She grabbed a branch, feeling pitch sticking to her hands.

"Go, go!" Jonny urged. "Climb up as fast as you can!"

Without heeding the sharp branches or noticing that Jonny had called her by her real name, Tatiana scrambled up with the speed of a squirrel. Jonny was hot on her heels. When they were far above the ground, they stopped and clung to the trunk like treed raccoons, their gasping breaths slowing.

They peered down through the pine needles. A pack of seven or eight snarling wolves circled the tree. Taking flying leaps, the wolves pushed up as far as they could go before sliding back down. Their claws dug at the bark and their jaws snapped ferociously.

Tatiana was sobbing softly and shaking all over. "Are we safe?"

Jonny swallowed, trying to hide his own fear. "I think so. That was close though. If we had waited a moment longer they would have caught us."

The girl shuddered. "I think Jesus heard my prayer."

Jonny looked at her. "Do you really think He could hear you praying with a bunch of wolves chasing you?"

Tatiana shrugged. "Gretchen says He can hear us anytime and anywhere."

"He must have good ears," Jonny concluded.

Tatiana was still watching the wolves below. "How long will we have to stay up here? When will they leave?"

"We might have to stay here all night."

"Really, Jonny? Oh, how awful." Tatiana wished with all her heart that she had obeyed Gretchen and stayed home in bed. She felt stiff and sore and cold and tired, and she kept thinking that she would wake up any moment and realize that this whole incident had simply been a nightmare.

The wolves paced around the tree howling, muzzles thrust upward. Jonny and Tatiana clung to the tree, shivering and drowsy, and wished for the wolves to go away or for someone to rescue them. As Tatiana grew more and more weary, Jonny took off his belt and lashed her to the trunk of the tree. In this uncomfortable position, she drifted in and out of sleep.

One time she woke up in bitter tears. "I'm such a stubborn, sinful little girl! I think I deserve to be fed to the wolves. I'm too wicked for anything else."

"You aren't wicked, Tatty," Jonny consoled her.

"But I am! Only righteous people will be saved, and I am so wicked, I ought to be thrown to those wolves down there."

Jonny laid a protective hand on the belt that tied her to the tree, just in case Tatiana decided to undo the buckle. "Hush. There are only a few more hours until morning."

Still sniffling, the girl fell back into a fitful sleep.

It was a little before sunrise the next morning when Tatiana awoke to find the wolves still at the base of the tree. Jonny was exhausted from staying awake all night, and Tatiana felt quite miserable as well. She had cut her hands climbing the tree, and the abrasions were starting to ache severely. "What if no one ever comes to find us and we die up here?" Tatiana wailed.

"Good morning to you as well," Jonny mumbled sarcastically.

"I mean it, Jonny. What if we die up here?"

"You'll most likely decay first since you're softer," Jonny predicted.

Tatiana shut her eyes to block out the picture. "Jonny Creek! Don't be cruel. It would be so horrible to die at the tender age of ten." She scratched fretfully at the sap that had dried on her wrist. "I think I should at least like to get married before I die."

"So you can make a widower of your husband?" Jonny questioned. "Anyhow, marriage isn't so great. My parents were married and they fought all the time."

"I wonder why."

He shrugged, "I don't know why married people fight. They shouldn't have anything to argue about since the husband's always right."

"Always right!" Tatiana screeched. "That is the biggest wagonload of tomfoolery I've ever heard! Gretchen says women have more common sense than men, so I'm sure they usually know best."

"Well, Mr. Smith says that women are very impressionable and easily swayed, so men have to keep strong opinions about things."

"I have strong opinions about things."

"I've noticed," Jonny grumbled. "Still, the man is the leader of the home and should have the last say about everything."

"Everything?" Tatiana shook her head. "What about things that relate to the kitchen and laundry? The wife would know much better when it comes to that."

"I disagree."

"Well, you're wrong."

"Well, you're wronger."

"Oh, be quiet."

"I won't!" the boy declared stubbornly, setting his jaw. "You can't order me around. I'll talk all I want."

Tatiana had reached the limit of the small amount of patience she possessed. She angrily shouted, "I hate you, Jonny!"

This silenced her young companion. He stared off into the sky with intense concentration and pretended indifference, but her words had stabbed deep into his tender heart. Did she truly hate him? In some ways, he thought of Tatiana as a puppy to be pestered and teased whenever he wished. She whined about it some, but she hadn't seemed to think any less of him for his abuse, and she still followed him around, wagging her metaphoric 'tail.' Now, upon hearing her feelings voiced, he felt remorseful, realizing that Tatiana was a sensitive creature with fragile emotions. Perhaps he should be more careful with his words instead of freely calling her any name that came into his head.

Jonny frowned. *Females! They are such complicated individuals.* He looked over at Tatiana, who dangled there and fiddled with the whipstitch around the hem of her hood. *How can she act so normal, as if she hadn't said those awful words? Is there no apology slipping through her lips? No sense of guilt in her selfish little heart?*

Tatiana kept her eyes lowered. She couldn't bear to look up into Jonny's golden eyes. How could she have said such a thing to him? It wasn't at all true. It had only slipped out in the heat of her anger; she had instantly longed to reach out and jerk it back in—but Jonny had heard it, and the look on his face had left Tatiana in complete agony. She wanted with all her heart to apologize and to tell her dear friend that she didn't mean it.

She glanced quickly at Jonny. He was sitting very still, gazing up at the sky. *He's as unfeeling as a block of stone. Boys! They are such callous creatures. He'd probably laugh at my apology because he wasn't even bothered in the first place. He's too hard-hearted to care for me at all.*

They sat there, rolling their contradictory inner dialogues over in their heads, until Jonny exclaimed, "Look at the wolves! They hear something." Sure enough, the wolves were acting restless. They got to their feet, and their ears pricked up.

The children strained their own eyes and ears, trying to discover what the wolves already knew. At last, Tatiana heard something. "It's a man! And he's singing! We're saved!"

As the traveler drew nearer, the song became more distinct, for the man was belting it out at the top of his lungs: "*When other helpers fail and comforts flee, help of the helpless, O abide with me!*" It was a familiar hymn, and the sound of it comforted Tatiana.

"Hello, sir!" Jonny shouted. "Please help us!"

A man came into the clearing and had soon assessed the situation. He pulled a rifle from the pack on his horse and shot one of the wolves, wounding it. The pack yelped in alarm and had soon dispersed. The man rapidly approached the tree as Jonny helped Tatiana undo his belt.

"Hello there!" the man greeted them, and Tatiana recognized him as the circuit pastor who sometimes came to visit Reverend Matthew. "I see those fiends had you two well treed. How long have you been up there?"

"Since last night," Jonny told him, scrambling partway down the tree and dropping the rest of the way to the ground. Tatiana was right behind him, half tumbling from the tree. She was soon wrapped in the pastor's warm arms. He lifted her gently and put her on his horse. Jonny attempted to convince the pastor to let him walk, but when the man saw the lad's condition, he insisted that the boy ride as well while he walked.

It turned out that their rescuer, Reverend Jeffrey Lyte, was scheduled to bring the sermon in church on Sunday. He was relatively young, in comparison to Reverend Matthew, and he had a swinging gait and an easy manner that cheered the exhausted children. He led the horse at a good pace, but glanced back often to check on them. He had a kind, homely face with a stubby nose. His protruding front teeth made him resemble a rabbit, but Tatiana's grateful eyes saw a prince.

Reverend Lyte took Jonny and Tatiana back to the parsonage, where Martha Matthew was only too glad to tend to the children's needs while the two ministers left to call off the search. While Mrs. Matthew bustled about, getting water for the children to soak their feet and fixing breakfast, she explained that all the townsmen were out searching for them.

Robert, Reverend Matthew's son, came downstairs while Jonny and Tatiana were eating and showed only minor surprise at finding the two of them at the breakfast table. Robert, who was about the same age as Jonny, was a very mild-mannered, courteous boy. He sat down and listened attentively to Jonny's rendition of their perilous night.

They had not quite finished eating when the ministers returned with Mr. Smith and Mr. Bergman. Tatiana rushed from the table into her father's arms. "You won't run away again, will you, my sweet?" Hans asked the question into Tatiana's stringy hair.

The happy little girl had buried her face into the front of her father's waistcoat. "No, Father, never," she promised fervently

CHAPTER THREE

A Redeemed Soul

The gloriously warm sunshine drew the congregation outside after services the next morning. Tatiana lingered near the church door, waiting for Reverend Lyte to finish speaking to everyone else. For the first time in a long while (or perhaps ever), Tatiana had listened to a church sermon. For some reason, Reverend Lyte's words had struck a chord inside her and had awakened a longing that Tatiana hadn't realized she possessed. During the service, the longing had grown into such a surging, powerful hunger that Tatiana felt that she absolutely had to speak with the parson.

When the last person in line had shaken the hand of the visiting minister, Tatiana trotted up the steps and said: "Reverend Lyte, I need to speak with you."

The young cleric was somewhat startled by this abrupt and unexpected entreaty, but he led the girl inside. "What is it you need to speak with me about, Tatiana?"

"Today you read from 1 Peter about a lion who tries to find us and eat us," Tatiana said soberly.

Jeffrey Lyte nodded. "Yes, in 1 Peter 5:8 the devil is compared to a 'roaring lion' that 'walketh about, seeking whom he may devour'."

"Like those wolves that wanted to devour Jonny and me?"

The parson seated himself on one of the pews. "It is much the same, only Satan wants to devour your soul, and those wolves only wanted your body."

"But we climbed a tree," Tatiana said thoughtfully. "They couldn't get us when we were in the tree." She raised her solemn eyes to the parson's. "Can Satan devour someone who is wicked?"

Reverend Lyte nodded, trying to decipher the meaning of all these questions. "Yes, he usually preys on the wicked."

His words seemed to open the floodgates; Tatiana let out a great gasp as if her lungs had suddenly failed her. "And I am so dreadfully wicked! I know because Gretchen and Rose say so and they never lie about anything. Even if I try to be good like my sisters, I am still impossibly sinful. The wolves might not have gotten me, but now the lion will." She was pacing frantically up and down the aisle, and Reverend Lyte got to his feet in surprise at her outburst. "All is lost! The wolves should have eaten me! Then maybe the lion wouldn't devour me. My soul is going to fall into Hell and be burned up at fast as my embroidery hoop!"

The parson had never heard this analogy before, and he puzzled over it. He was praying inwardly, thanking the Lord for Tatiana's open penitence. He opened his mouth to speak, but Tatiana broke into loud sobs.

"Jesus might have saved me from getting attacked by Jonny's guiding spirit and helped us get away from the wolves, but now I'm going to fall victim to my own sinful self! I feel just as lost as if I were still in the forest, only here there is no tree to run to for safety. I am undone!"

Poor Reverend Lyte could not have gotten a word in if he tried (and he did), until Tatiana stopped for a breath. "My dear child!" he exclaimed, taking the distraught little girl's hand. "The Lord most certainly will hear your confession. God is very quick to receive and comfort anyone who has a broken and repentant spirit." The parson dropped to his knees before Tatiana in order to look into her eyes. "I want to assure you, little sister, that there **is** a tree to run to for safety—the tree that Jesus died on to save us from the lion."

The parson's gentle words filled Tatiana's broken heart with hope. She raised her tearful eyes to the cross that hung at the front of the church. Suddenly, as if a veil had been yanked away, she understood what the death of Jesus meant for her—for anyone. She took a shaky step forward and knelt down.

"My dear," the parson continued, "all of us are impossibly sinful and wicked. God understood that no matter how hard we tried to be 'good' we could only fail. Therefore, he sent his only Son, who was perfect and innocent, to die in our place. Jesus has conquered the lion. If you ask Him, He will claim your heart as His own and protect you from the wiles of the devil." He rested a tender hand on Tatiana's quaking shoulder. "Do you wish to do that? Will you renounce the devil and give your heart to Jesus?"

"Yes, yes!" Tatiana cried, "I hate to think of what He will find there. I have a very dirty heart, but if Jesus still wants to have it after He sees what it is like, I'll be glad to give it up entirely."

And so Reverend Lyte and Tatiana came humbly before the throne of God to ask Jesus into the girl's repentant heart. The parson prayed first, and then paused to give Tatiana the floor. Her prayer could scarcely be uttered because of her rending sobs. The cleric was deeply moved as he listened to the little girl so earnestly pleading for God's grace, and tears were soon flowing in profusion down his own gentle face. When Tatiana at last wept out her 'Amen' she looked expectantly up at the parson.

"Is that all? Mustn't I do something more?"

Wiping his eyes, Reverend Lyte spoke. "Now you must remember that your heart belongs to Jesus. He has washed it clean, but you must endeavor to keep it pure. When you sin, come to Him and ask for mercy and forgiveness. Read your Bible and always strive to grow closer to God. Do you have a Bible, Tatiana?"

"I do, but it has thus far been intolerably neglected," the girl confessed, looking gloomy.

"Well, you can change that, can you not?"

Tatiana nodded sincerely. She was pressing a hand to her chest, marveling at the pulse that ticked against her palm. "It's clean now? All the wickedness is washed away?"

Reverend Lyte smiled. "You are right with God. He has forgiven you all."

"What about other people I have wronged?"

The parson was impressed by the young girl's insight. "You must search them out and ask for their forgiveness. If you are right with all men as well as with God, you will indeed be a rare jewel!"

"So many people!" Tatiana mused half to herself. "I think I must get busy right away!" Before dashing out, she took the parson's hand and shook it enthusiastically. "Thank you, Reverend Lyte."

"Thank the Lord, child. It is His doing—all of it." She was about to slip out the door when he called out, "And

Tatiana! I'll have you know that at this moment all the angels in heaven are exultantly rejoicing over you."

The girl's eyes stretched open in wonderment. "Over me? Oh, if only I could hear it!" Then she cast her eyes toward heaven and kept them thus raised almost the entire trip home. And if her sisters noticed, they did not make any comment. Strange behavior by Tatiana was as common as a nagging cough, and they assumed she would soon tire of this peculiar little game.

Stubbornness is not usually a desirable trait, but in Tatiana's case the one benefit of her sheer mulishness was persistence: when she began something, she held to it with wholehearted determination. She set out with an immoveable resolve to turn over a new leaf and be a different person than she had been for the past ten years.

With surprising dedication, she painstakingly read her Bible every day, said her prayers in the morning and before bed, and asked her family and friends for their forgiveness for any wrongs she had done them. Her penitent confession brought much bewilderment to those she spoke to. Her father was prouder of her than ever, her sisters were suspicious that this was only another of Tatiana's plots and she was trying to bring their guard down, and the townspeople were left scratching their heads. "That Bergman girl," they would murmur to each other. "She's a different child, that's for sure."

They didn't know that Tatiana had been using a checklist. She didn't want to overlook a single wrong because she wanted to be perfect and right with all men. By the end of the week, she had crossed off every name, save one. It was that of Jonny Creek.

It was not that she hadn't had the opportunity to speak with him—for she had. Something had always caught her tongue when she tried to get the words out. Tatiana had retained such pride in her heart that she could not humble herself before the person she most wanted to impress. Whether she admitted it or not, Jonny was that person. His approval meant more to her than anyone else's, and she would have stood on her head for an hour if she thought it would please him.

Her hasty words from the forest were still firmly lodged in the front of her mind. Even when she closed her eyes, it was as if she could see them spelled out in fiery red letters: "*I hate you, Jonny!*" Even as they talked and laughed together at school, Tatiana felt as if her vile words were hanging in the air between them, holding them apart. *Today. Maybe I will ask for his forgiveness today,* she told herself.

It was a brisk Thursday in November, and Tatiana was marching beside Rose on the way to school. Gretchen no longer attended school; she took care of the house and did mending for a few people in town. She earned a pittance for her careful labors, but she was proud of every cent she could earn on her own.

As they continued on their way, Rose asked, "Tatty, may I recite my Scripture verses to you? I need to say them today."

"Hmm, go ahead," Tatiana prompted, and then barely listened until she heard a certain word that stirred her interest.

"Now the works of the flesh are manifest, which are these; Adultery, fornication, uncleanness, lasciviousness, idolatry, witchcraft ..."

"Witchcraft!"

"Yes, witchcraft," Rose repeated patiently. "... hatred, variance, emulations, wrath, strife, seditions ..."

"What are 'seditions'?"

Rose's nose wrinkled cutely, as it always did when she thought hard about something. "I think it's making strife and starting fights. Now do stop interrupting, Tatty, and let me finish." Rose took a deep breath and launched back into the verse. "... heresies, envyings, murders, drunkenness, revellings, and such like: of the which I tell you before, as I have also told you in time past, that they which do such things shall not inherit the kingdom of God. But the fruit of the Spirit is love, joy, peace, longsuffering, gentleness, goodness, faith, meekness, temperance: against such there is no law. Galatians 6:19-23."

"So the first list is all things we are not supposed to do or else it will make our heart dirty, and the second list is all good things?" Tatiana asked.

"Yes. The fruits of the Spirit are all things you want in your life."

Tatiana tapped her chin. "I think I like Joy the best."

Rose smiled. "You need all of them, Tatty."

"I know, but Joy is still my favorite!" With a bubbling laugh, Tatiana ran ahead to the schoolhouse.

In general, Tatiana really enjoyed school. She had a busy mind that soaked up knowledge like fertile earth soaks up water. Socially, however, Tatiana was an outcast. A significant division existed between her and most of the other girls her age because Tatiana frightened them.

Samantha Culbertson, Arietta Jones, and Johanna Easley were an inseparable threesome. Katarina Siegfried—Tatiana's friend Kitty—would sometimes tag along with them as well. They were all very fine girls, though they did act a bit pretentious at times and liked to gossip. They were meek, gentle, ladylike, and graceful, with perfect manners. Every word that came from their pink lips was proper, and every action displayed flawless composure.

Tatiana, on the other hand, was loud, impetuous, and reckless. She seldom displayed any sense of propriety and did all manner of wild things (such as get chased by wolves). Tatiana's involvement with Samantha, Arietta, and Johanna went no further than being the subject of their gossip.

They were already whispering about her when she arrived. Johanna was the most boisterous of the three, if anything about any of them could be called boisterous. She was the unquestioned leader. "I still cannot grasp that Tatiana spent the entire night stuck up in a tree with Jonny Creek! It's so very barbaric."

"Don't I know it," Arietta agreed. "She's absolutely shameless at times!"

"It really is an abomination how those two are always running off together," Samantha sighed.

Johanna shook her head. "It cheapens a girl to run after a boy like that." Her two counterparts agreed with her wisdom.

The three young ladies were secretly jealous of Tatiana's rapport with Jonny. The lad seemed exotic and mysterious: two traits that made him irresistibly attractive to them. They called him a savage out loud, but each of them covertly longed to be the fortunate girl who would win the heart of the remarkable Jonny. And so they frowned and condemned Tatiana's impudence, all the while picturing themselves trapped up a tree with Jonny.

"Don't look now," Samantha whispered, "but she's coming."

"Who's coming?" Johanna questioned. She turned about and came face to face with Tatiana, who was standing there with hands clasped in front of her and an eager smile on her face.

"Johanna," she began sweetly, "I want to apologize for taking that slice of spice bread from your lunch pail. Yesterday I had been trying to think of what I needed to apologize to you about because I was absolutely certain there was something, but I couldn't think of it so I crossed your name off. And then it came to me this morning about the spice bread! I do hope you'll forgive me."

Johanna looked confused. "Wait, when was this that you stole my lunch?"

Tatiana tilted her head. "It wasn't your entire lunch, but I believe it was last January, unless it was the January before."

The three girls exchanged a look that expressed their superiority and their scorn for their eccentric schoolmate. They were gathered before the youthful penitent as one unit, lending confidence to each other. "And you're just now asking for my forgiveness?" Johanna questioned.

The dark-haired girl looked remorseful. "Yes, it is a pity that I'm so late. But I didn't know it was wrong until now and I'm trying to get all caught up. Will you forgive me?"

"Why does it matter?" Johanna asked flippantly, not expecting any great reaction from Tatiana.

"Why does it matter?" Tatiana cried in horror. "Why—because Jesus said we ought to forgive one another. He has forgiven me for every single wrong thing I ever did and has paid for me with His blood, so I think the least I can do is to forgive everyone who wrongs me and to ask for forgiveness for all the terrible things I've done.

And I pray that you will forgive me, because if you don't, you'll be creating a little wall between us."

Johanna, who was not a particularly spiritual person, laughed at Tatiana's earnest plea. "A wall? Why, how delightful! I happen to like walls very much." Then she turned to Samantha and Arietta, who snickered supportively, and the three linked arms and walked off.

Tatiana blinked several times at the blatant snubbing she had just received. Then she told herself very sternly not to get angry, asked God to help her forgive Johanna, and was comforted by the thought that God had seen the whole affair and would see justice served.

While the girls were shunning Tatiana, the boys were studying her closely. They found her to be a fascinating little creature and liked to find ways to provoke her, like a child trying to rile a caged rooster. The boys tormented Tatiana merely to see how she would react, and her reactions varied so much that they never grew bored with their game.

Fifteen-year-old Moses Drake, a tall boy with a mischievous streak, purposefully jostled Tatiana on their way out for break after lunch. "Oh, watch out for Wildcat Bergman!" he exclaimed, feigning horror.

Tatiana tossed her head. "Leave off, Moses! Go pick on someone else for once."

Moses brought his pointy chin close to Tatiana's shoulder. "Injun Lover."

Tatiana flushed and started walking briskly away, but he followed close on her heels.

"You're an Injun lover, Tatty. You're in love with a dirty Injun."

Tatiana froze and Moses grinned, knowing that he had hit the right vein. Then the little girl whirled around and struck the tall boy across the face with all her might.

He was too startled to move for a moment. She cried out in fury, "Be quiet, Moses Drake! You know that what you said isn't true! Jonny is the finest boy I've ever met, and he's a thousand times more honorable than you! A thousand times, Moses! You'll never be as good as him, no matter how hard or how long you try." Her eyes blazed as she shook her finger in the bully's face. "And he's not dirty."

By this time everyone on the playground was listening to the exchange. Jonny came out of the school just then and Moses spotted him. With his face a deep shade of scarlet, Moses called out: "Why don't you come get your little squaw over here, Injun? This little brat must be crazy. She doesn't have any idea what she's talking about."

Jonny flew down the porch steps and started punching Moses. Tatiana had never seen him so angry before. He fought like a wild animal, fearlessly taking on the older, larger boy. He was quick enough that he could dodge most of Moses' blows and get in plenty of his own.

The scuffle didn't last long because the schoolmarm, Miss Hartford, heard the commotion and came running, putting an immediate stop to the brawl. When she asked how the fight had started, a dozen fingers instantly pointed at Tatiana and Jonny. She ordered Moses to stay after school and write an essay, and she sent the other two home.

Expulsion, even for only a day, was an extreme form of punishment. It was very humiliating: expelled students were in utter disgrace. Somberly, Jonny and Tatiana pulled on their coats and got their lunch pails. Together, they left the schoolhouse and headed for home.

Tatiana had been trying to be brave, but she couldn't help crying just a little bit. Sniffling, she said, "I'm sorry for what Moses said about you, Jonny."

"Oh, I don't mind," Jonny answered, kicking a pebble in the road. "I know I'm a half-breed. I just can't believe what he said about you!"

Tatiana giggled. "And that hardly bothered me at all! Funny how we are so worried about each other and not ourselves."

Jonny rubbed at the nail scratch Moses had left on his chin. "You showed real spirit back there. I'm impressed."

Normally such words from Jonny would have made Tatiana feel all warm and happy inside, but she lowered her head. "No, I was wrong. I shouldn't have slapped Moses or said what I did to him. Rose just told me today that's called 'sedition.' I was stirring up strife, Jonny. Oh, how could I do it?"

She clasped her hands to her chest as if she'd been wounded there. "I didn't even think about it, but it's done. I've gone and got a horrid, dirty stain on my nice, clean heart." She began to cry harder. "I'm so sorry, Jesus! You've just finished getting it washed, and I'm already soiling it again. Please forgive me! Please take my sin away." She stared fixedly up into heaven for a few moments and then dropped her gaze with a contented sigh.

Jonny was staring at her as if she'd gone mad. She gave him a comforting smile. "I'm right with God now. I still have to apologize to Moses, and that won't be a bit of fun, but once I do that I'll be right with all men as well!" Then the memory of her unforgiven words to Jonny came back to her, and her face fell. "Well, I won't be quite right with all men, but almost."

Jonny shook his head slowly. "Tatiana, there are times when I'm convinced you've gone insane. When are you going to learn a bit of temperance?"

"Oh!" Tatiana exclaimed. "That's one of the fruits of the Spirit! My favorite one is Joy, and Rose says I have to learn how to use them all, but at least Temperance is at the very end of the list, so I shouldn't have to worry about that for a while yet."

Poor Jonny was squinting at her, trying to follow her busy stream of words. "Fruits of the Spirit, you say? Does it have to be a fruit? Could it be a vegetable? Like a potato?"

Tatiana skipped a few steps to keep up with Jonny's stride. "Well, I suppose they would have used vegetables if they ran out of fruits, but they obviously didn't, so fruits they are!"

Jonny thrust his hands in his pockets. "Well, I happen to think that Temperance should be a potato."

Tatiana snorted. "I think the world is fortunate that you didn't write the Bible, Jonny Creek."

The boy chuckled at this. "Probably so."

The following morning, Tatiana found a potato in her desk at school. She realized instantly who had put it there. She shot a quick glance at Jonny, who seemed thoroughly engrossed in reading his history book. She thought for a moment about pitching the vegetable at him, but then she recalled what the potato was supposed to stand for. Besides, she would rather not be sent home from school again. She slipped it back into her desk and got to work.

CHAPTER FOUR

Merry Times

By the next fall, Tatiana was a year older but scarcely a lick wiser. If she had, by some stroke of fate, accumulated any wisdom over the past year, she certainly didn't show it. She returned from school one afternoon to find Gretchen sitting before the big mirror in her bedroom, giving meticulous attention to styling of her amber hair. She was so absorbed in her toilette that she did not even notice her younger sister standing there.

"Why do you keep fussing about your hair, Gretchen?" Tatiana asked.

Gretchen jumped at the sound of her voice and the comb slipped, pulling a few strands of hair loose. "Oh, blast it all!" Gretchen moaned, "I'll never get it right!" She sat back with a sigh and gazed at her reflection in dissatisfaction. "I'm hopelessly plain."

Tatiana brought her head down to Gretchen's level and the sisters met each other's eyes in the glass. They were certainly opposites! Tatiana's shiny dark locks mingled with Gretchen's mousy brown ones. Gretchen's eyes were gray and her lips held no color, while Tatiana's eyes were a vivid blue and her lips were ruby red. Gretchen

43

had generally thicker, plainer features, while Tatiana had been blessed with fine, delicate bones. Gretchen sighed again in obvious envy of her young sister who showed promise of blooming into a great beauty.

"You look lovely, Gretchie. But I still don't see why you're so troubled over this."

"A certain young man has asked me to go buggy riding with him tonight," Gretchen explained lightly.

"Oh, really?" Tatiana was opening all the dainty glass bottles on Gretchen's dressing table and sniffing their contents. "Who is it?"

"Moses Drake."

Tatiana's hand jerked, and the bottle she was replacing rattled against the others with a loud clinking. She grasped the bottle in relief when she realized nothing was broken. "Moses Drake?" Tatiana gasped, "Gretchen, why on earth would you go courting with him?"

"He's a very polite young man, Tatty."

"Polite? Hah!"

Gretchen frowned and continued uncertainly. "And ... he asked me on Sunday night if he could call on me."

"Moses Drake? Does Father know you're going?"

"Yes, he gave his permission." Gretchen took the bottle Tatiana was still clutching in her hands and applied a bit of perfume to her neck and wrists.

"Do you even remember Moses from school?"

"He was a year older than me and a year behind in school work, I believe. But yes, I remember him. We never talked much, but he seemed nice enough."

"Moses Drake? Are we speaking of the same person here?"

"Yes, Tatty! You've said his name enough. Now, be a dear and fetch my gray boots."

Tatiana snatched up the leather boots, so upset that she hardly noticed her own actions. "Do you even want to go with him? Aren't you a little young to be courting?"

Gretchen began digging through the drawers in search of a pair of gloves. "Yes, I want to go. I'm fifteen years old. Some girls are married by this age!"

"Oh, stuff and nonsense! You can't get married now, Gretchen. You're much too—"

Tatiana cut off the rest of her sentence. Gretchen raised her forthright gaze to her sister's. "Much too what? Ugly? Is that what you were going to say?"

"No, Gretchie." Tatiana set the boots down and wrapped her arms around her elder sister's shoulders. Gretchen smelled clean and sweet, the scent reminding Tatiana of the times she had sat in her mother's lap. "I'm not ready to see you going out courting with young men because I want you to stay here at the house for always. I don't know what Father and Rosie and I would do without you. If you and Moses Drake get married and move far away, I don't know what I'll do!"

Gretchen sniffed and Tatiana saw in the mirror that she was crying. Gretchen rarely showed much emotion, and Tatiana wondered what had elicited this rare display. Gretchen bit her trembling lip and said, "I feel so afraid sometimes, Tatty. My body says I'm a woman and my mind tells me I'm still a little girl." She turned to look at Tatiana. Her gray eyes glistened with unshed tears. "I envy you at times, Tat. You're still so young. You can be free from worry and responsibility and can run into Father's arms whenever you wish."

"And you can't?"

Gretchen shook her head. "Father has estranged himself from me ever since I've become more grown up. It seems that at the moment when I need him most, he has pulled away. I wonder if he distances himself because he doesn't know how to react to me as an adult and a female."

Tatiana nestled her head against Gretchen's quaking shoulder. "Oh, Gretchen, you shouldn't be so heavy-hearted when you're being courted for the first time tonight. Aren't you excited?"

"Frankly, I'm terrified."

"Well, tell Moses he had better behave like a gentleman or he'll have me to contend with!" Tatiana declared, planting her hands on her hips.

Gretchen laughed lightly and rose from her chair. "Thank you for cheering me, little sister." She pulled on her white gloves and gave Tatiana's braid a tweak. "Whisper a prayer for me tonight."

"I will," promised Tatiana. Gretchen bustled from the room, leaving a swirl of rose water and sandalwood behind her.

After supper that same evening, Tatiana joined her father and Rose in the sitting room. Father was at his desk doing bookwork. Rose was curled up in the armchair knitting a scarf. Tatiana flung herself down upon the fireplace rug with her little red Bible, comforted by the click of the needles, the scratch of the pen, and the crackle of the fire. Tatiana was soon lost within the pages of the Word of God. She lay there contentedly, dragging her finger along the lines, until she stopped at one verse.

"What does 'Abba Father' mean?"

Hans thought for a moment and then said, "If I remember correctly, 'Abba' is similar to 'Daddy' in Hebrew."

"Daddy," Tatiana repeated. A smile crossed her face. The thought of calling God 'Daddy' warmed her heart.

Thinking of it reminded her of something. She rose and went to her father's desk. "Daddy?" she asked, tugging on the lapel of Hans's coat. She hadn't called him that for years; it had just slipped off her tongue.

"Yes, Tatiana?"

Tatiana sighed and rested her chin on the top of his head. "I think Gretchen needs you to be an Abba Father to her right now."

"Does she?" Hans mused, feeling a pricking in his conscience. Recently, he had felt very distant from his eldest daughter. She was so womanly, capable, and independent that it was easy for him to leave her to herself. He brought to memory the image of Gretchen's gentle gray eyes. She was so young and innocent. Without complaint, she bore so much responsibility on her shoulders.

Tonight she was going courting with Moses Drake, and he hadn't even been there to wish her well! She was growing up so fast. All three of his treasures were. They would be married and gone before long. How much time had he wasted being too occupied with work to focus on his precious girls? Tears came to Hans's tired eyes, and he scooped Tatiana onto his lap even though she was getting to be quite an armful. "I'm such a poor father to you girls," he declared.

"No, you're not!" Tatiana exclaimed.

Hans closed his eyes. "But I am! I have been absent during many of the times when you needed me most. I didn't cherish the moments I had with you, and now it is too late to ever bring them back!"

Rose laid down her knitting. "But you still have us, Father," she pointed out. "What of this present moment? Can you not cling to it tightly and still cherish the time you have with us now?"

"What a wise little flower you are, Rose!" Hans sighed. "Come here, my dear one!" And then he tightly embraced both daughters.

"It's a pity that Gretchen isn't here," Tatiana said, but hardly had she said the words when there was a clatter of horse hooves in the yard. Moments later, the door in the hall opened.

Tatiana bounced up and down as she greeted her windblown sister. "Welcome back, Gretchen! Was Moses a gentleman?"

Gretchen sighed and slipped her arm around her younger sister. "Moses Drake is a very fine boy, but I think I'm going to wait for the Lord to send me a true man, like our father. And I won't yield my heart to any other!"

Tatiana folded her arms. "I won't either! The man I marry should be gentle like the Holy Spirit, princely like Jesus, and an Abba Father like God."

"My!" Gretchen's eyebrows shot up. "Those are very fine credentials indeed! They are quite lofty, but do keep them that way. I'm sure there must be such a man somewhere in the world." And Gretchen thought on Tatiana's words many a time over the next week. Could there truly be such a man? And if so, could she ever find him?

Upon giving her heart to Jesus, Tatiana, a natural singer, began to sing even more, using her voice to share her joy. A redeemed heart that is full of the Spirit of God can hardly keep silent when an opportunity to sing arises, and Tatiana was no different. She often lifted her voice in praise as she went about her work, and she was singing now as she scrubbed the kitchen floor. "*My chains fell off;*

my heart was free. I rose, went forth, and followed thee. A-mazing love! How can it be? That thou, my God, shouldst die for me?" She raised her head to glance at Rose, who was bustling about the kitchen and springing from one island of dry floor to another. "How are the baked apples coming, Rosie?"

"Just fine!" her sister chirped. "I'm almost ready to put them in the oven."

"Did you put extra sugar on mine?"

"No ..."

"Could you, please? I like mine very sweet."

"Gretchen would say no, I'm sure." Rose laughed and added, "But I'm not Gretchen, so I suppose it won't hurt." She sprinkled two more pinches of sugar on top of one apple half and then opened the hatch on the wood stove and slid the pan inside.

"Saturdays are ever so fine!" Tatiana rejoiced. "I wish I could have a whole week full of them!"

"Even if you had to scrub the floor every day?" Rose asked teasingly.

Tatiana nodded emphatically and started to wash under the table. "Even then! Scrubbing isn't such a bad job. In fact, I almost like it. And as soon as I finish, I can go with Jonny to visit Beauty. Besides, if it was Saturday every day of the week, then Father would only work half days."

"And we'd be poor as paupers!" Rose finished with a laugh.

The back door banged open and Gretchen came in from digging the last of the potatoes. She had a bushel basket on her hip and a piece of paper in her hand. "Do either of you know why we might get a note addressed to someone by the name of 'Tamara'?"

"Me!" Tatiana cried, getting up so fast that she bumped her head on the table. "It's for me!"

Gretchen handed it over with one of her usual smirks. "Don't tell me you have an admirer who can't remember your name!" She reached into her apron pocket. "Oh, and the note came with a radish."

"A radish?"

The vegetable was dropped into Tatiana's waiting hands and she chortled with glee to see that the word 'Joy' had been carved into the vivid red skin.

Her two older sisters were watching her curiously. "Well, let's have all the news!" Gretchen pried, "Read your note!"

Tatiana was enjoying her position of power, so she primly announced, "I shall read it later at my own convenience!" Then she stuffed the paper down the front of her bodice.

This brought an outcry from both sisters. "Tatiana!" Gretchen wailed. "That is absolutely vulgar! Only barmaids and other loose women store things in their bodices!"

Tatiana stamped her foot. "Aunt Henrietta does!"

Gretchen looked flummoxed. "What on earth? Aunt Henrietta does not!"

"She does!" Tatiana crowed. "I saw her stow her reading glasses there."

"Upon my word!" Rose said softly, and all three sisters burst into mirthful peals of laughter. They were so engaged in their merriment that they did not even notice their father's arrival until he stepped into the kitchen.

"Well, well, well! What is so comical as to have you all laughing hard enough to wake the dead?" he teased.

The girls attempted to stifle their giggles. Hans surveyed the three of them fondly. Truly, they made quite a lovely sight.

Gretchen was looking windblown and sun-kissed. Her face was flushed from exercise, and her gray eyes gleamed with life. She wore her faded tan calico with a pattern of red flowers. The sleeves were rolled up on her strong forearms. Her hair was wispy and tousled from the outdoors; a few brown tendrils curled down against her temples, giving her a playful look.

Rose had been busy in the kitchen all morning, and her normally pale cheeks were rosy from bending over the oven. She had a smudge of flour on her face, and plenty more on her blue cotton dress and white apron. She had left her fair, wavy hair in a loose, thick braid that hung prettily over her shoulder. Her blue eyes shone with gaiety and her pink, bow-shaped lips curved in a sprightly smile.

Tatiana's gray dress was the most faded of all because it had been handed down to her from Gretchen, and at the moment it was looking considerably soggy. She was barefoot and messy, with her dark hair straying from the kerchief she had tied around her head. Her beggarly little face was smeared with dirt; her eyes danced with mischief.

Oh, but he loved them all! To Hans they looked like the most beautiful princesses that ever lived. They each carried a trait of their mother's: Gretchen had Elizabeth's gentle eyes, Rose had her golden hair, and Tatiana had her delicate facial structure. Overwhelmed with affection, he pulled them all to him in one great embrace.

His little family hugged him back, clinging closely for a few moments before Tatiana wiggled free. "Where are you off to, little bird?" Hans questioned.

Tatiana picked up her pail again. "I must finish the scrubbing so I can meet Jonny."

Hans nodded. "Well, you do that, then. Gretchen, I'll change my shoes and then come help you in the garden."

And so Tatiana hastened to finish her chores, did some minimal washing up to please Gretchen, and headed out to find Jonny. She sat for a while under a big chestnut tree on the edge of the commons. This was where she and Jonny usually met, but the minutes ticked by and there was still no sign of the boy. Tatiana was beginning to get frustrated when she remembered the note that she had carelessly shoved down her bodice. Making sure that no one was near, she dug it out and opened it. The note read:

Dear Tamara, I regret to inform you that I cannot meet with you in town today. Mr. Grable gave me a deadline for earning the money to buy Beauty and I need to have it by the end of December! This gives me very little time and I need to work as much as I can to try to obtain the cost.

But there is good news as well! Mrs. Smith is expecting a baby! I will have a little brother or sister by next June! That's what the radish is about. I decided that Joy should be a radish.

Sincerely hoping you stay away from any wolves,
Jonny Creek

Tatiana heaved a great sigh. Her Saturday had suddenly become a little less extraordinary, but she was not one to sit around pining about things that could not be. She skipped down to Kitty's house and knocked on the door.

Mrs. Siegfried answered it and politely told Tatiana that Katarina had gone to a tea party at Samantha Culbertson's house with Johanna Easley and Arietta Jones. "I'm sorry, dear. Have a good day!" Mrs. Siegfried said. Her words rang in Tatiana's head like a death knell.

Up until now, Tatiana had still been able to think of
Kitty as her friend. But going to a tea party that she had
never mentioned and Tatiana had never been invited to?
It was unthinkable! With hot feelings of self-pity burning
in her chest from this flagrant betrayal, Tatiana walked
down the street to where Samantha's tall, red-trimmed
house stood.

Brazenly, Tatiana walked in the open gate and tiptoed
through the flowerbeds, peering in the windows. At last
she found one from which she could spy on the girls'
cloistered gathering. Dressed up for the event in frilly
dresses and flowered bonnets, they all seemed to be
greatly enjoying themselves. Tatiana was on the brink of
tears. She felt that she had been wronged, neglected, and
mercilessly abandoned, and she might have done something reckless had it not been for a timely distraction.

"I say! Whatever are you doing, Tatiana?"

Tatiana spun about to see Robert Matthews, the minister's thirteen-year-old son, standing out on the street
with a fishing rod and pail. "What am I doing?" she echoed edgily as she stumbled out of the Culbertson flower-
bed. "I was just trying to see if the Culbertsons were
home. And what do you know, they are!" She laughed
nervously. Robert raised his eyebrow.

"By peeping in their windows? Surely there must be a
better way."

Tatiana joined him in the road with a heavy heart. *You
lied!* Her conscience declared, *and to the Reverend's son, no
less! Hurry and confess it! The longer you wait, the harder it
gets, just like with Jonny.* "I lied!" Tatiana blurted.

Robert looked at her with eyebrows raised. "I'm
sorry?"

"I lied!" Tatiana repeated. "I was actually peeping in the Culbertsons' windows because I was upset at the girls for having a tea party without me."

Robert tilted his head. "So ... now you're jealous?" he surmised cautiously.

Tatiana nodded shamefacedly, "Will you forgive me for lying?"

"Of course," Robert replied.

"Thank you! But I'm still feeling quite dismal," Tatiana complained. "I was already feeling bad because Jonny wasn't able to meet me. We were going to visit Beauty, but now he has a deadline to buy her and has to work extremely hard to earn enough money. He left me a sad little note saying that he couldn't come." Tatiana threw her hands up in the air. "This is turning out to be a very ill-fated Saturday. I might as well just go back home, scrub some more floors, and eat my Joy—I mean my radish."

Poor Robert was not able to grasp much of what the girl was talking about, but he was a very courteous young man who had been taught to make pleasant conversation, so he took a shot in the dark. "You sound like you're having a difficult day."

"I am!" Tatiana agreed readily. "Are you?"

"No," Robert replied honestly. "I'm going fishing."

"Oh, that does sound very fine," declared Tatiana. "I've only been fishing a few times, but I always enjoyed it. Pity you only have one reel, but I suppose we can take turns casting."

"Um ..." Robert raised his cap to scratch his head, feeling like a landed fish. He wasn't quite sure how Tatiana had suddenly invaded his private fishing trip, but there she was, skipping ahead of him with his pail on her arm.

Robert was not a dull boy, but he lived life at a slow, ambling pace; when Tatiana's whirlwind existence collided with his own, it made his head spin.

Robert's favorite fishing spot was in Owl Creek at a little bend in the stream where the water slowed and deepened. He led Tatiana there and settled himself on a log. "You may cast first if you like," he offered, proper gentleman that he was.

Tatiana consented readily to this and wildly cast the line out. She narrowly missed catching Robert's shoulder, but the hook miraculously landed in the water. Then Tatiana sat waiting for about half a minute before reeling the line back in and casting again. She did this several times and then handed the reel over to Robert saying: "You can try, but I'll warn you that the fish aren't really biting today."

Robert smiled knowingly. "We'll see." Once he had his line cast, he sat back and waited with languid, untiring patience.

Meanwhile, Tatiana was burrowing in Robert's tin pail. "What do you have this pencil and paper in here for?" she wondered.

"For drawin' on," he informed her, casting an easy glance over at her.

"Can I use a piece?"

"Certainly." Robert yawned. "Why don't you draw that blue jay up there? He's a jaunty fellow."

Tatiana eyed the bird. He certainly was jaunty, hopping and fluttering rapidly from branch to branch. She needed something a little more stationary. Her eyes fell on Robert, and she spread her paper on the flattest part of the rock she was sitting on and began to sketch.

Tatiana was quite good at sketching for her age. She would not be considered a very talented artist, but she could render a fairly realistic likeness of whatever subject she chose to portray. She lacked a rational method to her work and tended to start at a random spot. To draw Robert, she began with the strokes that would create the sheath of his hunting knife. Then she worked down to the frayed cuffs of his dungarees. After that she returned to his belt line and sketched upwards, ending with his face.

Robert had a pleasant face. It was solid and matter-of-fact looking. His forehead, cheekbones, nose, and jaw were situated in a pleasing manner that made his very appearance look undeniably good. Robert's appearance conveyed inherent goodness, in a way that couldn't be defined, but was more than skin, bone, soulful green eyes, and prominent eyebrows. Tatiana could imagine those eyebrows becoming as bushy as those of Robert's father with the progression of time, but presently they still looked nice.

Tatiana was almost finished with her drawing. Just as she leaned forward to get a better look at his notable eyebrows, Robert turned his head. He looked startled and asked, "Are you drawing me instead?"

"I am," Tatiana said, recreating his full eyebrows on the page. "I must say, you're really a very handsome boy." As Robert's cheeks colored, Tatiana cried out, "Oh, that blush is perfect! Keep it, just for a moment!" This required literally no effort at all for Robert at this point. Tatiana quickly put a little more shading on the face she had drawn. Sitting back, Tatiana looked over her creation with approval. "There! You look just like David: ruddy and with a handsome appearance. What do you think?" She lifted the page for his inspection.

Robert, unaccustomed to any form of compliment from a young female such as Tatiana, was feeling a bit overwhelmed. "Hmm, well, you're very good at drawing, Tatiana."

"Why, thank you! You're very good at sitting still, yourself," she replied generously. "And I very much appreciate that you invited me to go fishing with you, but I really should be getting back. I certainly wouldn't want to get chased by wolves or anything else of that nature!" She extended the piece of paper. "Would you like to keep it?"

Robert was very tempted to say yes because he thought the picture was nothing short of amazing, but he did not want to seem vain, so he graciously declined.

"Well, then, I will take it home and hang it on my wall along with all my other beautiful pictures!" Tatiana announced. This brought another blush to shy Robert's face, though Tatiana could not understand why. "And I suppose I will spend the rest of my afternoon reading my pretty red Bible and eating my little Joy radish. I hope you have a grand time fishing! Maybe if you wait long enough, you'll catch a shark!" Tatiana giggled at this, realizing how nonsensical it sounded. "But that would likely never happen. Goodbye, Robert!"

"Goodbye, Tatiana!" Robert called, drawing his eyes back to his line. For all the rest of the time that he remained there by the stream, his mind was kept busy mulling over all the strange things Tatiana had said and done. He concluded that she was both odd and wonderful.

CHAPTER FIVE

Trouble Afoot

I need one gallon of molasses and a bottle of powdered ginger, please," Tatiana told Mr. Weller. "Coming right up, miss!" he replied cheerfully, going to fetch the items. "Are your sisters planning to make ginger cookies?"

"That's my hope!" Tatiana replied. She leaned against the polished wooden counter and allowed her eyes to wander over all the lovely things in Mr. Weller's store. The shelves behind the counter were stocked to the ceiling with jars, canisters, and bottles—all full of good things to eat. Barrels of flour and crackers lined the back wall. Bolts of fabric were stacked on one shelf, and another was full of plowshares and other farm machinery. In the corner was a glass case full of shiny knives. The front window was inhabited by a row of dainty china dolls that Tatiana could have studied all day.

"Here you are, Tatiana." He told her the price; she dug out the coins Gretchen had given her. "Would you like to buy a peppermint stick with your penny in change?" he asked.

Tatiana would love a peppermint stick! The words 'yes, please!' were fighting to leap off the end of her tongue. *But the money is Gretchen's,* her conscience said. *She didn't say you could buy candy.* Oh, but the fat and glossy red and white spirals looked so enticing in the sparkling glass jar on the counter. *You know the right thing to do.* Tatiana straightened her spine and said clearly, "Thank you for asking, Mr. Weller, but I can't buy one today."

"Very well," the man said amiably, handing her a penny and wrapping her purchases in brown paper. "You have a good day, Miss Bergman."

"You too, sir!" Tatiana headed for the door and nearly ran into gruff Mr. Grable as he entered the store.

"Pardon me," he apologized, touching the brim of his hat.

"Oh, Mr. Grable!" Tatiana exclaimed, catching his coat sleeve. "Have you seen Jonny lately? He couldn't come to town last Saturday, and he hasn't been to church or school either. I haven't seen him since last Friday."

The elderly farmer frowned. "Didn't you hear, little one? Jonny was injured Saturday evening."

"Injured!" Tatiana gasped, "Is he hurt badly?"

"Jonny was helping out at the sawmill owned by Mr. Smith's father. I heard that Jonny's hand got caught in one of the belts and was pulled into the machinery."

Tatiana clasped a hand to her mouth. "Oh, how horrible!"

The farmer shook his head ruefully. "Poor lad lost two of his fingers and part of a third one. It sure is hard to see somethin' like that happen: young boy like that ... He'll struggle throughout life with learning how to cope with an injury like that. Like I always say, a sawmill's not a toy; it's not somethin' to have young boys playing around with. If the Smiths had kept that boy out of there, none of this would have ..."

Tatiana cut off the farmer's rant. "Thank you for telling me, Mr. Grable; now I must be going!" Then she flew out the door, clutching her parcels to her aching chest. All she could think of was Jonny and his agony. How could something like this happen to her dearest friend?

When Tatiana reached her house, she dashed inside and dumped the groceries on the kitchen table. Then the flustered girl ran to find Gretchen. "Gretchen, Gretchen, you've got to harness Jack! We must ride out to the Smiths' house immediately!"

Gretchen dropped the laundry she was folding. "In heaven's name, what's wrong?"

"Jonny's hurt! He got hurt terribly bad last Saturday. I just heard about it; I must go and see him right away, and it's a very long walk!"

Gretchen's shoulders sagged a little. "Tatiana Grace! That is not an emergency! He's been hurt since last Saturday, and he can survive without you there to coddle him."

Tatiana began to weep bitterly. "You don't even care what happened to Jonny! He'll probably die before I ever have a chance to say goodbye, and you're such a cruel old witch that you won't even let me go to see him one last time!"

"Hush, Tatty," Gretchen scolded. "You're working yourself into a tizzy over this. Of course Jonny is important, but if you see him and cry all over whatever part of him is hurt ..."

"His hand," Tatiana blurted.

"If you go cry all over his injured hand, it's not going to help him one bit."

"But I'm his only friend and he needs to see me!" Tatiana insisted, kicking at the laundry basket. "If you don't let me go, I'll steal a horse and go there all by myself!"

Gretchen firmly took hold of Tatiana's arm, and a dangerous glint shone in her eyes. "There will be no horse stealing done by anyone from this house while I'm in it. You will stay here if I have to lock you in the pantry for the rest of the day, is that clear? I won't have you off gallivanting around the countryside because of some foolish whim. We'll try to visit him soon, just not today."

"It's not a whim!" Tatiana shrieked, jerking against Gretchen's iron grasp.

"It is too a whim," Gretchen replied levelly. "I'll have Father deal with you when he gets home."

"When Father gets home soon he'll let me go see Jonny," Tatiana declared. "Father isn't unkind and heartless like you are!" Tatiana struggled again in her sister's confining clutch. "Let me go!"

"You'll run off as soon as I do."

Tatiana could not deny this.

"And don't count on Father being home soon," Gretchen said smugly. "Don't you remember he has to work this afternoon even though it's Saturday?" She brought a stool and made Tatiana sit in the pantry. The small space had a door that locked and only one window, too small for even Tatiana to wriggle through. Gretchen settled with her laundry basket directly outside the pantry door, ready to hear Tatiana's apology.

"How long must I stay here?" the unrepentant child angrily demanded.

"Until you realize your fault and are ready to make an apology."

"Well, you're the one who's wrong, so I won't be coming out," Tatiana sneered.

Gretchen shook out a dishtowel and folded it neatly. "That's fine with me, Tatty. Have a nice time." When she finished folding the laundry, Gretchen locked the pantry door.

"What if the house catches on fire?" Tatty yelled through the door.

"Then I will come and let you out," Gretchen replied calmly.

In a few minutes, Tatiana leaped up as she heard the door opening, thinking Gretchen had changed her mind. Without a word, Gretchen set a chamber pot inside the door and locked it again.

Stubborn Tatiana! How quickly her young heart could change from being soft and sensitive to even the smallest sin ... to being hard as stone. Tatiana's anger was like a blinder narrowing her focus, keeping her from seeing God's truth. Once she had cooled down a little, she realized how wrong she had been to make demands.

Although she flushed with shame and remorse, the last thing she wanted to do was admit her error to Gretchen. Because Tatiana had so passionately insisted that her sister was wrong, admitting that she herself had erred seemed as hard as asking Jonny's forgiveness for the terrible thing she had said to him.

So Tatiana sat, hating herself and nearly drowning in her own bitterness. She knew that all she had to do was confess, but for some reason it seemed like an impossible task. She would not, could not, humble herself before her sister or before God.

When the noon hour rolled around, Gretchen stepped in to speak with her sister. "Tatty," she spoke softly to the child huddled on her stool, "I have a plate of food for you on the table. Will you not apologize?"

"No," Tatiana said vehemently, lifting her haughty chin. "I have nothing to confess."

Gretchen shook her head sadly. "Don't let your heart become hard, Tatty. God always forgives those who come to him with a contrite heart."

Tatiana turned her head, signaling that she did not wish to hear anything that Gretchen had to say. Before she left, Gretchen held Tatiana's red Bible out to her. Tatiana refused to take it, so Gretchen set it on a shelf next to a big jar of pickles.

Tatiana's desire to live blamelessly had been strengthened in the last year as she studied her Bible and asked God and her community to forgive her sins. She wanted to confess this latest transgression, but pride and anger mingled with worry over Jonny and grief over his injuries made her mute. Didn't Gretchen understand how important it was for her to see that her friend was really all right?

She spent her entire day in the pantry, stuck in a pit of pride and stubbornness, with the hours crawling by. She could have used them to focus on pleasant or profitable thoughts, but instead she stewed in anger at Gretchen and self-pity for her own unfair treatment at the hands of her sister.

When it became dark, Gretchen brought an oil lamp into the pantry. Glancing over at the shelf, she said, "Please read your Bible, Tatty."

When Hans came home from work in the evening and stopped in to see the sad little prisoner in the pantry, Tatiana began pleading anew to be allowed to visit Jonny. Hans steadfastly supported the rules that Gretchen had established; Tatiana remained in the pantry. Her defiance seemed to cast a shadow over the whole house. Everyone, including the guilty party, was eager for the standoff to be over.

As the hours ticked by, the entire Bergman family withdrew to their beds, save for the staunch little rebel in the pantry.

Each time she began to nod off, her head would jerk back up. She would shake herself awake and plant herself more firmly on her stool. She thought of how terrible her family would feel if they found her dead in the pantry, withered away to a skeleton, all because they wouldn't grant her this one, simple request!

Exhausted and miserable, Tatiana turned her weary eyes to her red Bible where it lay unassumingly by the pickle jar. Stretching out her arm, she picked it up, turning it over in her hands. She parted the covers and let the Bible fall open. Her eyes dropped to the ninth verse of Proverbs 20: 'Who can say, I have made my heart clean, I am pure from my sin?'

The question seemed to cut like a sharp sword, straight to the depths of Tatiana's soul. What a question! Who, indeed, could claim a clean heart and purity from sin? "Not I," Tatiana whispered. Just the admittance of such a thing brought tears to her eyes.

She looked down at her Bible again. This time, a verse in the next chapter drew her eyes. Proverbs 21:2 read: 'Every way of a man is right in his own eyes: but the Lord pondereth the heart.'

Fear struck Tatiana as she read the words. "Oh, don't look! Please don't look, God!" She folded her arms over her chest, breaking into rending sobs. "Jesus cleaned my heart when I prayed with Reverend Lyte in the church, but I didn't keep it clean. I let it get dirty, and I let my own stubbornness make it hard."

She curled into a despondent ball on her stool, covering her face with her hands. "Oh, I am so ashamed! I pushed Jesus away and listened to my sinful nature instead. Please, Jesus, be merciful to me! I don't want a heart of stone. I want a heart of flesh that will love you more than anything else in the world."

Trembling, Tatiana cried out, "I was wrong, Lord! I was wrong the whole time! Please, please forgive me!" The child was so worn out from her emotionally draining day that she slipped from her stool to the hard floor of the pantry. "Clean my heart, Jesus, and I will try again to keep it clean," she pleaded, clutching her Bible to her breast. Then, as if her Heavenly Father had reached down and embraced her, Tatiana felt a divine sense of warmth and comfort. She lay back with a contented sigh. As she fell asleep, she whispered "Abba Father."

On Sunday afternoon, Mr. Bergman rode out to the Smith farm to check on Jonny and take the family a gift of food. Although Tatiana had apologized, her father left her at home; he finally was teaching her that she wouldn't get what she wanted by being demanding.

After watching her father ride off without her, she wanted to cry because she was missing Jonny sorely. As she entered the room she shared with her sisters, she noticed the picture she had drawn of Robert that hung beside her mirror. If only she could draw such a portrait of Jonny, she could gaze on his dear face anytime she wished.

Tatiana hurried to get out her paper and drawing pencils. Sitting at the dressing table, she closed her eyes just long enough to conjure his face in her mind; then she began to draw the place where his hair overlapped his ears.

After finishing her sketch, she studied it critically. No, it was wrong! It looked somewhat like Jonny, but it wasn't the Jonny she knew. This lad looked surly and mean. Pushing the page away, she started again, this time beginning at his mouth and going from there, picturing him calling her Tina or Tamara. But when she had finished this picture, Jonny looked foolish and dumb. With a sigh she began again. Tatiana drew a total of four pictures until she gave up in frustrated defeat. The next time she saw Jonny she would have to study him and see where she was going astray.

Finally, the following Friday, two weeks after she had last seen her friend, Jonny strode into school half an hour after class began. Miss Hartman raised her head to reprimand the tardy student, but then she saw that it was Jonny. She smiled and told him to have a seat.

Every eye in the school was trained upon the young man. The eyes of each student were drawn as if by a magnet to Jonny's left pocket in which his hand sheltered. As he walked by Tatiana's desk, she asked a hundred questions with her eyes—but the main question was, 'How **are** you, Jonny?'

With startling speed and sleight of hand, Jonny dropped something into her lap. She ducked her head and saw that it was a long, gnarly carrot on which he had written: 'Long Suffering.' Tatiana blinked. Long suffering indeed! He had certainly had plenty of it.

At recess, Jonny was the hub of attention. Everyone wanted to know exactly how the accident had occurred and what his hand looked like now. Jonny answered their questions brusquely and refused to withdraw his hand from his pocket. He remained slumped against the wall with his bangs hanging over his eyes like a curtain.

When the students finally cleared away, Tatiana came and slipped her arm through his. Jonny shot her a sideways glance and muttered, "It's in a bandage anyway, so there's nothing to see."

Tatiana looked down. "I wasn't going to ask to see your hand. I'm just glad you're back."

Jonny didn't reply, but he found her words very touching. Together they walked along the tree line behind the schoolhouse. "I hate it how people are treating me like an injured puppy! I don't want their pity! My hand is all they can talk about, and they are constantly cooing over how unfortunate I am! I am so wearied of hearing it."

"Well, then," Tatiana decided, "I shan't mention your hand at all."

"I'm glad it was my left hand and not my right." Jonny continued, "But I'll still have many limitations. Do you know how difficult it is to button a jacket with one hand?"

"No, I suppose I don't."

"Or even something as simple as tying my shoes! That took an awful long time today. I'm not sure what I'll do now if I can't do a man's work. I'll never be able to raise the money to buy Beauty." He sat down dejectedly on a rock.

"Jonny, I thought you said you didn't want pity," Tatiana reminded him gently.

Jonny blinked as if he hadn't realized what he'd been talking about.

Tatiana continued: "I think you can learn how to use your hand and work just like you always did." She knelt so she could peer up into his downcast face. "No one will pity you as long as you don't make a victim of yourself."

Jonny nodded slowly. "Yes, your words are true, Thelma." He pulled his bandaged hand from his pocket. His thumb and index finger protruded from the wrappings and the rest of his hand looked very stumpy and short. "This is my hand now, and I need to learn to use it as best I can." He looked at Tatiana who had a strange expression on her face. "What?"

"Thelma," she repeated, "That's the worst name yet!"

Jonny began to laugh. "Well, I happen to like it."

"Oh, heaven forbid!" Tatiana complained.

Jonny was looking at his hand again. "Mrs. Smith says I might be able to remove my bandages for a while tomorrow or the day after. I wonder if my hand will look very bad."

"Jonny Creek!" Tatiana exclaimed. "Stop fretting over your silly hand! Oh, and put your head up. I need to study you."

"Study me? Is there a test?" Jonny inquired.

Tatiana leaned forward and thoughtfully considered the lad's puzzled face. "No, I was trying to draw a sketch of you and was having the hardest of times. Ah, that's it!"

"What's it?"

Tatiana tapped his chin. "Your chin and cheekbones are very prominent. I've got to fix that in my drawing. And I had your eyes wrong. They need to be a little crinklier so it looks like you're trying not to smile, because that's usually what you're doing."

Jonny snorted. "Nice to know I have crinkly eyes!"

"Oh, I think they're lovely."

Jonny laughed again, throwing his head back and showing his straight, white teeth. Tatiana admired how his whole face lit up when he laughed. "You're always so kind, Tatty," Jonny said, "I think you would call a toad 'lovely'."

Tatiana shook her head. "I only call things 'lovely' if they honestly deserve the title. But I can find beauty in many humble things as well." She stretched her arms out before her. "Except for my hands."

"What's wrong with them?"

"They are so very small and white. Gretchen has strong hands, and Rose's are slender, but mine are only very pale and short," Tatiana concluded sadly.

"I'll wager mine is shorter!" Jonny declared. "My left hand anyways." He tugged her to sit beside him and looked at her hands. They were indeed very small. The skin over them was so thin, delicate, and pale that it was halfway transparent. Jonny could see the blue veins running from the base of her fingers and twining up her wrists. For some reason this jarred the young man. She was such a fragile girl! She had such an insubstantial covering of skin shielding her from the elements. Right then and there he resolved to be her loyal protector. Never would he allow any harm to come to this dear girl! Nothing would touch her—at least not on his watch.

The school bell beckoned them back to class. As they approached the schoolhouse, Tatiana watched Jonny transform back into the sullen boy who had learned not to trust people. His shoulders sagged, his hands were shoved into his pockets, and his face took on a joyless expression. Why did he hide the real Jonny? Tatiana found it very curious, but she could not bring herself to ask him about it.

CHAPTER SIX

The Christmas Ball

Rose! Tatty!" Gretchen's voice echoed from the hall and brought her sisters running to meet her. The eldest Bergman girl had just come in from running errands, and she was cold and breathless. Snowflakes dotted her black wool pelisse and clung as shiny, wet droplets to her eyelashes. "See what Mrs. Weller gave us as an early Christmas present?" She held up a generous evergreen wreath adorned with a crimson bow.

This elicited squeals of delight from the younger girls. "How kind of her, the dear woman!" Rose exclaimed, "I'll have to take her some mulled cider and spice bread before the season is over."

Tatiana was dancing about in excitement as she gleefully claimed: "I daresay, this is the finest wreath I've ever seen! Quick, Gretchen, let's hang it on the door!"

When the wreath was in place, Tatiana stood gazing at it in the softly falling snow. Since the silly girl had dashed outside without shoes or coat, she was shivering from cold, but her heart was so warm she scarcely noticed. "It makes our house look so very festive, Gretchie. I think I could kiss Mrs. Weller right about now!"

"I dare you to run down to the store and do it!" Rose taunted. Tatiana howled and tugged at her sister's apron strings.

71

Gretchen removed her bonnet and coat and fixed her hair in the mirror that hung by the door. "I have another surprise for you girls," she announced, pulling an envelope from the pocket of her coat.

"Who is it from? What does it say?" Tatiana cried as she hopped and frolicked about like a newborn calf. "May I open it?"

Gretchen smiled at her sister's antics and handed the letter to Rose. "Rose shall read it to us since she is waiting so patiently."

Eagerly, Rose opened the envelope and withdrew the missive. As she began to read, her voice rose in excitement. "Mr. Hans Bergman and his daughters Miss Gretchen Bergman, Miss Rose Bergman, and Miss Tatiana Bergman are all invited to come to the Annual Christmas Ball, which will be held at the home of Conrad and Julia Easley, on December 13th at 7:00. Join us for the dancing and other festivities. Signed: Conrad Easley, Esquire." Rose lowered the letter with a dreamy sigh. "I love the Christmas Ball, especially the dancing."

"I love the food," Tatiana added. She then tugged at Gretchen's arm. "May I run down to Mr. Grable's and tell Jonny about the Christmas Ball?"

Gretchen nodded. "I suppose you may. You haven't been overly naughty today. Just make sure to bundle up warmly! It's chilly out."

Swathed in warm winter clothes, Tatiana trotted out of the house and headed for the lane that led to Mr. Grable's farm. She loved the feel and sound of her boots crunching through the thin layer of snow on the ground. The frosty blanket of white that covered everything added magic to the day. Gazing about in amazement, Tatiana breathed in great gulps of cold air.

She crossed the meadow to get to the back stable where she found Jonny dutifully shoveling out the stalls. "Hello, Jonny!" she called, running over to the fence.

"Hullo," he replied, continuing his work. The lad was dressed in a ragged work coat and a dirty cap. His face was bright from the biting cold and his breath came out in frozen clouds.

"What are you doing, Jonny?"

"Making French rolls," he answered sarcastically. "What does it look like I'm doing?"

"Mucking out the stall?" Tatiana guessed.

"Yes. I need to get all this cleaned out before it freezes."

"Oh." Tatiana watched him work for a bit longer and then asked, "Did you get an invitation to the Easley Christmas Ball?"

Jonny shrugged. "I probably won't be invited at all. No one wants an Indian at a Christmas ball."

Tatiana climbed over the fence and stood outside the open stall Jonny was cleaning. Beauty shared the stable yard with Tatiana. "Oh, don't say that, Jonny. I'm sure you'll be welcome there." Tatiana reached into her coat pocket and pulled out a carrot. She broke off a short piece.

"What's that for?"

"Oh, I brought this carrot for Beauty, but I think I might give a piece to you as well since you seem to be in such a foul mood!"

"Oh, why thank you!" Jonny said, setting aside his shovel, taking the carrot chunk, and tucking it in a pocket. As he did, Tatiana noticed his injured hand.

"I thought you had your bandages off by now!"

He glanced down at his injured appendage. "Well, I did, but I somehow broke it open again."

"Oh, gracious!" Tatiana wailed. "Your poor hand! You mustn't work so hard, Jonny. Doesn't it pain you to do that?"

He hefted another shovelful of soiled bedding. "Yes. But if I don't keep working I'll never earn Beauty in time. I have 'til the end of the month, and I still have three and a quarter dollars to go."

At the mention of her name, the stunning yearling pricked up her ears. Tatiana turned to the pretty horse and offered her the remaining part of the carrot. Beauty came forward timidly and gently took the carrot from Tatiana's open palm with her warm lips. While Beauty devoured the carrot, Tatiana gazed admiringly up into the animal's trusting black eyes.

Tatiana had never been overly fond of horses and did not have a natural ease with them, as Jonny did, but she had a special love for Beauty that stemmed from Jonny's devoted affection for the animal. Tatiana slowly raised a pale hand and ran it from Beauty's forelock down her long, smooth nose. She tenderly stroked the velveteen end of Beauty's nose. The horse huffed a soft breath into Tatiana's palm. "She's wonderfully tame," Tatiana observed.

Jonny leaned his shovel against the stable wall and climbed to sit on the fence. "In the stable, she is. But she hasn't been saddle-trained yet. She would likely go wild if you tried to ride her right now."

Feeling courageous, Tatiana edged closer to the horse and leaned against Beauty's strong neck. "Oh Beauty," she sighed, "I **so** hope that Jonny will be able to buy you so he can train you and ride you." The horse looked at Tatiana as if the beast understood what the girl had said.

Jonny still sat on the fence and munched amiably. "Say, this is a good, sweet carrot, Thelma. Is this my long-suffering carrot?"

"No, I don't believe so."

Jonny studied his snack. "Maybe it's his brother."

Tatiana smiled. "I got it from our root cellar though."

"Or maybe just some distant relative," Jonny decided. He took off his cap and dusted the snow from it before putting it back on. "So, you mentioned this Christmas Ball. What's it like?"

Tatiana was all too eager to tell him about it. "Well, the house is all decorated so that it looks like a palace—and really the Easleys are very rich so their house nearly is a palace. And there's lots of delicious food, and music and dancing late into the night!" Tatiana picked up a rake and pretended to twirl about the snow with it. "And all the ladies wear their finest dresses and all the men look so handsome in their suits! It really is the best night of the year!"

Rather than being impressed, Jonny looked quite underwhelmed with Tatiana's description. "Hmm, I'd say the bad outweighs the good on that one. Fancy houses, dancing for hours, and dressing up aren't my cup of tea. Maybe I'll just stay home."

"But you must go, Jonny! Who will dance with me if you're not there?"

Jonny shrugged as if it were not his affair. "What about Rose?"

Tatiana shook her head. "I'm sure Rose will have a crowd of beaus following her around. And I will have no one at all!" Tatiana looked so dejected that Jonny regretted his careless words.

"I might come after all, Tatty," he decided. "And you mustn't look so sad. See, I have a gift for you!" Reaching to his throat, he removed the necklace that had been hanging there. Jonny had made it himself out of horsehairs that he had collected and a flint arrowhead with a hole bored through it. He had braided the hairs together with contrasting colors and then added the arrowhead. He had not originally made it for Tatiana, but he had felt silly wearing it himself. "Merry Christmas," Jonny said as he handed the rustic jewelry to the girl.

Tatiana was delighted with the necklace. She looked at it approvingly and put it on. In Tatiana's eyes, it was just as precious as a string of pearls. "Thank you, Jonny. I'll wear it always!"

Jonny felt flattered and a bit guilty for the undeserved gratitude. "Oh, it's nothing," he said, snatching up the rake and getting back to work. His ears felt hot and his face burned. What kind of gift giver was he, to give his best friend one of his castoffs that he no longer wanted? He determined to find a way to give sweet Tatiana a good, proper gift—the kind of gift she deserved.

On the night of December 13, the Bergman home was in an ebullient state of chaos. While outside the night was clear and crisp and peaceful, indoors, mayhem ruled. The three Bergman girls were running to and fro in a rush to be presentable by 7 o'clock, while Hans Bergman watched it all in quiet incredulity and thanked the Lord that the Christmas Ball came no more than once a year.

Rose flew down the stairs in search of a pair of gloves and nearly collided with Gretchen, who was trying to find suitable footwear. Tatiana called dismally from their bedroom: "Gretchen, my curls undid themselves and I look like a mop!"

A tiny scream came from Rose in the kitchen. "Oh, NO! I snagged my sleeve! Gretchie, can you mend this?"

It was in times such as this that Hans sincerely wished he had sons instead of daughters. Fortunately, he had been generously endowed with patience, and the good man simply checked his watch for the hundredth time and folded his arms to wait.

Gretchen surveyed the wreckage of Tatiana's curls. "Oh, dear. This does look disastrous."

Tatiana looked at her reflection gloomily. "I don't see why Rose has to have all the pretty waves and I get left with hair that's as straight as a horse's tail!"

"But horse's tails can be pretty!" Gretchen claimed as she ran a brush through Tatiana's hair. "In their own ... peculiar sort of way."

"And that's all I'll ever be!" Tatiana moaned, "Peculiar!"

Rose hurried into their bedroom and began undoing buttons. "Oh, what do I wear, Gretchen? We should be leaving now and I haven't the slightest clue what to change into!"

Gretchen finished with Tatiana's hair and scurried to the wardrobe. She reached to the back and pulled out a dark pink dress. "Try this. I wore this when I was younger, so it should fit."

Rose changed, kicking out of the torn dress as the new one floated over her head. Gretchen helped her fasten it, and then Rose gauged her reflection in the mirror. "It's rather baggy about the waist, wouldn't you say?"

Gretchen's quick gray eyes flickered about the room. "Aha! Tie this sash about your waist!"

"But ... but ..." Rose spluttered. "That's a curtain sash!"

"And none will ever be the wiser! See? You look dazzling!" And she did. Rose had spent much time on her golden hair and had braided it intricately and wound it about her head. The pink dress set off her rosy skin.

"And I?" Tatiana piped up, "How do I look?" Tatiana was attired in a blue silk dress that had belonged to her mother when she was a child and had been carefully preserved since then; it was still beautiful.

"You are very lovely as well," Gretchen assured Tatiana, patting her hair. "And I am looking plain, as usual. But I suppose it is best that way. A rock in a colorful wrapping is still a rock, and I will not aspire to be what I am not, nor ever will be."

The girls were about to head downstairs when Rose gasped, with her hands spread against her thighs. "My petticoat! Gretchen, I must have pulled off my petticoat with my torn dress!"

Gretchen shook her head. "Mercy, well, it's too late now. Come as you are, Rose."

Rose's face was pale. "But I feel dreadfully indecent!"

"No one will ever know your mistake. Honestly, I can't tell. Just avoid standing in intense light and all will be well."

"Dressed in a curtain sash and lacking proper undergarments!" Rose groaned. "It will be a wonder if I can ever show my face after tonight!"

"Oh, hush," scolded Gretchen. "Now come along, girls. Father has waited long enough."

The girls descended the stairs and met Hans at the door. He complimented each of them, lingering at Gretchen. "You look as heavenly as an angel, my darling," he told her, laying a kiss on her pale cheek. Gretchen closed her tender eyes and drank in his words. No one could make her feel as beautiful as her dear father did, when he thought to do it.

The family rode together to the Easley estate. When they entered the great house, they stepped into a bustling hive of lively activity. The girls immediately started to make their way through the crowd in search of their friends. Tatiana looked all about for Jonny, feeling disappointed because she could not spot him. Hadn't he come? Had he chosen to stay home after all? Or, horror of all horrors, had Conrad Easley not invited him because he would rather not have an Indian at his Christmas Ball?

It was then that Tatiana spotted a slim, dark figure slouched against the wall in a shadowy corner, sipping a glass of punch. She sighed with relief and started in that direction. But her progress was interrupted by a light touch on her arm. She turned. Robert Matthew was gazing at her with his kind green eyes and a warm smile.

"Hello, Tatiana."

She swallowed her surprise and replied with a shaky "Good evening."

"I was beginning to wonder if you would ever arrive, Miss Bergman," he admitted. "And I wanted to ask if I might be your partner for your first dance."

Her first dance? With Robert Matthew? Tatiana was so taken aback she could hardly answer. She had envisioned the evening as being the same as in previous years when she had run off to play with the other children. She had expected the only difference to be Jonny's attendance. She had imagined sitting on the sidelines with him, giggling about the ladies' hairstyles and trying to spot lint on the gentlemen's jackets. She had thought that later in the evening, she and Jonny could do a bit of dancing on the edge of the floor so as not to bother anyone.

But an official dance? So early in the evening? With Robert Matthew? It almost made her dizzy just thinking about it. Tatiana was quick to recover from her shock, summoning a bright smile to her face and responding with a cheery: "Thank you, Robert! I would be delighted to!"

When the next dance began, Robert gently took Tatiana's hand and led her out onto the floor. It was a simple dance that Tatiana had seen many times, so it took very little effort for her to follow the steps. She and Robert were one of the youngest couples on the floor, and just the sight of them provoked many an amused smile. The youthful pair did not notice this, however, because Tatiana was focused on the steps of the dance and Robert kept his gaze on his lovely partner.

When Tatiana at last thought to look up, she was startled to find Robert's gaze so intensely settled on her. Blushing girlishly, she tried to think of something to talk about. "You have a very nice suit, Robert. I don't think I've ever seen you wear it before."

"No, it's new."

"I see. My dress is very old. It belonged to my mother as a child."

"It's lovely."

"Thank you." And after this short interchange, Tatiana, for perhaps the first time in her life, could not think of anything to say.

When the music ended, Robert prepared to lead Tatiana from the dance floor, but the head violinist called out: "Anyone who is presently on the dance floor had better not dare leave! Anyone else want to join? Do it now, because next we will have the Virginia reel!"

This brought a cheer from everyone. The bouncy reel began to play and everyone hurried to form lines. Robert and Tatiana exchanged looks and threw themselves into the speedy dance. Afterwards the violinist announced the next dance and Robert caught Tatiana's hand. "Oh, this next one is so much fun! Shall we dance just once more?"

Tatiana was laughing and panting and having so much fun that all she could manage was an eager nod. So once more she was spun across the floor in the arms of Robert Matthew, while Jonny Creek looked on in envious silence.

When that dance was over, she went to find Jonny who was exactly where she had last seen him. He was sipping his fifth glass of punch. "Hello, Jonny!" she said merrily, stepping up beside him.

"Hello, yourself," he muttered, staring down into his drink.

"Aren't you having a fine time?"

The boy raised his miserable amber eyes. "I should have stayed home."

"Oh, Jonny," Tatiana sighed, "but then you couldn't watch all of this!" she motioned with her arm toward the grand activities going on in the spectacular room.

"I didn't come to watch you dance with Robert Matthew all evening," Jonny growled.

Was that what was eating him? Tatiana wondered. *Could he possibly be jealous?* "Well, then, let's dance! This set will be over before too long."

Jonny shook his head. "I won't dance with you if you prefer him."

"But I don't, Jonny!" Tatiana cried, "You're my best friend and nothing could ever change that! Won't you come?"

"Oh, go find that pampered baboon and dance with him," Jonny replied curtly.

"He's not a baboon. And it's you I want to dance with, Jonny, not him," Tatiana answered sternly. "I won't have you sitting here wretchedly in the corner all evening looking like someone who's just fallen off the prison wagon! Up with you now!" With these words Tatiana fastened her grip upon Jonny's arm and attempted to pull him to his feet.

Jonny did not help her in the least, but hung like a dead weight. But Tatiana was stubborn and she worked with all her might at tugging him away from the wall. She had made a slight bit of progress and this gave her hope. She yanked with all her might and at this same fated moment, Jonny wriggled his arm free.

This resulted in Tatiana being launched backwards and staggering into the refreshment table. As she fell her elbow caught the edge of the punch bowl. To her horror, the entire reservoir of hot punch washed down on her. Fortunately, the punch had been sitting out long enough to cool a bit. Had it been its original temperature it might have severely scalded the unlucky girl.

Although she wasn't hurt physically, Tatiana was not only wet and sticky but also tremendously humiliated. She rose shakily from the pool of punch. Her mother's beautiful silk dress was ruined. Her gaze was drawn upward: before her was a sea of staring eyes. Everything, including the music, had halted. Tatiana wished with all her heart that the earth would just open up and swallow her so that she would not have to experience such degradation.

Then Gretchen was at her side. Sweet Gretchen! Tatiana wanted to melt into her elder sister and disappear altogether. Gretchen took the bedraggled girl's arm and led her toward the door. The music resumed then and all the guests returned to their celebration. Tatiana was in tears by the time she and Gretchen had reached the kitchen.

Gretchen explained to the kitchen staff what had happened. One worker went to clean up the sticky mess by the refreshment table while the rest set about trying to clean Tatiana. The girl huddled on a wooden chair in someone's warm housecoat while one of the maids tried to save the dress. She still sobbed when she thought of what a disgrace she was. Her dignity was in shreds. Tatiana thought of a hundred ways she could have done things differently.

While she sat there, Hans came to the kitchen to check on her. "Tatiana," he said, sighing at the site of his disheveled daughter. "I'm sorry to see you like this, but maybe it will teach you to be more careful of your actions." He patted the black, wet hair that now smelled strongly of ginger. "I was planning to save the last dance of the evening for you, Tatty, but I suppose that will have to wait until next year. I'll come for you when it is time to go."

For the rest of the evening Tatiana sat in the kitchen and talked to the cooks. She normally would have enjoyed such a chat, but now she morosely thought about everything she was missing out on because of the embarrassing mishap.

It seemed like an eternity before she could finally climb into the carriage for the ride home, now wrapped in a carriage blanket so the housecoat could be returned. She took her dress along. It had been irreparably stained, but Tatiana could not stand to part with it just yet.

She hadn't seen Jonny after the mishap, but the next morning Tatiana found a split radish on the front step with the word 'sorry' carved into it.

She held it for a moment, thinking of Jonny and his behavior the previous night. "You *should* be sorry, Jonny Creek!" she said. "Apologize all you want, but you'll be no friend of mine! Ha!" and with this she hurled the vegetable as far as she could. It landed in the street and rolled to a stop. With that Tatiana retreated back inside with a loud slam of the door.

Only moments later Jonny came striding down the street leading his hard-earned Beauty behind him. He had made the last payment for her and she was officially his! The lad was so happy that he felt he could fly. He was eager to show off his purchase. Then he stepped on something. Lifting his foot, he saw the radish and knew immediately that Tatiana had thrown it there. *I'm sorry, Tatty! I am—honest! Can't you please forgive me?* The words traveled no farther than his throat as he stood in the street; it hurt that she had rejected his apology by vegetable.

Beauty snorted. Jonny reached back to pat her soft nose. He had one proud beauty secured on his lead; would he be able to tame the other one?

CHAPTER SEVEN

Growing Pains

Tatiana and Jonny were growing up. That growth might have caused a natural drifting apart, as boys and girls begin to feel awkward with each other, but for them the punch bowl incident at the Easley Christmas Ball caused a sudden break. Tatiana was too stubborn to grant Jonny her forgiveness, and Jonny would not humble himself enough to ask for it. Tatiana began to seek out the companionship of the young ladies she had so long ignored.

At thirteen, she was beginning to blossom socially as she began to leave childhood behind. She had been accepted into the circle of friends with surprising ease. Much of her speedy reception was due to the fact that Tatiana knew everything there was to know about Jonny, and the girls peppered her with questions. With the exception of Kitty—who thought young Mr. Creek was rather barbarous—the girls found him absolutely fascinating. Johanna, especially, was strongly attracted to him; she had long ago decided that she and Jonny were destined for each other.

One afternoon Tatiana and her friends had gathered at Johanna Easley's house for an embroidery party. They sat chatting in the family's lavish parlor, with giggling punctuating their conversation.

"You'll never guess what happened to me on Sunday night," Kitty said. "I passed by Daniel Weston, and he winked at me!"

"Truly, Kitty?" Arietta gasped. "Was it an honest to goodness wink? Maybe he had something in his eye?"

Kitty shrugged, "It looked much too intentional to be anything but."

"Ooh, la, Kitty, you've made me break my thread! Some pillowcase this will be!" Johanna exclaimed. "It is my point of view that Daniel Weston is nothing but trouble."

"I agree," Samantha added softly.

"If only," Arietta added, "he weren't so devilishly handsome." She sighed.

"A crime, isn't it?" Johanna licked her thread and poked it through the eye of her needle. "All the best looking ones are always the worst."

Samantha leaned toward Tatiana, who had been silently sitting on the far end of the sofa. "Have you decided what yours will be, Tatty?"

Tatiana turned her hoop to give Samantha a look. "I'm going to put the Fruits of the Spirit on my pillowcase, I believe."

Samantha sighed wistfully. "Oh, if only I had thought of such a grand idea! Mine is turning out to look horridly stupid. You have such talent, Tatty."

Tatiana's dark eyebrows shot up. "Why, I've scarcely begun!"

"Yes, but what I can see is well done. Yours is likely to be the most beautiful of all."

Tatiana ducked her head modestly and smiled to herself. If only Samantha could have seen the way she had hurled her embroidery hoop into the fire only a few years ago! But much had changed since then, and Tatiana felt more like a mature young lady than the spoiled child she had been at ten.

"You've been quiet, Tatiana." Johanna directed everyone's attention to the unobtrusive young girl. "Have you no stories of any romantic escapades to entertain us with?"

Tatiana raised her blue eyes from her work. "No, I'm afraid I have none. I haven't really had any opportunities for such things."

"Not even with Robert Matthew?" Johanna prodded.

Tatiana looked up in surprise. "With whom?"

"Robert Matthew, of course. Anyone can see he's nearly wild about you."

Color stole across Tatiana's cheeks. "No, I never noticed."

"Nothing to be embarrassed about, Tatty!" Johanna exhorted, "He's a fine young man—though not as fine as Jonny Creek, I might add."

"Oh, heavens, Jo, you're so delightfully brazen!" Arietta said.

Johanna flashed Arietta a teasing smile and continued. "He's gotten so manly looking lately! And he's just filled out so nicely. He doesn't look at all like the skinny lad he used to be. I'm starting to think that he looks quite fine!"

"Have you lost your mind, Johanna?" Kitty gasped. "You forget the boy is an Indian!"

"Half Indian," Johanna pointed out.

"Half is hardly different than full when he has savage blood flowing through his veins," Kitty insisted. "I'm shocked that you could even consider him."

"What would your parents think?" Samantha wondered.

Johanna reached out and clasped Samantha's hand. "In mercy's name, DON'T tell them!" Her penetrating gaze moved over each of the girls gathered there. "The only reason I bared my soul is that I trust all of you. I have faith that you will tell no one of my feelings toward Jonny."

"It is so very romantic!" Arietta sighed. "She and Jonny are just like the star-crossed lovers of old!"

"Jonny would make a fine Romeo, would he not?" Johanna asked.

"I think not!" Kitty exclaimed. "The boy is a savage. You will bring shame to your entire household, Johanna. Your parents raised you to be a refined young lady. What can you be thinking?"

Johanna shook her head sadly. "But love is blind, Kitty. If you could only feel as I feel, you would understand. I must have him, Kitty, or I fear I shall wither away and die of a broken heart! Recently, all I can think of is how perfect we'll look together and that we were meant for each other. With him on my arm, I'll be the talk of the entire town!"

"Goodness!" Tatiana cried, and her outburst startled her companions so much that they all fell immediately silent. "You speak of Jonny as if he's some trophy to be won! As if, once you have him, you can shine him up and put him on display for all to see. Handsome or not, he isn't meant to be treated as some object to be drooled over. I only wonder if you care for him any more than you would a prize-winning stallion at the fair!" Tatiana's eyes burned with righteous anger; the girls stared at her in shock.

"And you, Kitty! Do you think he had control over his own birth? He cannot help what family he was born into, nor what he looks like. Give the lad a bit of grace! He is a person, you know. He's a person with normal feelings, wishes, and dreams. And Indian or white, he deserves to be given the respect that every human being does."

During her heated address, Tatiana had risen to her feet. When she finished, she stood there uncomfortably for a moment, trying to decide what to do. "I'm sorry for my outburst," Tatiana said mildly, "But I felt that it needed to be said." She meekly began to gather her things. "I suppose I will be going home now."

It was eerily quiet as Tatiana headed for the door, with none of the normal farewells. The silence made her heart heavy. Then she heard a rustle behind her and turned around. It was Samantha who stood there with an understanding look in her gentle brown eyes. "Do you mind if I accompany you home, Tatiana?" she inquired.

Tatiana wanted to sing and dance for joy, but instead she briefly touched Samantha's hand. "I would be most grateful."

The two girls walked together with Tatiana stamping along in her high-heeled boots and Samantha tip-toeing softly in her slippers. Really, everything about Samantha was soft, from her big brown eyes to her thick chestnut curls and her soft curves. Tatiana thought Samantha was absolutely beautiful, with her full figure that differed so much from her own.

Tatiana was still thinking about the events that had just occurred when Samantha spoke: "I've noticed something, Tatty."

"And what is that?"

"It just seems that you're …" Samantha's brow puckered as she thought of the right words. "You're somehow different from the other girls. You don't act like them or talk like them, and it's a good difference. What is it?"

Tatiana skipped a happy step. "It's because I'm a Christian."

The girl paused thoughtfully. "Well, aren't we all? We all attend the same church."

Tatiana picked up a pebble to cast into last year's tall, dry grass. "Going to church does no more to make you a Christian than going to Johanna's makes you an Easley." Her strong, confident words were earthshaking for Samantha, who had been taught all her life that going church and behaving well were the only steps needed for her salvation.

"I don't understand."

The eager young believer prayed silently for the right words. "It's not complicated, Sam. You've heard about Jesus dying on the cross since before you could walk. You know the story."

"Yes. Jesus died for our sins," Samantha recited, her brown eyes questioning.

"So did you repent of your sins and ask Jesus to take them away?"

"N-no ..." Samantha shook her head. "I thought repenting was just for sinners."

Tatiana raised her eyebrows. "And who do you think sinners are?"

Samantha shrugged. "Bad people who do terrible things, like murderers and thieves."

"I'm a sinner," Tatiana said frankly, her finger pointing at her own small chest.

Samantha gasped and moved away from Tatiana as if she feared contamination. "What did you <u>do</u>?"

"Everything," Tatiana replied. "I coveted other people's belongings, I was disrespectful to my parents, I lied, and I harbored hateful feelings toward my sisters. And worst of all, I failed to give God the proper love and re-spect that He deserves. I was selfish enough to love other things more than Him."

Samantha looked pale. "Well, I've done some of those things."

"See, Sam? You're a sinner as well."

"Oh, unholy day! Promise you won't tell my mother, Tatty!"

Tatiana smiled. "I promise."

Samantha covered her eyes in distress. "Well, what must I do?"

"You must repent of your sins and ask Jesus to wash your heart clean. Without Jesus our hearts are impossibly stained."

Tatiana suddenly pointed off to the left. "The old Tip-pin Mill! Just look at that place! That is what I envision my heart used to look like."

The Tippin Mill was a dilapidated structure that hadn't been used for nearly fifty years. It was engulfed by ivy and beginning to list to one side. It looked gloomy, crumbling, ethereal, and otherworldly. Many children whispered that the place was haunted; no one dared go near it.

"And then Jesus cleaned out all the dirt and cobwebs?" Samantha guessed.

Tatiana shook her head. "My heart was so rotten and decrepit that He gave me an entirely new one."

"What does it look like?"

Tatiana tilted her head back to look at the sky. "A tem-ple. It is a temple of shining, white marble. And inside it is an altar on which I must sacrifice myself at the begin-ning of every day." Samantha looked horrified. Tatiana continued blithely. "I must drag my selfish, greedy, willful desires—kicking and screaming, mind you—over to the altar and offer them up. It is only then that Christ can truly work through me; only then is my temple rightly pure."

Samantha blinked. "It sounds rather frightening."

"Frightening, yes. But it is so very beautiful at the same time. It is such a joy to proclaim that I am crucified with Christ! At first it seems like a difficult sacrifice, but it is nothing compared to what He suffered, and even less compared to the glory we will see in Heaven. What do you say, Samantha? Will you come to Him?"

A big tear ran down Samantha's round cheek and dropped from her chin. "Yes. I want Jesus to make my heart His temple. I've been unhappy for so many years and I never knew why. Can we pray right now?"

Tatiana closed her eyes, thanking the Lord for Samantha's willing spirit. "Yes. Now would be perfect." Tatty took the girl's hands as they stood in the road, tearfully pouring out their hearts before their Savior.

When Samantha had finished, Tatiana wrapped her up in a hearty embrace. "I-I feel different already," Samantha declared.

"Good!" Tatiana told her. "You're a new creation, Samantha. Jesus picks up our broken, sin-warped hearts and molds them into a temple fit for His Spirit to dwell in! Is He not altogether lovely?"

"He is wonderful!" Samantha declared. "And I shall never forget it."

Tatiana smiled. "God bless you, Samantha."

"And you, Tatty! Thank you!"

The girls parted at Samantha's house. Tatiana continued home with a light step and an even lighter heart. It wasn't until she was lying in her bed that night that she had a very sobering thought. Her hand stole up to touch the arrowhead that still hung around her neck. *What of*

Jonny Creek? You never did forgive him for spilling punch on you, and you never asked forgiveness for saying that you hated him all those years ago. What a hypocrite you are, Tatiana! You preach the power of repentance and forgiveness to Samantha Culbertson while you have unconfessed sins of your own that are fouling up your heart! Shining white marble indeed!

For about an hour Tatiana tossed and turned and didn't get a wink of sleep. *Tomorrow,* she told herself, *tomorrow I will talk to him.* Finally, the girl gave herself a shake. *Tatiana, you—you whited sepulcher! You can't keep putting things off until tomorrow because you never get them done!*

She kicked back her covers and stood in the middle of the dark room. *But it's so late! It's the middle of the night; you'll get in trouble if you go now!* Tatiana's mind made one more excuse, but she quashed it once and for all by hissing aloud: "Be quiet, you dastardly thing! Must you always try to ruin everything? I'm going, and that's that."

Tiptoeing so as not to wake her sisters, Tatiana pulled a dress on over her nightgown. She tugged on her boots without bothering to lace them and simply tucked her ties inside her shoes. She wrapped Rose's warm shawl about herself and slipped out of the house. It was drizzling lightly as she ran to the stable to get Jack. The horse snuffled curiously at her and whinnied softly. "Shhh! Not a peep, Jack!" Tatiana urged, stroking his nose, "I need you to be very quiet and obedient for me tonight."

Good old Jack was a carriage horse, not a saddle horse, but he would have to do. She didn't have a saddle, but she tied a blanket onto his back and climbed the planks on the wall to get high enough to mount. She was halfway on when Jack decided to move away from the wall. With a squeal, Tatiana slid down and clung wildly to his slippery side. She got a handful of Jack's dark mane and managed to haul herself up. "There!" she whispered, once she was safely astride. She nudged Jack toward the gate and leaned over to unlatch it.

Once out of the stable, Tatiana kept Jack at a slow walk as they left the yard, keeping him on the grass so his hooves wouldn't clack on any rocks. She paused after latching the garden gate just long enough to send a wistful look back at her bedroom window. Then with a kick of her high-heeled boots, Tatiana prodded Jack into a canter that carried them swiftly out of town.

By then, the light drizzle had turned into a full-fledged rainstorm that intensified until it had become a down-pour. Still, Tatiana rode without turning back. "Please, God," she prayed, "keep me and Jack safe and help us find Jonny's house." She prayed this over and over and over again until she had long since lost count. It all blurred to-gether into a time of wind and darkness and rain and the solid mass of horse that rose and fell beneath her.

Jonny awoke to the sound of rain hammering on the roof of the cabin. It was shaping up to be quite a storm! Well, we can use the rain, he thought sleepily. He won-dered if the Smiths had arrived safely in Shrewsbury be-fore the storm hit. Then he stretched out his long arms, arching his back and letting out a big, satisfied yawn. Now to get back to sleep!

The boy had just closed his eyes again when he heard a faint tapping sound. He stopped and listened carefully. *Is someone knocking at the door? Of course not! No one would be fool enough to be out on a night like this! ... But there it is again!*

Getting up, Jonny strode through the dark house and flung open the front door, just to convince himself that no one was knocking. He nearly jumped out of his skin when he saw a small, dark figure huddled on the porch.

He squinted. Why, it was Tatiana! He immediately slammed the door shut and ran to his room to pull trousers on over his nightshirt. Then he returned and opened the door again. The bedraggled girl was still there.

"Jonny," she whimpered, sounding pitiful enough to melt the heart of an ogre.

The boy put his hands on his hips. "Well, now, what do we have here?"

"Jonny!" The girl said his name through another sob, and Jonny realized that she was not at all in the mood for jokes.

"Come in and get warm, Tatty," he invited, standing aside. She took three steps in and stood, shivering and dripping and looking very pitiful indeed. Jonny hurried to get a towel for her and then crouched to add wood to the glowing bed of coals in the fireplace. "I'll see if I can find you something dry to wear in a minute," he told the drenched maiden.

"Jack's outside," Tatiana whispered. She mopped her face and wrapped her hair in the towel, feeling better without the wet strands dripping down her back.

"Don't worry. I'll see to him." Satisfied with the fire, Jonny jumped to his feet. He lit a lantern for himself and a candle for Tatiana. He headed out into the rainy night with his lantern lighting the way; it was so dark he was amazed that Tatiana hadn't gotten lost.

Tatiana crept closer to the fire. She took off her boots and stockings, set them on the hearth to dry, and then looked around. She was in a large room that was a combination of kitchen and parlor, with a door on each side as well as at the front and back of the room.

Jonny soon came back in with rain spotting his white shirt and shining in his black hair. He put a pot of water for coffee on a hook in the fireplace, to save lighting the kitchen stove. He took a lantern with him through the door on one side of the room. He soon returned without the lantern and gestured to the doorway. "I put one of Mrs. Smith's work dresses on the bed in there," he said. "If you need any other—er, articles of clothing you can look in the dresser."

Tatiana slipped into the bedroom and gratefully peeled off her soggy, mud-splattered layers. Rose wasn't going to be happy about the condition of her shawl. Tatiana dried herself with the towel and changed into Mrs. Smith's worn housedress. Once wearing the dress, she felt that she could once again think logically.

Looking at the feminine touches around the room, she realized this was the bedroom of Jonny's foster parents; she wondered where they were. She finger-combed her damp hair and bundled her wet clothes into the towel. *Time to get on with asking forgiveness.*

As soon as she stepped out, Jonny took the wet clothes and candle from her, pressed a steaming mug of coffee into her numb hands, and offered her a seat by the fire. He hung her damp clothes on a wooden clothing rack and then sat down next to her. "Are you feeling better?" he asked.

"Yes, very much," Tatiana told him. She was overwhelmed by his kindness and hardly knew how to respond.

Then Jonny noticed her bare feet and rushed to find stockings for her. He settled in the chair across from her and propped his foot on his knee. "May I ask what you are doing all the way out here in the middle of the night?"

Tatiana took a sip of her coffee. "I came because I needed to apologize to you."

"To me?"

"Yes, to you. I never told you how sorry I was for arguing with you in the tree when the wolves had chased us."

"In the tree!" Jonny cried. "But that was years ago! And we've had fights since then."

"I know, Jonny, I'm getting to those. I'm also sorry for telling you I hated you, because that wasn't at all true. I don't hate you."

"Good to know."

"And I'm sorry for the time I yelled at you for pulling my hair."

"I don't even remember that..."

"And I'm sorry for being so angry at you when the punch spilled on me at the Christmas Ball..."

"That was more my fault than yours," Jonny blurted. "I'm the one who made you fall over. You had a right to be angry about that."

"Hush, Jonny, it's still my turn to confess."

Jonny smiled. "It's all right, Thelma, you don't need to confess every cross word you've ever said to me. That's all in the past."

"But if I don't confess them, how can you forgive me for them?"

Jonny reached over and took her hand. "Tatiana, I forgive you for all the wrongs you've done me and I'm sorry for all the things I've done to you. Will you forgive me?"

"Yes," Tatiana said softly, blinking in amazement. Could it really be as easy as that? One brief sentence and all past wrongs were redeemed? Yes, of course! Jesus had done the same! In one night He had paid the price for all the sins of the world! Tatiana put her hand to her mouth to hide her vast grin. Forgiveness was such a magnificent thing!

The two sat quietly for a while, and Tatiana glanced around the snug cabin. "Where is your family?"

"They went to Shrewsbury to visit Mrs. Smith's sister. They took little James too."

"And left you all alone?"

"I asked to stay," Jonny said, getting up to tend the fire. "I don't mind being alone. Besides, I've got Beauty to take care of. And you now," he added with a chuckle.

Tatiana scowled. "Just what is so funny?"

"I still can scarcely believe you came out here at night, in a storm, to apologize to me. You could have done it tomorrow!"

"That's what I kept telling myself, but I never got it done. What if you died tonight and I never had a chance to ask your forgiveness?"

"Well, I hope I don't die tonight."

"And I hope so even more," Tatiana replied, for she worried about Jonny's soul. The boy fell silent. Tatiana surveyed him as he crouched there by the fire. Johanna had mentioned that he was growing up, but Tatiana had not noticed it until now. Jonny had indeed changed. He was fifteen now and he was more of a man than a boy. *When did his shoulders become so wide?* Tatiana wondered, *and when did his face become so strong and defined?*

And it wasn't just a physical change; Tatiana noticed that Jonny carried himself with newly acquired dignity and strength. He wasn't the same foolish lad she had known. The girl slid lower in her chair. Here Jonny was, all grown up and sounding so wise, and she was still just Tatty. He had become a man, while she was still a silly little girl.

Tatiana had always enjoyed being the baby of the family and had never been in any hurry to grow up. Now,

though, as she watched the firelight flicker on Jonny's in-
telligent features, she had a sudden longing to become a
woman. She wanted to be a woman who could captivate
the young man kneeling at the hearth—for he was unwit-
tingly captivating her.

When Tatiana finished her coffee, she rose from her
chair. "Well, I had best be going," she announced. "Thank
you for your hospitality."

Jonny leapt to his feet. "Oh, certainly not! Tatty, I can't
let you venture back out into that storm! I can think of a
thousand horrible things that could happen to you out
there, and you'll catch pneumonia at the very least. You're
lucky you didn't get hurt on the way."

Tatiana shook her head. "No, I must go. Father will be
worried sick if I'm not home by morning." She suddenly
remembered her promise to him that she wouldn't run
off again. *Oh, no,* she thought, *now I'll have to ask him for
forgiveness as well.* She had felt such an urgency to make
amends with Jonny that she hadn't considered the possi-
bility that her absence would be discovered before she
could get home.

"Tatiana, I insist."

"But I can't!"

"You can."

"No, really, Jonny..."

"What of poor Jack?"

"He'll be all right."

"What of yourself, Tatty? You'll suffer more than that
old horse! Have you forgotten already how chilled you
were just a few minutes ago? You still look pale. Your father would not want you to become ill or be hit by a falling tree limb. Wait until daylight."

Tatiana huffed and went to the door. Jonny walked
over and leaned against it. Tatiana lifted the latch and

pulled with all her might. She glared up angrily at her af-
fable obstruction. Smiling at her, he said, "Pull all you
want, Thelma. There's no punch bowl to fly into."

Tatiana gave a furious cry and stamped her foot.
"Jonny, you beast! You can't keep me here!"

"Au contraire, mademoiselle! I can stand here all night
if need be."

"You rogue!"

"You realize I'm only looking out for your safety. Your
father trusts me to take care of you; I don't want to disappoint him."

"Devious villain!"

"Such names! Will you be asking my forgiveness in a
moment?"

Tatiana, too angry to listen to reason at this point—or
even to hear what he said—countered: "Rapscallion!"

"Shall I make a warm pallet for you by the fire?"

"Impudent scoundrel!"

"I'll take that as a *yes*," Jonny concluded, taking Tatiana's arm and firmly leading her back over to the fire.
Tatiana was thoroughly ruffled and frustrated at her lack
of leverage against this new, muscular version of Jonny.
She sat dejectedly and watched while he prepared a cozy
little bed for her.

"See, now doesn't this look nice?" he coaxed, as one
would with a small child. "You can sleep here where it's
warm, and I can take you into town first thing tomorrow
morning."

Tatiana folded her arms and refused to speak to him.

Jonny rose and lifted the oil lamp from the table.
"Sleep well, princess." *Princess?* Jonny thought. *Why did I
say that? Maybe because she's acting as spoiled as a little princess.* On his way back to his room, Jonny paused once to

look back at Tatiana. Angry or not, she looked unquestionably adorable. She hadn't grown rapidly the way he had, but she was a little taller and more graceful. Jonny always marveled at how dainty Tatiana was, like a fairy. *Like a troublesome little angel! And I'm nothing but a great, clumsy oaf!*

As soon as Jonny had retreated to his room, Tatiana sprang to her feet with an insolent toss of her head. Who does he think he was, keeping her here against her will? For a moment, the old, bad Tatiana stamped around the room, trying to think how to get back at Jonny. She considered jamming a chair under his door, but dismissed that idea—it wouldn't stop *him* for long. She knew if she tried to leave, he could be out his bedroom window and to the stable before she could reach her horse. Besides, riding through the storm had been miserable. Then she remembered she was here at Jonny's because she had felt compelled to ask his forgiveness before it was too late. She didn't want to have to worry about that again; it was bad enough that she had called him names when he was just trying to keep her safe and that she had broken her promise to her father. She swallowed hard. How difficult it was to keep a clean conscience. Tatiana went over to her warm pallet on the floor and was soon sound asleep.

She woke to Jonny's voice in her ear, telling her to wake up. For a moment she felt disoriented, and then she remembered her late-night ride. She blinked until her eyes focused and saw Jonny gazing down at her with an amused look on his face. With a squeal she jerked her blanket up over her head to hide her messy hair.

"Thelma, you silly duck! What are you doing?" Jonny laughed.

"Go away."

"Put the blanket down."

"No."

Jonny rolled his eyes. "How about you make us some breakfast?"

Tatiana lowered the blanket until her eyes showed. "You said we would leave first thing in the morning."

"So I did, but you can't ride on an empty stomach." He looked sternly into the blue eyes that peeped over the edge of the flannel blanket. "I'm going to saddle the horses," he informed her. "It's finally stopped raining, and it will be dawn soon. There should be some biscuits in the larder," he added. He rose from his crouch and loped to the door.

Tatiana stood up and shook her head to wake herself up. She felt sore and exhausted from her cold ride and short sleep. She ran her fingers quickly through her hair and smoothed it over her shoulder. Her own clothes were mostly dry, so she changed and then investigated the larder. She set out ham, cold biscuits, and apple butter. By the time Jonny returned, she had sliced the ham and was setting out plates and silverware. He had meant for them to take a biscuit to eat as they rode, but it was still early, so he didn't stop her.

He had never noticed it before, but Tatiana's movements had a particular rhythm to them. As she put slices of ham on their plates, split the biscuits, and added apple butter, it was almost as if she were listening to some unheard tune and all her actions were part of a dance. Jonny was so enthralled by this that he very well could have watched her all day, but the simple meal was ready. Besides, he had promised to get her home early. He was proud that he had gotten up an hour before dawn after having his sleep interrupted.

As the two sat down to eat, Tatiana asked, "Will you pray, or shall I?"

Jonny looked at the floor. "You go ahead."

Tatiana prayed with all the zeal and fervor a thirteen-year-old girl can possess. Most of her prayer was exclusively focused on Jonny and the perilous state of his soul. When she finally uttered 'Amen,' Jonny sat staring at his food in silence. He had been deeply moved by her words … and frightened as well. He finally picked up his stuffed biscuit and bit into it thoughtfully.

They rode back to town as the sun rose in the east. Jonny convinced Tatiana that their horses should race. The two youths urged their mounts to go faster, galloping down the wagon track that ran alongside the Smiths' fields. Beauty won easily. After Jonny gloated, Tatiana complained that it wasn't fair to race a yearling against a tired old horse like Jack.

The two of them were laughing and breathless when they met Hans Bergman on the road at the edge of town. He was riding a borrowed horse and searching for his roving young daughter long before Tatiana had expected him to discover her absence. The disappointed look on the man's face was enough to wipe every smile from Tatiana's. "Tatiana!" he cried.

The girl reined Jack in and half tumbled off her horse in her haste to get to her father. Hans dismounted as well and pulled his youngest close to him for a moment. Then he pushed her back far enough to look her in the eye. "You've done it again, child. You can't just run off whenever you have an urge to. You are getting too old for these shenanigans, and I am getting too old to withstand them."

Hans's dark eyes observed Tatiana gravely. "You are a young lady now, Tatty, and it's time you acted like one. There will be no school for you today. You will stay home and work as a punishment."

"Yes, sir," she said, her face flushing red from the shame of being reprimanded in front of Jonny. A rebuke from her father was never pleasant, but to have Jonny hear it! Oh, that was a hundred times worse! She hung her head as her father nodded to the boy. "Jonny, thank you for keeping her safe."

Jonny gave Hans a polite nod and touched the brim of his cap. Then, without a word, the boy gave Beauty a touch with his heels and rode off. Chastened and humbled, Tatiana allowed her father to boost her up onto Jack and turned the animal toward home.

CHAPTER EIGHT

Friend or Foe

The spring had certainly come in as a lion, but now, a few weeks later, it was displaying its lamb-like disposition. The day was fair and warm. Tatiana drank in the sweet, clear air like nectar, taking great, greedy breaths as if she could catch every playful breeze in her lungs. The trees all along the lane were exploding with new growth. The tiny new leaves were a vibrant green, and as they fluttered in the wind they seemed to whisper their own peculiar praises to the Lord. It was all so miraculously breathtaking that Tatiana began to skip along and sing as she went.

The girl was returning from a visit with Johanna Easley. She had been surprised that Johanna had invited her, and even more surprised when she learned the occasion. Now she could scarcely wait to arrive home and tell her sisters her exciting news.

Tatiana breezed through the gate, spun around three times in the yard just for the pure joy of it, and then went dizzily careening inside. "Gretchie!" she cried, whipping her shawl from her shoulders. "Rosie-Posie! You'll never guess what I'm going to do!"

She dashed into the kitchen and halted in her tracks to see the unexpected guest. "Why, Samantha! What are you doing..." Her words were cut off as she suddenly groaned. "Oh, no, I completely forgot about Bible Study, Sam! I'm ever so sorry! Did you wait long?"

"About half an hour," Samantha answered good-naturedly. "I was beginning to doubt you would come at all. But I had Gretchen to talk to for most of that time, so it wasn't an unpleasant wait."

The back door squeaked and Gretchen came in with a basket of laundry on her hip. When she saw Tatiana, an exasperated look crossed her face. "Well, I see Her Royal Highness has decided to grace us with her presence! What a lovely hostess you make, Tatty, skipping off and completely neglecting your guest." Gretchen set the basket down with a thump and pushed some stray hairs back with her wrist. "Could you not at least inform me when you're plan to race off on one of your frivolous excursions to who knows where? Or do you think yourself too important for such trifles?"

Tatiana was about to answer when a child's crying floated from the upper floor. "Ach, James!" Gretchen pumped water into the sink to wash her hands. "He didn't nap for long."

"James?"

Gretchen shot Tatiana a peeved look. "Yes, James. I'm watching him for Mrs. Smith today and tomorrow so she can help Mr. Smith and Jonny with the planting. If you had been here this morning you could have helped me with him." Gretchen shook the water from her hands and dried them on her apron. Just before heading upstairs, she leaned close to Tatiana, her normally soft gray eyes flashing fire. "And I suggest you sincerely apologize to Samantha for your inexcusable behavior!" Gretchen hissed. She gave a gentle slap to Tatiana's cheek to emphasize her words, but Tatiana flinched as though she had been struck a hard blow.

"Come, Samantha!" she said, taking her friend's arm. "Let's go out in the yard for our Bible study. I see no reason to linger indoors with such cantankerous company." Then a smile came to her face as she remembered her news, and she leaned over to whisper in Samantha's ear. "Besides, I have something to tell you."

The girls sat under a stately old lilac bush. With her face alight, Tatiana clasped Samantha's hands and announced: "Johanna has invited me to do a poetry recitation with her! Mrs. Easley is holding an exquisite tea party for all the ladies of the town, and Johanna and I will be performing in front of all of them!"

Samantha smiled kindly. "How thrilling! Have you decided on a piece yet?"

"Well, I didn't have one in mind really, but Johanna suggested *The Destruction of Sennacherib* by Lord Byron. I read it and think it's absolutely perfect! The words are so powerful, and there are just enough stanzas to be divided evenly."

"Divided?"

"Yes. We're doing it together since Johanna didn't want so much to memorize. I will do the first two stanzas, Johanna will do the next three, and then I will finish. Oh, I can hardly wait to practice it! Johanna says she will have me over again later this week for practice. It sounds like such fun!" Tatiana took sudden notice of Samantha's expression. "What's wrong? You look as if you were standing before a crypt with such a face!"

Samantha shook her head, her rich brown curls swaying. "I have a terrible feeling about it, Tat. Johanna doesn't share the limelight with anyone, and I can't help but suspect that she's planning something against you."

Tatiana laughed at the ridiculousness of Samantha's warning. "I spent the morning with her. She was all smiles and compliments. I've seen Johanna's bad side, and this wasn't it. I think she's finally accepted my friendship and wants to do something to deepen it."

Samantha's deep brown eyes were full of gravity. "I know Johanna. I've known her since we were still in diapers, and even then she wouldn't share her toys. She's craftier than a serpent, Tatty. If you want to recite a poem, find one on your own and perform solo. You have the talent as well as the confidence to pull it off, but don't team up with Johanna."

Thoroughly offended, Tatiana jumped to her feet. "You know what I think, Samantha? I think you're resentful that Johanna prefers me to you! I think you're full of nothing but green-eyed jealousy!"

Samantha raised an innocent face toward her accuser. "I've been burned by Johanna countless times, and I can promise you that I'm not jealous." She licked her pink lips nervously. "But I know of someone who is."

"Who?"

Samantha patted the grass beside her and Tatiana obediently sat. Her brunette companion reached over and played with one of the gathers on Tatiana's skirt. "Johanna is very envious of you."

"Of me?" Tatiana cried incredulously. "Why on earth would she envy me? Johanna has both of her parents still alive and she lives in the finest house in town! Why, Johanna has everything she could ever want!"

Samantha smiled wisely. "Not everything. You have what Johanna desires the very most."

"Oh, balderdash! What is that?"

"Jonny Creek."

"Jonny! Pffft! Samantha, I don't have him! We are good friends, and that's all."

"Are you sure that's all?" Samantha persisted.

Tatiana lifted her chin haughtily. "Yes, Samantha. If Johanna wants to have that stubborn boy, I'll gladly give him to her. I'd even bedeck him in holly and put an apple in his mouth if she'd find that more attractive."

Samantha snorted. "I think she finds him plenty attractive as he is!" The girls giggled and Samantha shook her head. "The girl doesn't know what to do with herself. She's always gotten anything she set her heart on, until now."

Tatiana stretched. "Well, Jonny's not a toy that she can ask her parents to buy."

"Right. Truthfully, she would be in deep trouble if she so much as mentioned him to her parents!" Samantha's chocolaty brown eyes sparkled. "I find it dreadfully funny that Johanna used to call Jonny a 'savage half-breed' and now she's hopelessly in love with him. It's better than Shakespeare!"

"How, again, did she justify it?" Tatiana questioned.

"Well, to me she said: 'Someday, my child, you will look into a similar pair of dark eyes and have your heart instantly stolen away!'"

Tatiana laughed. "What nonsense! Dark eyes! Jonny doesn't even have dark eyes! They're golden."

Samantha grinned mischievously. "She's probably never held his gaze long enough to find out!" Both of the girls fell mirthfully back on the grass and had a nice long round of giggling, healing their earlier discord.

When they finally had to stop for a breath, Samantha reached out and took Tatiana's hand. "I just do hope you'll be careful around Johanna. Keep your guard up and don't let her do anything sly."

"I will, Sam." Tatiana sighed, resting her head on Samantha's shoulder and enjoying the coolness of the grass. "I'll blink one eye at a time around her, if need be. But don't you worry your pretty head about it."

Samantha sighed into Tatiana's silky hair. "One can only try."

"My!" Gretchen's voice carried gruffly across the yard, startling both girls. "I see you're quite busy studying out there!"

Tatiana and Samantha exchanged comradely glances and reached for their Bibles.

"I am thankful for what I have," Tatiana told herself in a lecturing tone. "I'm happy with my place in life and I am perfectly content!" She said these words as she rounded the stone wall that encircled the Easley property, and then sighed at the difficulty of being content while her eyes swept the Easley estate.

To Tatiana, Johanna was a princess in a castle. Tatiana liked to imagine herself in Johanna's shoes. Every time she visited the Easley home, she drank in the luxury of her surroundings and imagined herself as a wealthy young heiress. Tatiana was not overly extravagant and normally felt comfortable, even fortunate, with her situation in life. It was only when she got a potent taste of what she did not have that a materialistic hunger rose inside of her and her contentedness transformed into covetousness.

Miriam, the quiet, middle-aged maid, answered Tatiana's knock. Miriam took pleasure in the girl's simple, artless sincerity. "Good morning, Miss Tatiana! Come to visit Johanna, have you?"

"Good morning, Miss Miriam!" Tatiana replied with charming naiveté. "I certainly have. Will you let her know I'm here?"

"Gladly, miss," Miriam responded, curtsying graciously. Tatiana curtsied back, and the maid pursed her lips to hide her smile.

Johanna soon flounced into the entryway and greeted Tatiana. Her words were as sweet as honey, but she retained a haughty air about her. "Let's go and practice in my private chambers," she suggested, taking Tatiana's arm. "Miriam, please bring up some refreshments for us in a little while."

The maid curtsied again as her eyebrows rose in response to Johanna's tone. She was accustomed to Johanna putting on airs in front of her guests, but it never ceased to annoy her.

The girls went upstairs to Johanna's rooms—the cosseted child had two, a spacious sleeping room with an even larger sitting room adjoining it. They settled into red plush chairs in front of the sitting room fireplace.

Tatiana's wide blue eyes took in the gilt-framed paintings that featured idyllic, pastoral scenes. The lamps on the walls were made with fine glass and fastened in intricate holders. A thick Persian rug in blue, green, and rose cushioned the oak floorboards. Johanna's collection of china dolls covered an entire shelf in a cabinet and bested the selection at Weller's General Store. "Oh, Johanna," Tatiana said yearningly. "You live a life I've only dreamed of. You must feel like the most fortunate girl in the world!"

Johanna cast a lazy eye about her. She seemed to consider the chintz curtains, rich wallpaper, and fine furniture with scorn. "There are others that are richer."

"Don't you consider this to be an uncommon amount of wealth?" Tatiana persisted. "How could you want for more?"

"If you were rich, you would understand," Johanna said dismissively. "It is never enough. There is always something else to be had. Father is never content, and I'm afraid I take after him in that respect." As Johanna toyed with the necklace that hung around her neck, Tatiana asked about it curiously.

"It's made with an amethyst, my birth stone. Father gave it to me on my last birthday."

"It's beautiful!" Tatiana breathed. "How wonderful to have something like that as your very own! No one's ever given me a necklace before." Then Tatiana remembered Jonny's gift. She recalled the look in his golden eyes as he had handed it to her and realized how dear he was to her. Her hand stole to her chest and she could feel the arrowhead through the thin fabric of her dress.

"Well, we should practice," Johanna suggested, pulling out a sheet of paper. She handed it to Tatiana.

The girl looked over the poem and sighed. "These words! Lord Byron could work magic with his pen, that's for certain. Each line is so rich that I think I could almost taste it!"

"You're quite a poet yourself, Tatty," Johanna teased. "Why don't we begin by reading our parts? You may start." Both heads were soon bent over the page.

❖❖❖

"Hold my hand, Rose! I'm so nervous I think I'll be sick!"

"I pray it isn't catching," Rose sighed, taking her sister's damp fingers. "You know your parts backwards and forwards, Tatiana. And with your natural flair for drama, I'm sure your performance will be spectacular. Stop fretting so!"

Tatiana pulled out her handkerchief and mopped her brow. "I can't help it! I've never stood before an audience before. I just know I'll make some terrible blunder and ruin the entire evening!" The carriage jolted to a stop at the Easley gate. Tatiana moaned. "Oh, and here we are already! I tell you, Rose, I shall be amazed if I survive the afternoon!"

"I shall rejoice when it is over," Gretchen muttered. "I have heard more than my share of this nonsense. I think the poem would be more aptly named *The Destruction of Tatiana.*"

"Oh, Gretchie, don't be smart," Tatiana scolded, groping for the handle on the carriage door and nearly tumbling out. "This means a lot to me."

The three sisters trooped into the Easley mansion and threaded their way through the swarm of laughing, chattering women. Tea tables circled with padded chairs were arranged in the Great Hall, and the Bergman girls were soon seated at one. Gretchen and Rose conversed pleasantly with the two other women at their table, but Tatiana could only stare miserably at the platform at the end of the room that had been erected for the afternoon's entertainment.

Once all guests had arrived, the first performance began, with several townspeople taking a turn on the stage. A mother and daughter played a violin duet, another woman played the harp, and then Arietta sang a beautiful rendition of *'Flow Gently, Sweet Afton.'* Mrs. Easley then took the stage.

After applauding Arietta a little longer, she announced, "And now, to finish off the afternoon's excellent entertainment, Miss Tatiana Bergman will be reciting a poem for us!" She stretched out her hand to beckon Tatiana forward.

Why didn't she mention Johanna? Tatiana wondered as she got to her feet. She went up to the stage with leaden steps. Her feet felt like they might fail her at any moment, but somehow she managed to climb to the stage. Mrs. Easley flashed Tatiana a bright smile and touched her arm as she walked past. Then Tatiana was left standing alone, with all eyes on her.

As for Tatiana, she was desperately scanning the crowd for Johanna. Then she saw her friend. She was seated comfortably with Kitty and Arietta. Tatiana looked directly into Johanna's eyes with an expression of pleading confusion. A tiny smile curved cruelly across Johanna's face, and Tatiana saw the glint of triumph in the girl's eyes.

It was then that Tatiana realized Johanna's intentions. She felt her face burn as she realized that Johanna's only goal had been to shame her. Johanna did not love her, did not care for her, and did not want to be her friend. Remembering Samantha's kindhearted warning, she recognized her own foolishness. She had been so gullible! Blinded by Johanna's wealth, Tatiana had carelessly opened herself up to pain. Johanna, trampling on Tatiana's innocent admiration and trust, had purposefully tried to disgrace her! The flagrant rejection settled like a heavy stone in Tatiana's chest.

All this flashed through Tatiana's mind in a matter of seconds before reality intruded. She was still standing in the middle of the stage before half of the town. They were expecting something of her. Opening her mouth, Tatiana spoke. At first her words came out in a little croak, but she soon recovered her voice and spoke the first word of Lord Byron's poem about the attempted siege of Jerusalem:

"The Assyrian came down like the wolf on the fold,
And his cohorts were gleaming with purple and gold;
And the sheen of their spears was like stars on the sea,
When the blue wave rolls nightly on deep Galilee."

Tatiana recited another stanza and then paused. The next three stanzas had been Johanna's verses to recite. Lifting her chin, Tatiana continued, for she had memorized the entire poem. Her face bore a look of complete devastation, but her audience attributed this to her superb theatrics. As she spoke, Tatiana kept her eyes solidly fixed on Johanna, letting her betrayer see her heartbreak.

"For the Angel of Death spread his wings on the blast,
And breathed in the face of the foe as he passed;
And the eyes of the sleepers waxed deadly and chill,
And their hearts but once heaved, and for ever grew still!"

Through the entire poem, Tatiana held her audience spellbound. She poured herself into the words, voicing the horror and the wonder of the unearthly massacre that Byron had depicted. By the last stanza, audience members had edged forward on their seats with eagerness. Tatiana didn't disappoint them.

"And the widows of Ashur are loud in their wail,
And the idols are broke in the temple of Baal;
And the might of the Gentile, unsmote by the sword..."

The young exhibitionist lowered her voice to a reverent whisper,

"Hath melted like snow in the glance of the Lord!"

Ducking her head, Tatiana bowed slightly to signal the end of the piece. Thundering applause rippled through the Great Hall. Tatiana curtsied prettily and then stepped gratefully down from the stage.

As she walked back to her table amidst the ovation, her gaze flitted once more to Johanna. The girl that Tatiana had thought was her friend sneered at her. Tatiana had escaped embarrassment and had come through the fire shining like silver, but the shiver that danced up her spine told her that she would have to be more careful next time.

CHAPTER NINE

Raising and Falling

I can sense it, Gretchie," Tatiana declared, tucking her arm through her sister's as the carriage lurched through a large dip in the road. "Today is the day. Some dark, handsome stranger will come to the barn raising and be so overcome by you that he will propose within the evening!"

Hans was swaying along in mirthful silence on the driver's seat. Usually, if he kept quiet enough, his daughters almost completely forgot about his presence and would carry on all kinds of humorous, sisterly conversations. For Hans, it was a highlight of being their father.

Gretchen laughed shortly. "Tatty, you silly thing! You know I've given up on marriage, nineteen years of age and only one time courting! I am happily doomed to spinsterhood."

"I suppose I shall join you," Rose sighed.

"Nonsense!" Gretchen cried. "You're as precious as a jewel. Someday a good, wise man will look past all those silly girls, see what a beauty you are, and fall deeply in love with you."

Tatiana, gazing dramatically heavenward, announced: "And I shall become a nun."

After a moment of surprised silence, her sisters burst out laughing. "Tatiana, you goose!" Gretchen chortled. "Whatever gave you the thought?"

"And we're not even Catholic!" Rose pointed out practically.

"I think it would be wonderfully romantic to be a nun," Tatiana continued, "excepting for the Catholic part. Just think, Gretchie, how wonderful it would be to dedicate your life entirely to the service of God and give your love to no other. Wouldn't it be blissful to be able to declare: 'My Maker is mine husband'?"

Gretchen said 'humph' in a way that said she wasn't impressed. "That's probably all I'll ever be able to say."

Tatiana tugged Gretchen's elbow. "Oh, don't act like it's a punishment, Gretchie! I think it should be an unimaginable honor!"

Gretchen sighed and stroked her little sister's hair. "It is doubtful that you will ever have that honor. You probably will be married before either of us. You've already got half the boys in town pursuing you!"

"I do not!"

"You practically do," Gretchen insisted, "and you're only fourteen!"

"Yes, and I still look like a little girl," Tatiana pouted.

Gretchen squeezed Tatiana's hand. "Your time will come, Tatty. You won't be thinking about it, and one day, all of a sudden, you'll be so beautiful that all the young men in town won't be able to stop looking at you."

"And they'll drive their buggies straight into the ditch!" Rose finished cheerily.

"All right, you three!" Mr. Bergman called, "What do you say we pick up this young gentleman?" The carriage slowed as Mr. Bergman reined Jack in. Jonny Creek was walking beside the road. Hans offered him a ride. Jonny declined and Hans questioned: "You are going to the Weston barn raising, aren't you?"

"Yes, sir," Jonny replied. "I left Beauty at the smithy for new shoes. But I think I'll keep walking. It's not much farther, and I enjoy the exercise. But thank you for offering, sir." Jonny touched the brim of his cap and nodded toward the three girls. "Good morning. I'll see you ladies there."

"Oh, Father, can I walk with him?" Tatiana asked quickly, before Hans could flick the reins again. "Is that all right with you, Jonny?"

The boy nodded. Mr. Bergman eyed him. He normally would not allow his daughters to walk with a boy, but Jonny was different. Hans felt a kinship with the lad and trusted him so much that he had no trouble granting his permission. Tatiana happily scrambled down from the carriage with a helping hand from Jonny. Gretchen and Rose exchanged glances. "She's never going to become a nun!" Gretchen whispered. Rose giggled her agreement.

Hans clicked his tongue and flicked the reins; the carriage wheels turned and Tatiana watched it move forward as she began to walk with Jonny. Jonny wore a smudged pair of buckskin trousers with black suspenders, a faded blue shirt, and a wide-brimmed felt hat. He carried a broad ax over his shoulder.

Beside him, Tatiana bloomed like a flower in a soft lavender dress adorned with frothy white trim. She had a basket of dinner rolls on her arm, and her head was covered with a straw bonnet that was decorated with freshly picked violets.

As Jonny shortened his stride so she could keep up, he asked, "Is there a reason you wanted to walk with me?"

"Other than wanting to spend time with my dear friend, there is not," Tatiana replied. "Though I did want to show you something." She waved her hand at Jonny. "Look away, please! It's in my garter."

"Oh, bosh!" Jonny sighed, looking off toward a field of corn ready for harvest. "I dislike you putting on these airs, Thelma."

"They're not airs, Jonny. I'm trying to behave like a lady."

Jonny scowled at the corn. "Well, if behaving like a lady means that you simper into your handkerchief and stare at a man's shoes when he talks to you, like Johanna and her bunch, I'd rather you not become one at all!"

"Well, I'll try not to be like that. But you must admit that I can't remain a little girl for all my life. You've changed, Jonny. Why can't I?" She tapped his shoulder. "You may look now."

He quickly faced her. "How have I changed?"

Tatiana smiled sagely. "You're a man now, Jonny. You're a man who occasionally slides back into being a little boy again. And I'm just a little girl who is desperately trying to be a lady."

An earnest look crossed Jonny's face. "You've always been a lady, Tat. Even as a young girl when you were chasing me across the commons, you were like a spurned little princess. I've never thought of you as anything **but** a lady." Tatiana fell silent because she was choking up. Jonny, not realizing the effect his words had had on her, asked, "What were you going to show me?"

"Oh, it's something I found." Tatiana sniffed loudly and held up a small gold necklace that was inset with an amethyst. "Beautiful, isn't it?"

"I should say so!" Jonny reached out to study the jewelry more closely. "I wonder whose it is."

"Oh, I know whose it is," Tatiana said. "It's Johanna's. I'm returning it to her at the barn raising."

"Why don't you just keep it, Thelma? The Lord knows she's treated you poorly enough all year."

"Because that would be stealing."

"Not if you just found it lying on the ground."

"But I know it belongs to her. Therefore, to take it would be theft."

Jonny sighed and fingered the handle of his ax. "Well, Tat, you're a better person than I am. I would probably keep it just for spite."

"She thinks a lot of you, you know," Tatiana pointed out.

Jonny lowered his head. "Hmm, I know it." He looked uncomfortable and squinted up at the sky. "Perfect weather for a barn raising, don't you think?"

The conversation turned to lighter talk, and the two friends had soon arrived. Most of the volunteers had arrived first thing in the morning and had begun trimming and squaring logs and putting together sections of framework. Mr. Bergman usually worked all Saturday morning, but had taken off at mid-morning that day. Jonny had risen early to work for pay before arriving to help the Weston family.

Jonny began trimming more logs while Tatiana watched him, but he was soon called over to help raise and join the first big sections of wall. Soon men stood high in the air on the wide beams, outlined against the blue sky. Even at forty feet above ground, they moved about confidently, talking and laughing as if they were on a stroll down Main Street.

Tatiana finally headed for the Weston house with the basket of rolls cradled in her arms. The kitchen was crowded with women busily preparing the meal. They shooed her back out as soon as she dropped off the basket of rolls. Johanna didn't seem to be among the crush of women.

Heading back outdoors, Tatiana spotted Johanna talking with Kitty and Arietta under a maple tree. Taking a deep breath, Tatiana crossed the lawn. The girls had been talking in low tones and they stopped when she drew near and looked at her guardedly. Clearing her throat, Tatiana spoke kindly and clearly: "Hello, girls! Johanna, could I speak with you for a moment?"

"I'd like to speak with you as well, Tatiana Bergman," Johanna said coolly. "Shall we take a turn around the garden?" The girl nodded toward the well-tended Weston garden that was at this moment scattered with bright orange pumpkins and squash.

"Let's," Tatiana agreed, falling into step beside Johanna. She pushed her straw bonnet back from her face.

"Are you fifteen now, Tatiana?" Johanna asked abruptly.

"Not yet, no."

Johanna nodded. "I had forgotten that you were almost a year younger than me. I'm surprised that your father considers you old enough."

"Old enough for what?"

"To court, obviously."

"To court! I'm sure he wouldn't!"

"Then however could he be so blind to the matter?"

"What matter?"

Johanna frowned. "Let's not play games, Tatty. I saw you and Jonny Creek arrive together."

Tatiana felt flustered. "Yes, but we were only walking together. It didn't mean anything."

"Didn't mean anything! Rubbish! I know what you're trying to do, Tatiana Bergman! You claim that you and

Jonny are only friends, but you are blatantly stealing him from me. You know how I feel about him, and you decided that the best way to hurt me was to claim him!"

Tatiana's face grew hot. She stumbled on the uneven ground. "That's not at all true! I don't—"

"This is because of that silly poem, isn't it?" Johanna exclaimed bitterly. "Oh, you're a sly one, Tat. I know you think of this as the perfect revenge, but I won't stand for it. Jonny and I were destined for each other, and I will **not** go down without a fight."

"I'm not going to fight you, Johanna," Tatiana said as steadily as she could. "Jonny has the freedom to love whomever he chooses, and I will not attempt to sway his decision in any way."

Johanna's eyes shone in triumph. "Is that so? Is that a promise, Tatty? I won't promise any such thing. I will try to sway him every way I know how. Is that still all right with you?"

Tatiana swallowed, "It pains me, but I can do nothing to stop you." Tatiana was shaking with suppressed anger. The chain of Johanna's necklace was biting into her palm. She longed to slip it back into her garter and keep it, just for spite. It would serve Johanna right to never see her necklace again! *You can't do that, Tatiana. That would be wrong. Jesus was treated unfairly, but He didn't cave in to sin, so neither must you! Use your self-control and pull yourself together. Go on, give her the necklace!*

Raising her head, Tatiana stiffly extended her arm. "Johanna, the reason I ... I needed to ... I—I found this."

Johanna gasped and lifted her necklace from Tatiana's open hand. "I thought it was gone forever!" She suddenly glared at Tatiana. "You stole this, didn't you?"

Tatiana was taken aback for the second time in the span of a few minutes. "No! How could you even think that? I found it outside the schoolhouse."

"Liar! You always loved this necklace. You picked it up when I wasn't looking."

"Then why would I return it to you?" Tatiana questioned. "Why must you always assume the worst in me, Johanna? I am not out to steal your necklace or your loved one. All I ever wanted was to be your friend!" A tear slid down Tatiana's face. "What do you have against me?"

"More than I have time to explain at the moment," Johanna replied haughtily, fastening the necklace about her neck. Then the proud girl sashayed off. Tatiana gulped back sobs.

The house door slammed. Samantha came out carrying a pitcher of ginger water for the men. "Tatiana!" she called when she spotted her friend. "What are you doing back here?" As Tatiana approached her friend, Samantha frowned, "Why, you're awfully pale! Are you feeling all right?"

"As well as someone can feel when they've been despised and rejected," Tatiana moaned.

Samantha sympathetically touched her friend's shoulder. "I'll have to hear it all later. I hope the rest of your day takes a turn for the better."

Tatiana nodded soberly and turned toward the house. "I'll go get some cups."

The women began bringing the food outside and setting it on a long table in the yard. Tatiana organized the serving dishes on the table. Feeling warm from her labors and from steam rising from the hot food, she undid her bonnet ties. Only moments later her bonnet was swept from her head. Whirling around, she came face to face with Daniel Weston.

The grinning young man was standing in a playful pose, her bonnet held high out of her reach. His dusty cotton shirt and sandy hair were damp with sweat, as was the hat dangling from his other hand. His forest green eyes were sparkling with glee; his teasing smile made cute dimples appear in his cheeks. Although he was undeniably handsome, Tatiana had never quite trusted Daniel.

"Give me back my bonnet, Mr. Weston."

"Mr. Weston is my father's name, Tatiana. To you, I'm just Daniel."

Tatiana wasn't in the best of moods to begin with, and Daniel wasn't improving things. "I don't see how you can say what you are to me, sir. Now will you please return my bonnet?"

Daniel leaned against the table and crossed his ankles. "Well, let's see ... I suppose I might be convinced to, for a small fee."

"That is my bonnet, Mr. Weston. I don't owe you anything."

"Oh, I assure you, miss, that it won't be a difficult price. It will only cost you a bit of your time." Daniel gave her his most dashing smile, the one that caused most girls to blush. "My only request is that you reserve me a dance tonight in the new barn."

"I will not offer favors in return for what is rightfully mine!" Tatiana cried adamantly. She made a sudden grab for her bonnet. Daniel swept it away from her, laughing.

"Just say 'yes' and it's yours!" He chuckled. "Is dancing such a chore?"

Tatiana's eyes flashed. "Yes, if it's with a ruffian such as you!" She reached again for her bonnet.

Daniel remained undaunted. "What a fiery little vixen you are! I daresay, if you weren't so young I would—"

The boy stopped talking abruptly as Hans, who had come up behind him, sank a strong hand onto the back of Daniel's neck. "Do tell, Daniel! What would you do? Give her bonnet back." Daniel shakily handed it to Tatiana. Then Hans gave the young man a hard shove that nearly sent him to the ground. "I'd better not catch you heckling my daughter ever again or I'll take the strap to you myself. And if you don't apologize, I'll be telling your father and he'll be sure to whip some sense into you as well."

"I'm sorry, Mr. Bergman."

"To her, boy, not me," Hans growled.

"I-I'm sorry, Tatiana," Daniel stammered. "I sure didn't mean anything. It won't happen again." The lad clapped his hat onto his head and fled.

Father and daughter exchanged meaningful glances. "Thank you," Tatiana whispered.

Hans touched Tatiana's smooth chin. "Be careful, my little dove." He stooped to pick up a coil of rope.

Tatiana touched his sleeve. "We'll serve the meal soon; you could just wait."

"No, I won't stand idly by. Five or ten minutes of work now will finish the job that much sooner." He strode back toward the partly completed barn.

Tatiana looked down at her bonnet. The violets tucked into the brim were wilted and crushed. Tatiana threw them onto the ground, pulled her bonnet back on, and knotted the ties tightly under her chin. She returned to the house for more food. She was carrying a pan of baked ham toward the table when she heard a shout from the barn.

"Hans!"

She looked just in time to see her father falling from the roof of the barn and slamming into the ground. "Daddy!" she screamed. The dish crashed to the ground.

Tatiana tripped on her skirts as she dashed to her father's side, arriving before anyone else. Hans Bergman lay still. His eyes were closed. Tatiana's heart thudded with fear. She snatched his warm hand and held it against her cheek. "Oh, Daddy!" she wept, "Oh, God, please let him live!"

Tatiana shut the bedroom door softly behind her and descended the stairs to the kitchen. A cloud seemed to have settled over the Bergman house. The girls went quietly about their work without their usual singing and chattering.

Gretchen looked up from chopping apples for sauce. "Is Father still resting?"

"Without a stir," Tatiana replied. "It has me worried. He's been mostly asleep for three days now! And when he does wake up, he seems hardly conscious of his surroundings. Will he always be like that?"

Gretchen brushed some hairs from her forehead with the back of her arm. "I'm sure he won't. The more rest he gets, the faster he will heal. And if his backbone is fractured, like the doctor said, it is better if he stays perfectly still."

Tatiana settled on a stool near the fire and wrapped her arms around her knees. "I was just sitting there watching him sleep, and he looked like a dead man. I had to feel his chest to make sure his heart was still beating! It frightened me so much, Gretchen, I had to leave the room. I can't imagine what I would do without Father."

"Neither can I." Gretchen worked silently for a while. Her face showed her fatigue. The dark circles under her eyes and the weary slump of her shoulders testified to the fact that Hans's injury was wearing on her.

Gretchen tossed more apples into the kettle on the stove and handed the spoon to Tatiana. "Here, stir this." She stabbed another apple from the bushel basket. "Father won't be able to return to work for quite some time. We'll have to find a way to cope without his paycheck for several months. I haven't been getting very much sewing business lately, and Rose doesn't get a very substantial salary for working part-time at Weller's either."

Tatiana stirred thoughtfully, staring at the apple mush in the kettle. "I need to find a job!"

Gretchen's knife slipped. "Tatiana, that's not what I meant at all! You need to go to school. You're a smart girl, Tatty. I don't want you dropping out early like Rose and I did."

"I can read, Gretchen. If I need to learn something, I can find a book about it. I wonder if Reverend Matthew would pay me to clean the church ..."

"All I know is that Robert already does it for free," Gretchen noted. "But really, Tatty, I don't want to see you sacrifice your education. I'll find a way to make enough money to get us through until Father is recovered."

"I just ..." Tatiana bit her lip. "I feel such a sense of duty—of obligation. I'm going for a walk, Gretchie. I need to pray." She gave the apples a vigorous stir and set down the spoon.

Tatiana threw on a shawl and headed out. "Dear God ..." she began to pray. She suddenly stopped as she noticed the Jersey cow that was grazing just outside the fence. She marched over to the animal and grabbed the frayed rope that hung around her neck. "Whose are you, hmm, boss?" Tatiana petted the cow's smooth nose. "You're certainly very tame." She ran her hand down the bumps in the bovine's back and then a thought came to her mind. "I'll wager you belong to Reverend Matthew! He's mentioned owning a Jersey. Come along, pet!"

Tugging her captive along, Tatiana started toward the Reverend's house, praying as she walked. "Dear God, I'm so worried about Father. Please heal him. Help everything that's broken inside of him to knit back together. Give him strength, Lord. And help Rose and Gretchen ... and help me, God. We don't really have anyone to take care of us right now, and we need your provision. Show me how I can find a way to make money for our family. I want so badly to help, but I don't know what to do."

Tatiana prayed in this manner for the entire walk to the parsonage. She alternated between talking to God and talking to the cow. The Jersey had very large, understanding eyes; Tatiana found comfort in telling the creature her troubles. The cow lifted her big ears and seemed to be carefully listening while knowingly chewing her cud.

Robert Matthew was whitewashing the front yard fence when Tatiana arrived. He jumped up when he saw her coming and wiped his hands on a rag. "Good morning, Tatiana! I see you found Agnes. She's a sly one. I didn't even notice that she had escaped."

"Agnes, hmm?" Tatiana said, giving the cow a friendly slap. "She's a good listener."

"I apologize for the trouble she caused," Robert said, suddenly looking shy.

"It was no trouble. I was going for a walk anyway, and she was pleasant company."

Robert smiled, which made his face look very mature. Jonny hadn't been the only one growing. Robert was looking more adult as well. "How is your father?"

"Not well, I'm afraid." Tatiana sighed. "He has been sleeping constantly. The doctor reported that he might have some internal injuries. He has a broken leg, several cracked ribs, and maybe even a fractured backbone."

"Oh. That's worse than I had expected." Robert looked at the ground for a moment and then raised his eyes. "Is there anything I can do to help your family? I would be willing to offer my services until your father is well enough to return to work."

Tatiana was touched by his generosity. She was tempted to accept! Robert was exactly what they needed. But no, Gretchen would never take charity from anyone. Then another idea came to her mind: "Actually, Robert, I was wondering if you know of anywhere I could find work?"

"You?" He was taken off guard. "You're quitting school?"

Tatiana lifted her chin. "I am considering it. I know your father has lots of connections. I thought he might know of someone who would hire me."

"I can ask him," Robert said, stroking Agnes' head. "I'm sure he would be happy to recommend you to someone."

Tatiana let out a long breath. "Thank you."

Robert was still looking at her with his calm, green eyes. They were almost the same color as Daniel Weston's, but somehow Robert's were gentle and kind. Robert's paint-splattered fingers fiddled uneasily with the knife that hung from his belt. "I ... just wanted to tell you that I think you're very brave. God go with you, Tatty." He extended his hand as if to shake hers, but at the last moment he instead reached and tucked a strand of her hair behind her ear.

Tatiana shivered and stepped back. No one except her family had ever touched her in such an intimate way. Robert's own face bore such an expression of surprise and confusion that Tatiana suspected that his action had startled even himself. Tatiana felt a peculiar flutter in her chest. It was like a mixture of happiness and pain. "Goodbye," she whispered, slipping away.

She walked quickly toward home, blinking back tears. The strangest thing was that she didn't even know why she was crying. "Oh, Abba Father!" she wailed, looking up at the gray sky. "Why does life have to be so difficult and confusing? I think I would give anything to be a little girl again! I'm not ready to grow up." She wiped her nose on her sleeve. "I used to think I had all the answers. And now, with all these emotions and feelings, I don't even understand myself anymore!" She shook her head as more tears ran down her face. Closing her eyes, she prayed: "Be my Rock, Lord."

CHAPTER TEN

Leaving Home

The train rocked and rattled. Tatiana rested her head against the window and watched the green Pennsylvania hills rolling by. It made her heart sick to think that every turn of the train wheels was carrying her farther from home.

Tatiana was looking particularly grown up today, wearing one of Rose's dresses. Dark pink chrysanthemums stood out against a gold background. The stylish dress had puffed sleeves, a tapered bodice, and a full skirt with a wide ruffle at the hem. Over the dress, Tatiana wore a tweed jacket with the same rose and gold colors of the dress.

Rose had insisted that Tatiana take the outfit, claiming, "It will look better on you. I haven't the coloring for it." For the first time ever, Tatiana's hair was pinned up. Gretchen had helped her comb her black locks into an attractive upsweep and fixed it into a thick twist on the back of her head. To top it all off, Tatiana planned to wear Gretchen's finest hat, but for now, it rested on the seat beside her because she felt silly wearing it.

The only downside to Tatiana's mature appearance was the unwanted attention it was attracting. She had already escaped from two overly zealous dandies that morning. A young gentleman sat across from her now, but she made a point of not looking at him. She was busily repeating her last conversation with Reverend Matthew in her mind.

"The Lord must have brought you to our house yesterday, child!" the Reverend had proclaimed. Tatiana had smiled, thinking of Agnes. Perhaps it was true: there was no reason that God couldn't use a Jersey cow. *"I have a friend who is in a dire situation at this very moment!"* he continued. *"Ananias Wolfe has just recently lost his dear wife and is left with two very young children. One is about three years of age and the other is an infant. He lives in Philadelphia and is a good Christian man."*

"A penny for your thoughts."

The man's voice jerked Tatiana from her reverie. The young gentleman leaned forward in his seat, studying her. "Pardon my interruption, miss, but you look so grave. Are you always so burdened?"

Tatiana sighed and fingered the brim of Gretchen's hat. "No, I am not. At the moment I have some very heavy matters pressing upon me."

"Heavy matters! Tsk, tsk!" the young man said. "You look much too young to have to worry about such things. How old are you?"

Tatiana, who knew a prying question when she heard one, shifted her eyes back to the train window. "Old enough to leave home but young enough to hate doing it." She glanced at the man again. Clean-shaven with neatly combed hair, he wore a cream-colored cravat and a stylish suit coat that was cut short in the front. "Are you a college student?" she asked.

"I am," he replied, pleased with her guess. "I'm studying to be a doctor at the university in Philadelphia."

"Oh." Tatiana looked at him through misty eyes. "There's probably no help for me though."

Her comment was unexpected. "For you? What do you have?"

"A broken heart."

The gentleman politely held back his amusement. "No, I'm afraid time is the only remedy for that, miss. Are you leaving behind a spurned lover?"

Tatiana raised an aristocratic eyebrow. "Only my dear family and all my friends."

"Well, now you can say you have met a new one." The young man held out his hand.

Tatiana refused to take it and put on a haughty look. "I don't call someone a friend when they are merely a nameless passenger who happens to be sitting across from me in a train car!"

"Then I should make sure that I am no longer nameless," the young man replied, with a bow of his head. "Charles Culbertson, at your service."

"Culbertson!" Tatiana exclaimed, "Would you happen to know a Samantha Culbertson?"

"Would I? She's my cousin!"

"And my dearest friend," Tatiana finished. Her weak tolerance of this man changed instantly into a bond—a loose bond, of course, but at this moment Charles was the only security Tatiana had. She began to pepper him with questions. They passed the time in pleasant conversation, and it wasn't until the train was pulling into the station that Tatiana remembered what she faced. She stiffened her spine, pulled her two bags from under the seat, and put on Gretchen's hat. She clasped the bags nervously.

"You're white as an All Hallows Day ghost, Miss Bergman." Charles observed. "Will you be all right?"

Tatiana licked her lips and rose to her feet. "Yes... yes, I'll be fine."

"Allow me to carry one of your bags," Charles ushered Tatiana off of the train and onto the bustling platform. "Do you know who's coming to meet you?" he questioned.

"I would assume Reverend Wolfe or else a member of his household."

"Well, perhaps I'll wait with you until someone arrives for you," Charles said, pulling out a pipe.

"Oh, you needn't trouble yourself," Tatiana told him. "I'll just wait until some of this traffic clears and see if I can spot him."

"It's really no trouble," he informed her. "I wouldn't think of leaving you here. It's getting late."

"Mr. Culbertson, please. I appreciate your chivalry, but I need to learn independence at some point. I might as well start now."

Charles seemed to understand. He bid her a polite farewell, saying that he hoped they would meet again. As he disappeared into the crowd, Tatiana held back her rising anxiety. She had a strong urge to call him to her, but she bit back the words. She told herself that once the crowd dwindled, she would be able to spot Reverend Wolfe easily.

A few minutes later, the crush had eased, but Tatiana was still waiting. She eyed the remaining people, trying to discern which one of them might be her new employer. She felt a gentle touch to her elbow and jumped. Standing silently beside her was a tall, gangly man in plain, dark clothes. "Are you Mr. Ananias Wolfe?" Tatiana cried eagerly.

The man hesitated and then nodded. He stooped and picked up both of Tatiana's bags and headed toward a nearby carriage. Tatiana hurried along at his heel, prattling of her relief in finding him. "I was beginning to worry no one would ever come for me! I've never really been away from home before, you see." She climbed into the carriage beside her new employer. The man clucked at the cream-colored horse, which then moved forward. "I hope I get accustomed to living in Philadelphia. Just from what I've seen so far it looks frightfully big! I think I'll miss all the trees and the open skies the most. I'd never even been on a train before today," she continued, "and if it wasn't for Charles, I would have felt so much worse about it."

Her driver had yet to utter a word. Tatiana looked at him curiously. He was younger than she had expected, but his weary eyes and pinched face kept him from looking youthful. His brown eyes were close together and his teeth were crooked. He had a jagged scar beside his eye, making her think he had suffered a powerful blow there. His rough appearance signaled a hard life. Tatiana wondered what he had done before the ministry called him.

His hands on the reins were calloused and peeling. Tatiana tucked her own soft hands under her skirt. "Well, sir, I am so very sorry about the loss of your wife. It must have been horribly tragic, losing someone you loved so dearly. I, of course, have never lost a spouse, but my mother was carried away to Heaven when I was young. It is a terrible experience."

The man said nothing. Not even a 'thank you' or a 'yes, it certainly is' escaped his lips! Tatiana was rather disgruntled by this, but she tried again. "What are the names of your two children, Reverend Wolfe?"

The man looked at her, but then his sorrowful brown eyes reverted back to the road and he did not reply. Instead he flicked the horse with the small carriage whip, urging it on faster.

Tatiana broke out into a cold sweat. "Sir," she said in a frightened bleat, "have I done something to offend you? Please let me know if I've done anything that might bring you displeasure. I would be satisfied with even the most minimal of answers."

Her silent companion blinked slowly but said nothing. Convinced that she was being shunned for some unknown misdemeanor, Tatiana slid lower on the carriage seat and inwardly prayed for the Lord's guidance.

They wound their way through long cobblestone streets flanked by tall buildings. The echoing clip-clop of the horse's hooves sounded like a death knoll to Tatiana. Each new street they turned into appeared to be darker than the one before because the fog kept getting thicker. Shadowy people peeped out as they rolled by. Laundry dangled in ghostly rows from clotheslines strung between buildings. A dog barked at their carriage wheels. Tatiana could hear the chug of factory machines somewhere in the distance.

They came finally to an area where the houses were bigger and farther apart. The carriage rolled to a stop in front of an imposing two-story house surrounded by a high wrought-iron fence. Her driver sat looking expectantly at Tatiana until she nervously rose from her seat. She reached for her bags, but the man grunted and shook his head. Actually, that small, guttural sound comforted Tatiana ever so slightly. It was the first vocalization she had heard since embarking on this carriage.

Leaving her bags, she climbed fearfully down to the street. She walked over to the gate, lifted the latch, and listened to a mournful groan as she opened the portal. She looked over her shoulder at her driver. He gave her a quick nod and then drove the carriage down a small lane on the far side of the house. Shivering, Tatiana made her way through the barren yard to the front door. She stood looking at the big brass knocker that looked like the head of a roaring lion. Then she lifted the handle and tapped three times.

She waited, listening for footsteps within, but heard nothing. After a bit she knocked again. She waited anxiously, bouncing nervously on her cold toes. "Oh, Father," she whispered. "What am I to do? I need you to help me, Lord. Help me not to fear."

The door opened. Tatiana flinched in surprise. Her silent driver stood there, somewhat out of breath. Her bags were at his feet. She stepped inside; he shut the door after her. The house's wide foyer was even gloomier than outdoors. A single oil lamp on the table lit the space; heavy drapes covered the windows. The table and a hat rack were the only furnishings in the foyer, but several doors broke up the space. The most remarkable feature of the room was its double staircase. One flight curved along the left side of the room and the other flight mirrored it on the right. It was impressive, but at this moment it only served to intimidate Tatiana even more. This house felt nothing like home, and the air itself seemed to carry an inhospitable chill.

The man picked up Tatiana's bags and started up the left wing of stairs. Tatiana had no choice but to follow him. He went down the hallway at the top and knocked on a door. "Come in!" a voice barked. The man opened the door and motioned Tatiana inside.

She stepped in timidly. The room appeared to be an office. A broad-shouldered man sitting at a desk was bent over a stack of papers, writing furiously. A fire was dying in the nearby hearth. The man finished a sentence, emphatically punctuating it with a stab of his nib, and looked up. He noticed Tatiana, whipped off his spectacles, and stared at her. "Miss Bergman?"

He hadn't spoken very loudly, but his voice still seemed to fill the room, a deep, hollow sound that lacked even a hint of joviality.

The man rose to his feet and seemed to tower over her. Physically, he appeared to be in his early thirties, but a mature, commanding air made him seem older. He was well built and robust looking; his expansive chest filled his black coat quite nicely. He had thick brown hair and a broad, strong face that would be handsome if it were less dour.

She somehow managed a half-hearted curtsy. "Yes, sir, I'm Tatiana Bergman. And you are?"

Her question seemed to offend the man. "Who am I? I'm your new employer, Miss Bergman. Ananias Wolfe."

Tatiana frowned. "Then ... then who was the man who brought me here?"

"Malchus Hemmings. My servant."

"Why did he claim to be you?"

"Would you have gone with him if he hadn't?"

"If he had explained who he was, I would have!" Tatiana declared, reaching the end of her patience. After holding back her frustrations the entire way home, she could contain herself no longer. "I've never met someone **so** rude as to refuse to speak even one word of courtesy to a young girl who is away from home for the first time ever! I was frightened and alone, and he wouldn't so much as answer my questions! I was very much insulted by this cavalier treatment! Why would you keep such a man?"

Ananias Wolfe's green eyes glittered. "Miss Bergman, Malchus Hemmings is mute. No matter how much he wanted to answer your questions, he was unable to."

Everything suddenly became clear to Tatiana. She cried out in horror, "Then I have terribly wronged him by my words to you!"

Reverend Wolfe waved his letter in the air to dry the ink. "Then I suppose an apology is in order." He folded the paper and slid it into an envelope. "My children are currently staying with my sister but she will be bringing them here tomorrow morning. Aside from caring for them you will also be in charge of cooking the meals, cleaning the house, doing all the laundering, and attending to any other domestic needs that should arise. Do you understand?"

The man looked at Tatiana expectantly. She exclaimed, "I wish I didn't! Reverend Matthew said you were seeking a nursemaid for your children, but you're apparently expecting much more than that. Why didn't you just advertise for a wife?"

The man raised his eyebrows and scribbled the address on his letter. "Simply because one cannot very well advertise for a wife, now can he?"

"Such deception!" Tatiana raged. "I didn't expect to face such blatant trickery from someone who claims to be a minister of the Gospel!"

"Claims to be!" Ananias Wolfe straightened from his desk so violently that Tatiana took a step back. "You have a sharp tongue and a wild spirit, Miss Bergman. But I trust that under my instruction your tongue will soon be controlled and your spirit will be tamed. I will forgive your disrespectful comments this once, seeing as you have had a long, tiring day of travel. But hereafter, you will address me with the deference that is befitting to a man of my station, or else you will suffer the consequences."

He studied her for a minute. "Furthermore, I expect you to wear something other than that outfit or any similar clothing during the time that you are here. I won't see anyone in this household parading such frippery. Must I remind you, Miss Bergman, that this is a house of mourning? I will have Malchus leave a few of my wife's dresses outside your door."

Tatiana clutched her flowered skirt in disbelief. "But I—"

"Your room is in the hall to the right of the stairs, third door on the right." Reverend Wolfe informed her, sitting once again at his desk. "Have a good night, Miss Bergman."

Tatiana did not trust her 'sharp tongue' to give Reverend Wolfe a civil reply, so she held it as she left the room. She forced herself to close the door softly, though she would have loved to give it a sound slamming. She followed Reverend Wolfe's directions and had soon found her dark little room. Hurrying inside, she flung herself upon the high bed and burst into tears.

Knock! Knock! Knock! Tatiana sat up and looked around in confusion. She had sobbed herself to sleep in her sprawled position across the bed. She was still in her clothes and still wearing her shoes. She felt so tired! She lit a candle; with a glance at the tall clock that had scary dragons molded into its edging, she saw that it was only five in the morning. Who would be disturbing her so early? Staggering to her feet, she tried to smooth her tousled hair. She went to her door and opened it just as wide as the width of a single eyeball, and peeped out.

Malchus was standing there with several drab, black dresses over his arm.

"Malchus," she said softly. "Do you have need of something?"

He handed her a note and she quickly read the scrawled handwriting: *Breakfast is served at 6 o' clock sharp.*

Realization set in. "Ah! And I suppose I am expected to fix breakfast? Am I?"

Malchus nodded.

"Is that so?" Tatiana was not at all happy with this arrangement. Malchus handed her the dresses and she took them grouchily. "Well, now. I'll fix breakfast, all right." She retreated to her room and shut the door behind her. "And I wish I could fix that Reverend Wolfe while I'm at it!"

Then, just as it always did, Tatiana's faithful conscience interceded and scolded her for her harsh words. *What was I thinking? Reverend Wolfe is my employer and, for the time being, my authority. Who am I to disrespect him? And Malchus! Oh, I forgot to apologize! Blast!*

She struggled into one of Mrs. Wolfe's old dresses. The dark fabric seemed to drain every tint of color from Tatiana's face; her fair complexion held a deathly pallor. She glanced in the mirror and shook her head. "Mercy! This dress could make even a healthy person look ill." She braided her dark tresses and wrapped them about her head like a halo. Then she ventured downstairs to find the kitchen.

It was a fine kitchen. It was not as cozy as the kitchen at home, but Tatiana assumed this was only because it lacked the warm presence of her dear sisters. She started poking about in the pantry and the kitchen door banged. Malchus strode in with his arms laden with firewood. Then he bent over the cold hearth and worked to kindle a flame.

Tatiana brought out a bowl of eggs and the end of a ham. She located the flour bin and began to mix up a batch of rolls. She kept glancing at Malchus's thin back as he knelt over the fire. His worn, dusty coat hung loosely on him and the fabric was torn at the shoulder, showing a white shirt underneath. Once the fire was going, the young man rose and headed for the door.

"Malchus," Tatiana said quickly before the opportunity was lost. "May I talk to you for a moment?"

The man looked uncomfortable. His brown eyes darted about in his homely face, making him look like a stray mongrel. He pointed toward the door.

"Yes, I understand that you must go, but it will only take a moment."

The servant started edging away.

Tatiana walked briskly over to him. "Wait, Malchus. You can't go out yet, see? Your coat has a tear." The man twisted his neck, trying to see, and Tatiana continued. "It's cold and rainy outside, and if you go out with a torn coat, you're bound to get consumption, or something of the like. Sit down, and I'll mend your coat."

Malchus eyed her for a moment, then removed his coat and handed it to her. He sat obediently on a stool and watched her sullenly. Tatiana fished in her pocket for needle and thread and got to work on the coat.

"I want to apologize to you, Malchus. I was angry last night because you wouldn't answer my questions. I didn't know you couldn't speak, and I was frightened and didn't act like myself. And, I confess, I feel so ashamed of my awful behavior! I spoke badly about you to Reverend

Wolfe until he explained. You seem to be a fine young man. Will you forgive me for wronging you?"

Malchus raised his shaggy head and looked at Tatiana with surprise. No one had ever asked him this before; truthfully, no one ever really bothered to ask him much of anything, and he wasn't sure how to respond. So he gave no response at all.

Tatiana felt disappointed. Her fragile soul was constantly awash with driving, compassionate emotions. To meet someone who was so stoic and impassive was extremely vexing to Tatiana.

She quickly mended Malchus's coat; the servant took it and left the room. Tatiana finished preparing breakfast and carried it out to the dining room. She, Reverend Wolfe, and Malchus were the only ones at the table. They ate in silence. Tatiana was still too angry at Reverend Wolfe to initiate any conversation with him. Reverend Wolfe preferred to eat without speaking. And Malchus was, of course, unable to contribute anything to the conversation.

All that could be heard was the scrape of silverware on plates, the ticking of the grandfather clock, and the sounds of chewing. Reverend Wolfe ate voraciously with lots of lip smacking. Malchus ate almost as quietly as he did everything else, with an occasional cough. Tatiana chewed timidly, making less noise than a caterpillar munching leaves.

Reverend Wolfe finished his food and laid down his spoon. "Tatiana."

The girl looked up expectantly, eager to hear what he had thought of her first meal.

"Have you never heard the passage in Timothy that clearly says: '... women adorn themselves in modest apparel, with shamefacedness and sobriety; not with broidered hair, or gold, or pearls, or costly array ...'?"

Tatiana blinked. "Yes, I have heard it. But I don't understand why ..." She glanced down at herself. "I am wearing your wife's clothing, may she rest in peace. There is nothing immodest about it!"

"I speak of your broidered hair, child," the minister boomed, his face turbulent. "What do you mean by braiding it in such a fashion? Why must you flaunt yourself so? Who are you trying to impress, hmm? Is it Malchus? He is a loyal, godly servant, Miss Bergman. He will not fall prey to your wiles."

Tatiana gripped the edge of the table. "Reverend Wolfe, I am not flaunting myself. And I am much too busy to even think of pursuing Malchus. Now, please excuse me."

Tatiana rose to clear away the dishes. Reverend Wolfe barked, "I did not give you permission to leave the table, Miss Bergman."

The girl sat down with a thump. "May I leave the table, Reverend Wolfe?"

The man sat for a while without reply, studying a portrait on the wall. The clock ticked and Tatiana dug her fingernails into the seat of her chair. Malchus stared down at his plate. Finally, Reverend Wolfe yawned. "All right, you may both be excused."

Tatiana gathered up as many dishes as she could carry. Once back in the kitchen she set them down with a clatter and angrily undid her offensive braids. She shook her hair out with a toss of her head and leaned despondently against the kitchen table. "Oh, God, help me," she prayed.

While she entreated her Lord, Malchus quietly brought in the rest of the dishes, poured hot water and soap into the dry sink, and rolled up his sleeves.

A few hours later, Reverend Wolfe's younger sister arrived. She was a slim, auburn-haired young woman who had an elegant, oval face and a noble, aquiline nose. She looked so much different than her older brother that Tatiana never would have guessed them to be siblings. The woman introduced herself as Sarah Wolfe.

Sarah shifted the infant she held in her arms. "Of course you're eager to meet the children. This little one is Naomi. And this little shaver..." she turned to look down at the little boy who clutched her skirt, "is Tobias. But we call him Toby most of the time." She held out baby Naomi. "Would you like to hold her?"

Tatiana had held pitifully few babies in her life. She took the infant with bated breath. What a tiny, delicate creature she was! Tatiana relished Naomi's slight weight in her arms. The girl studied the child closely, taking in the dark lashes that lay on her chubby pink cheeks. Her skin was like velvet and her perfectly formed fingers were a testimony to her Creator's handiwork.

Sarah took off her coat and pulled a jar from her pocket. "I've been feeding her goat's milk since it tends to be easier on the stomach than cow's milk. I can bring you fresh jars every Lord's Day. I'll warm some up now for her." She headed for the kitchen with Tobias trailing behind her.

Tatiana looked down at the baby once again. "Oh, Naomi! Did you know you're a treasure straight from Heaven? I promise I'll take good care of you."

When Sarah returned with Naomi's bottle, the two women sat in the parlor and talked. Tobias drowsed on his aunt's lap.

"How did Malchus Hemmings come to work for your brother?" Tatiana asked Sarah.

Sarah stroked Tobias's light brown hair. "Ah, I'm sure Malchus does have quite a story. I've only heard bits and pieces, but the boy had a terrible childhood. He was born into a very poor family, and he was terribly mistreated because of his inability to speak. My brother was very generous to the young man in hiring him. I must say, the two of them have a very special bond."

Sarah sighed, her earnest face sad. "Still, I pity the boy. He has never known true love. He was born into adversity and was suckled on hate. By the mercy of God he has found refuge here. I pray that somehow he has escaped the snare of bitterness."

"Is he a Christian?"

Sarah shook her head. "I do not know. He is a good boy. Yet, so much of his life lies in secret; I haven't an inkling of the state of his soul."

"Well," Tatiana resolved, "I shall make an effort to show him every kindness I can manage."

Sarah's face grew solemn. "I know your intent is good, but beware of my brother. He could find fault in even the holiest of saints. Promise me you will be careful."

Tatiana looked into the woman's serious gray eyes. "I promise."

CHAPTER ELEVEN

Faithful Service

It didn't take Tatiana long to fall in love with her adorable young charges. Naomi was the first to steal her
heart with her cloudy blue eyes and her sweet breath, and
Tobias didn't take long either. The three-year-old was the
epitome of cuteness, with brown puppy-dog eyes and
silky soft hair. The little boy was startlingly well behaved
and hardly ever caused the least bit of trouble. Tatiana put
up with all the other trials of the job, just to have the
pleasure of caring for the two children.

Tatiana dipped a comb into a basin of water with a
little splash and ran it through Toby's fine hair. The boy
scrunched his shoulders up as the water dripped onto his
ears and neck. "It's cold!"

"Oh, I know it's a bit chilly, Toby, but can you be a
brave boy for Tatty? I want you to look handsome for
when we go to church."

"Church?"

"Yes, we're all going to church this morning. Do you
like church?"

The boy frowned and swished his fingers in the water.
"No. I wanna stay home."

"Well, you have to come," Tatiana said matter-of-factly, planting a kiss on Toby's damp forehead. "I enjoy going to church."

"I don't like church. Daddy yells too much."

"He yells? That's silly, Toby."

The boy shook his head. "He does!"

Tatiana knelt to button the boy's vest and straighten his shirt collar.

"Good morning!" Reverend Wolfe's rolling bass made Tatiana jump. The reverend leaned against the door-frame of Tobias's room and calmly fastened the top button of his dark coat. "I've been meaning to ask, Miss Bergman: how are my children behaving for you?"

Tatiana brushed water droplets from her skirt. "Oh, very well, thank you! Naomi is a little angel, and Toby is a very obedient, mild-mannered child. I must say, sir, that your wife must have been an excellent mother."

For the first time since Tatiana's arrival, Reverend Wolfe expressed something akin to pleasure at her words. "Yes," he replied, his lips hinting at a smile. "She was indeed."

Tatiana looked up at him in wonder. How his face changed when it bore an agreeable expression! It softened all the lines in his forehead and around his eyes and mouth and made him look years younger. Why, he even seemed somewhat handsome!

However, Reverend Wolfe's smile only lasted for a moment. Then his frown returned. It was the expression that he was most familiar with and he resorted to it naturally. "Did you braid your hair before pinning it up, Miss Bergman?" He asked, glaring down at her.

"No, sir," she answered honestly, bowing her head to reveal the knot on top. "I twisted it up as simply as I know how."

"Hmm, very well. Come down as soon as you are ready."

Tatiana generally loved church, but this Sunday she found it nearly unbearable. She sat on the hard pew beside Malchus, holding Naomi on her lap and listening with trepidation. Normally she found the Sabbath day refreshing to her body and soul, but today, listening to Ananias Wolfe's strident voice raging over his congregation, she only felt like he was stirring up a tempest inside of her.

She now understood the meaning of Tobias's words "Daddy yells too much." She wholeheartedly agreed with him. She had come seeking to worship the Lord, and she felt that the Reverend Wolfe's harsh bellowing was drowning out the Holy Spirit's presence. The minister was preaching fire and brimstone—explaining the torment of unsaved sinners with poorly masked delight. Tatiana sank lower in her seat and wished his sermon would end.

She thought about his sermon all week. She could only wonder if he had been moved by God to preach it. She was curious to see what his next sermon would be. The next Sunday rolled around; Tatiana sat miserably as he preached basically the same thing: the downfall of the unrighteous.

On the carriage ride home, Reverend Wolfe asked Tatiana what she thought of his preaching.

Tatiana held her breath for a moment. What was there to say? Did she dare tell him the truth? She cleared her throat. "I find it rather hard to listen to."

Reverend Wolfe chuckled. "Convicting, is it?"

"Perhaps to some," Tatiana allowed. "I find that I leave the church with a heavier heart than when I came in. You speak a rather despairing message."

His face became cold; his green eyes narrowed. "It is a message that must be told."

"And I agree with that, sir! But, once it is told, mustn't you continue on to the good news? After describing the depravity of man and the horrors of Hell, must you not proclaim Christ's redeeming plan of salvation? You explain the problem, and leave out the remedy. You speak of the disease, and forget the cure. We are all doomed without our Great Physician, and yet you leave your flock in constant fear and despair!"

"The fear of the Lord is the beginning of wisdom," Ananias Wolfe quoted.

"But perfect love casteth out fear," Tatiana replied. "Conviction of sin is futile unless it is followed by repentance and justification. We serve a just, righteous God, but He is also a God of love. He is a God of compassion—a God who laid His life down for sinners. He is a God who is faithful and just in forgiving us of our sins and cleansing us from all unrighteousness. He is a God who clothes us in garments of praise and anoints us with the oil of joy! He is a God whose mercy is new every morning. Will you deprive your flock from ever seeing His innate goodness?" Tatiana raised her pleading eyes to Reverend Wolfe's face. His expression was one of devastation, and his hands were shaking. Apparently he had never been told anything like this before.

"I will think about what you said, Miss Bergman," he said in a tremulous voice. After that he remained silent for the rest of the trip home. Tatiana wondered if he truly would do as he said.

❖❖❖

Weeks slipped by and Tatiana found contentment in her work. It also gave her satisfaction to be able to send her paychecks home to her family, knowing it was helping her father and sisters. One day well into November, Tatiana heard a knock at the door. She wiped her hands, lifted Naomi from her blanket on the floor, and hurried to the foyer. Opening the door, she looked up into a familiar face.

The young man swept off his cap and bowed smartly. "Miss Bergman."

"Jonny!" Tatiana shrieked, giving him an awkward hug as she held the baby on her hip. Her excitement overwhelmed her manners as she clung to her childhood friend. "Oh, Jonny, it's so good to see you! Oh, just let me smell you for a moment!"

"Smell me?"

"Yes. You smell just like home. It's been so long since I've breathed fresh country air or smelled the dusty scent of dry hay. Oh, it's heavenly!" She stepped back and noticed she had left a white mark on his suit coat. "Oh, I'm sorry about the flour," she said, brushing it away. "I'm fairly well coated in it. I'm making apple dumplings today. But come in, Jonny! What brings you here?" She caught his arm, gazing up into his brown face.

Jonny stepped inside and glanced curiously about the wide foyer. "Mr. and Mrs. Smith brought James into town to see a special doctor about his lungs. They're afraid he has tuberculosis."

"How awful! I pray it's not that."

"Yes." Jonny turned his cap in his hands. He seemed to have grown even taller since Tatiana had last seen him. "Anyway, I just thought I'd stop in and see how you were doing. Has all been well for you here? You're dressed as if you're headed to a funeral."

"Only by decree of Reverend Wolfe," she answered, kissing Naomi's soft, dark hair. "I adore the children, but their father is a complete bear at times. I sometimes wonder why Reverend Matthew ever recommended him to me if he knew what sort of man Reverend Wolfe is."

Jonny frowned. "I can't imagine he wanted you to be unhappy. Perhaps he just never got to know Reverend Wolfe very well. "

"He called him a friend. He would have only had to listen to the man preach! That alone should have aroused his suspicion." Tatiana shoved a few stray hairs from her forehead with the back of her wrist. "Any news from home? How is Father?"

"He is improving … slowly. He caught influenza a few weeks back—I'm sure Gretchen wrote you about it—and that dramatically slowed his recovery. But he is doing well under the care of your sisters. Robert has been helping out around your house quite a bit."

"Doing what?"

"I'm not sure exactly. But I think he enjoys the responsibility." Jonny slipped his finger into Naomi's tiny hand and she clutched it tightly. "Have you heard about Moses Drake?"

"Moses? No."

"Folks say he's gone bad—left the straight and narrow, they say. He took to drinking and causing trouble around town. Then I guess he ran out of ways to make mischief around there and ran off to the city. This city."

Tatiana shook her head. "And to think that Gretchen once courted that scoundrel! I'll have to watch that I don't run into him while doing my errands. How is Samantha?"

Jonny scratched his head. "She's doing well, as far as I know. I think she misses you." He shoved his hands into his pockets. "I guess everybody misses you, Thelma. It's strange not seeing you skipping around town every day."

Tatiana sniffled. "Every morning I wish I were home. I keep my eyes squeezed shut, just hoping and praying that when I open them I'll be looking up at the cracked plaster ceiling in our bedroom at home. But then I have to face the facts. I'm here, and I probably will be for quite a while longer."

"You've always been a fighter, Tatty." Jonny told her, putting his strong hand on her shoulder. "Stay brave."

Before Tatiana could reply, the front door opened and Ananias Wolfe stomped inside. He saw Jonny and froze. "Who's this?" He bellowed, "Who is this stranger that has intruded into my house?"

"H-he's a friend of mine, Reverend Wolfe."

"A friend of yours!" he sneered. "And what is he doing here? This isn't a tavern, Miss Bergman. I won't have you entertaining all your gentleman callers and flaunting yourself like a brazen hussy. Go to your room!"

Tatiana's face paled. "I am not a child, Reverend Wolfe. I am a paid servant and I will not be treated like an errant youngling."

"Even though that is exactly what you are?" Reverend Wolfe barked. "I will treat you as you deserve to be treated, and I will reward you according to your actions. You are behaving like a disobedient child, so I will treat you as such. Go to your room!"

Tatiana's face was hot with shame, but she boldly returned Reverend Wolfe's glare. "I will not!"

"You dare to disobey me?"

"I dare, and I will dare as long as you continue to degrade me! All I ask is a little respect, sir, and I will gladly obey you. I darn your socks, make your bed, wash your dishes, and mop your floors without complaint and without a word of thanks from you. All I request is to be treated reasonably."

"Ungrateful child!" Reverend Wolfe spat. "I feed you, house you, clothe you, and pay you! You should be beyond content with such. You should be thankful that I am not going to turn you out this very hour!" He waved a hand at Jonny who was standing nearby with a shocked expression on his face. "Don't just stand there gawping, boy! Off with you!"

"Sir, I insist that you explain why you are treating my dear friend in such a despicable way," Jonny replied, planting his feet firmly.

"You, a stranger, would insist..." he was nearly choking with anger. "You would insist to me in my own house? I will have you removed!" Reverend Wolfe exclaimed. "Malchus! Come here!"

Undaunted, Jonny continued. "Tatiana is the kindest and most thoughtful and honorable young woman I know. She deserves your courtesy and your respect. If I hear that she has been mistreated at all under your roof, you will have me to contend with."

"Malchus!"

The lanky servant entered from the outdoors and eyed Jonny with a quiet curiosity.

"Remove this trespasser!"

Malchus stared at Jonny but did not make a move. He looked at his master as if he could not believe what he had been ordered to do.

"Reverend Wolfe," Jonny spoke again, "if it comes to a physical contest between your servant and me, I believe I can foresee the outcome, and you won't like it."

"Malchus!" Reverend Wolfe roared.

Malchus stepped forward tentatively and reached for Jonny's arm. Jonny grabbed the young man's hand instead and shook it firmly. "Jonny Creek. I hope you have a good day, sir." He bowed toward Tatiana, and lowered his voice to a whisper. "Can I not take you away from this place, Tatiana?"

For a moment, she was tempted to say a loud 'yes,' but then she remembered the precious Wolfe children and the money she needed to send to her own family. "No ... no, Jonny. I will stay."

Jonny nodded, respecting her decision. "Then good day, and best of luck to you." To Reverend Wolfe he said nothing, only offered a brisk nod. Then he made his way out of the door.

Tatiana slammed a pan of cornbread down on the wooden kitchen table. "Malchus, I just don't understand how you can tolerate that horrid man!"

Malchus poked more wood into the stove and then turned to look at her. His deep-set, brown eyes told her he was listening.

"He's stubborn and proud and willful! He always has to have things his way or else he gets upset. He's bossy and demanding about everything. And he's always blathering on and on about his ridiculous opinions, as if everyone actually wants to hear them! I'll never understand him!" She glanced at Malchus. "And just what are you smiling about, young man?"

Malchus's eyes danced as he looked at her and raised his eyebrows.

"What? You think I'm like that?" She slammed the door of the pantry. "Well, maybe we're more alike than

I'd like to believe, but I still think he's absolutely impossible." She sniffed the air. "Malchus, could you taste that soup for me and see if it's done?"

Malchus did as he was told, taking a loud slurp of the soup. Then he shook his head, sprinkled some salt in, and gave it a few stirs.

Tatiana sliced the cornbread into thick squares. "Do you ever feel stifled, Malchus? Do you ever feel like God must have some greater plan for your life—like you're just squandering the time He's giving you doing tedious little jobs that don't really matter?"

Malchus thought for a moment and nodded.

"Is there anything you've always dreamed of doing?"

Malchus picked up his hat and put it on. He picked up a half empty flour sack and slung it over his shoulder, pantomiming shielding his eyes from the sun.

"You'd like to travel?"

Another nod. Then he pretended to put a ring on his finger and another ring on the finger of someone else.

"You want to get married?"

He nodded again. His skeletal hand rested on his heart and his expression was sad.

Tatiana had learned little bits and pieces about her mysterious coworker. But this was the biggest revelation yet. Slipping beside him, she touched his arm. "Someday, Malchus, you'll meet a lovely, sweet young woman who will love you more than anyone else in the world."

He raised his bushy eyebrows at her. Motioning to himself, he grimaced and made a face.

Tatiana laughed. "You aren't ugly! To be honest, you aren't the handsomest either. But you have a face that's easy to take a liking to. You're a fine man."

Malchus smiled slightly. Whenever he smiled, his face lit up and his eyes shone. He mouthed the words: 'Thank you.'

Still watching him, Tatiana felt she couldn't delay asking any longer. "Malchus, are you a Christian?"

Her simple question electrified the young man. He nodded emphatically, motioning toward Heaven and then pointing to his heart. Then his face became questioning and he pointed at Tatiana.

"Yes, I'm a Christian too."

Tatiana watched in amazement as the young man raised his arms in praise to God. Then he grasped her hands and twirled her joyfully about the kitchen. Tatiana could not help but laugh as she wondered at his animation. Praise the Lord for this brother in Christ!

Malchus suddenly stopped at the sound of heavy footsteps approaching. He let go of Tatiana's hand and turned abruptly toward the fire. Crouching beside it, he used the poker to stir the coals. Tatiana busied herself stirring the soup. The door opened violently. Reverend Wolfe tromped in. "Did I hear laughing in here?" he growled.

Malchus looked up as if he was surprised and Tatiana said: "Laughing, sir? Not here. Perhaps you heard Tobias in the other room."

The surly man scowled. "I find it hard to believe that my son would laugh like a boisterous young girl. Malchus! Was she laughing?"

The young man raised his eyebrows and said nothing.

"Humph." Reverend Wolfe stared hard at Tatiana for a moment and then stormed back out.

Tatiana stirred the pot furiously. "Intolerable man!"

She heard a chuckle from the hearth. "Malchus, you can laugh? I don't think I've heard a sound out of you since I arrived! You have a wonderful laugh though."

The young man beamed, and even with his yellow, crooked teeth, it was one of the most beautiful smiles Tatiana had ever seen.

The following week Malchus became terribly sick. He was weak and feverish, and he refused to eat anything. Tatiana scurried to keep up with Malchus's chores as well as her own. Now she carried a steaming bowl of broth up the stairs.

Ananias Wolfe met her mid-flight. "Where are you going, Miss Bergman?"

"The children are both in bed so I thought I might take some soup to poor Malchus."

"I can take it to him."

Tatiana edged back. "I haven't seen him at all in the past two days. I'd like to know how he's doing."

"He's doing fine."

"But…"

"I won't tell you again, child. You may not see him." Reverend Wolfe's jaw was tensed. The stringy tendons of his neck stuck out like the roots of a banyan tree. With his teeth set, he looked frighteningly like his namesake, the wolf. Tatiana could imagine him as an evil, dog-like creature intent on causing her ruin. "I know the deceitfulness of your heart, Tatiana Bergman," he said in a low, dreadful voice.

"And what, exactly, is that?"

"I know you are trying to ensnare Malchus with your feminine wiles. You will make him believe that you love him, and then you will break his innocent heart. Malchus is a good, honest boy, and I won't allow you to tarnish his purity."

Tatiana felt her blood pulsing angrily in her temples. "I am astonished that you would have such a depraved opinion of me, Reverend Wolfe. I want only good for Malchus. He is my friend and my brother in Christ, and I have treated him as nothing more and nothing less."

It was as if he had not even heard her words. "I will take the soup, Miss Bergman. You can go find some other ignorant soul to prey upon."

Clenching her jaw to stop an angry retort, Tatiana shoved the bowl into her employer's hands. She ran to her room and put on her wool cloak. She had to get out of the house for a while! She felt that another moment behind those dark, confining doors would drive her mad. The sun was setting and a cold, gusty wind whistled through the streets, but Tatiana went out anyway. She stalked out the drive and slipped through the gate. The rage that burned in her heart was so hot and urgent that she hardly noticed the biting cold.

Never before had she been so completely livid. As she hurried down the foggy lane, she was unaware of her surroundings. A beggar tugged at her skirt, but she hardly seemed to notice him. She walked for some time with angry thoughts roiling in her mind.

As her temper began to cool, Tatiana was able to think clearly enough to pray. Her prayer began as an angry tirade before God, telling Him all about Reverend Wolfe's unkindness. By the time she was done praying, however, she was no longer angry. She humbly asked the Lord for forgiveness and turned toward home. Truly, Jesus was the best friend she had ever had.

CHAPTER TWELVE

Surprise Visitor

What a poor job I've done keeping my heart pure and 'unspotted from the world'! Tatiana thought as she plunged a gray shirt into the steaming tub of water and rubbed it viciously against the grooved washboard. *How could I allow myself to become so consumed by the things of this world? I must fix my eyes on Jesus, or I will be burdened down by the sin that does so easily beset me!*

Tatiana's hands had turned bright red from the hot water, and her knuckles were raw from scraping the board. Soapsuds glistened like pearl bracelets on her forearms. Dark strands of hair clung to her damp face. She rinsed the shirt, wrung out as much of water as she could, gave the garment a brisk flick to smooth out wrinkles, and hung it on the clothesline that had been strung across the misty kitchen. Below the clothesline, an echoing line of drips marked the floor; she would have to keep mopping them up. She hoped the weather improved soon. With a sigh, she reached into a bucket where dirty diapers were soaking; she had been saving the odorous task for last.

"Now I know how Gretchen must have felt doing all the chores around the house," she murmured to herself. "Only, I'm sure Gretchen probably handled it much better." Smiling remorsefully, Tatiana vowed inwardly to never again run off and leave Gretchen with all the housework.

I was such a careless, unthinking, selfish child! It's a wonder that my family could even tolerate me! Well, I suppose all my responsibilities here have cured me of my laziness. As she was thinking this one of her 'responsibilities' came trailing into the kitchen.

Tobias walked over and swished his hand in her rinse water. "Are you 'bout done?"

Tatiana smiled at the little boy's curious, round face. "As soon as I finish washing these diapers."

"Ew, they stink!"

"So they do, Toby. That's why I'm washing them."

The boy poked at the bubbles on Tatiana's arm. "Naomi's awake."

Tatiana wrung out the diaper she had just finished rinsing and hung it up. "I'll go get her then."

"Malchus has her."

Tatiana smiled. "Well, God bless him." She tugged open the kitchen window, shivering as a blast of cold air hit her. She took a jug of goat's milk from the wide sill outside the window and warmed enough to fill a baby bottle.

Malchus soon entered the kitchen with little Naomi in his arms. He waited while Tatiana filled the bottle and tested the temperature on her wrist, and then he settled into a hearthside rocking chair to feed the baby. Tatiana went back to her laundry, but she glanced up several times to study them.

What a sweet picture they made! Naomi was sucking contentedly with a hand resting on Malchus's arm. Her tiny fingers opened and closed against his tanned skin as she gazed up at him with trusting eyes. The firelight danced on his serene features. As he gazed lovingly down at the child, he looked more like the young man he was. *Malchus is so gentle with her!* Tatiana noticed. *He is truly a rare gem of a man.*

"You know, Malchus, it's nearly Christmas," Tatiana pointed out. "I can hardly wait! It's my very favorite time of year!"

"What's Christmas?" Tobias piped up, drawing on the stone floor with a charred piece of wood.

Tatiana stared at the child in consternation. "Why, Christmas is a time when we celebrate the birth of Jesus!" She whipped around to look at Malchus. "Doesn't Mr. Wolfe keep Christmas?"

Malchus shook his head sadly.

"But what could he possibly have against it? Isn't he glad that Jesus Christ came to earth to live with mankind?"

Malchus shrugged.

"Should I ask him about it?"

The young man's eyes widened. That was his warning look.

Tatiana smiled. "I think I shall! I'm quite curious to see what excuse he could possibly have to ignore the birth of Christ."

Malchus dramatically covered his eyes with his hand. Tatiana laughed. "You silly! He's not going to eat me." She looked at the young man again. "Don't be so sure? Is that what you're thinking? Someday, Malchus, you will learn how to stand up to that cantankerous man."

"Christmas is to be a time of remembrance." Reverend Wolfe had declared when Tatiana innocently asked him what preparations she should make for the holiday. "Christ came to earth to die, and His birthday should be kept with all respect and gravity. I will not engage in any giddy, frivolous celebration that causes me to forget the true reason for this special day, and I will not approve of any member of my household doing so either."

Tatiana repeated his words glumly to Malchus and said once again that she couldn't understand how he had dealt with Reverend Wolfe for so many years. Malchus held up three fingers to show that he had only been there for three years. Tatiana nodded. "But three years of that man would be enough to drive me into insanity! I think I'm halfway there already."

Malchus laughed heartily.

Christmas morning came with little fanfare in the Wolfe home. In the week preceding it, Tatiana tried hard not to feel bitter when she passed by carolers in the street; their faces were rosy and their eyes shone with the excitement of the season. Their merry singing lifted her spirits, but only temporarily. All too soon she had to leave the bustling streets that were full of laughing people, jingling sleigh bells, and store fronts adorned with evergreen branches to return to Reverend Wolfe's gloomy domicile.

"It's not about decorations and gifts," she told herself as she marched resolutely through the snow. "The true joy of Christmas is in the gift of Jesus Christ to the world."

Yet her mind continued to wander back to the jolly Christmases she had at home with her family. Her father would come in with an armload of packages wrapped in brown paper. Gretchen would be making a delicious

Christmas feast. Rose would be hanging their stockings over the hearth. The high point would be the Christmas Ball. Tatiana sighed. She reminded herself to be thankful. Some people had never experienced a Christmas celebration in their life, and she had had at least fourteen! Even if she never had another good Christmas in her life, she was more fortunate than most.

As she neared the gloomy Wolfe home, Tatiana began to sing 'Joy to the World' just to encourage herself a little. She was singing lustily as she stepped in the door and nearly collided with Reverend Wolfe. Under his frigid glare her felicitous words died on her lips. With a heavy heart she slipped past him and went to check on Naomi.

Christmas morning was spent in the parlor. Reverend Wolfe read the account of Jesus' birth from the book of Luke, immediately followed by the passages describing His crucifixion. Tatiana rocked Naomi and tried not to listen to the merry voices of happy townsfolk passing by outside.

When Reverend Wolfe finished the reading, he excused them both, telling Malchus that he could have the day off. "And Tatiana, I request that you stay with the children today. I need to prepare a sermon."

Again, Tatiana quashed the bitterness that was rising in her bosom. *Please Lord! Give me grace to handle this! I wanted so very much for this to be a special day.* Taking Tobias's hand she led him toward the kitchen. Malchus was already there, putting his coat on. He caught her sleeve as she started past him. With a lopsided grin he reached deep into his coat pocket and pulled out an orange and held it out to her.

"Oh, Malchus! Thank you!" Tatiana held the vivid fruit to her nose, breathing in its exotic fragrance. "I have

something for you too." She went to the pantry and returned with a package wrapped in paper. Malchus looked
stunned; he held it dumbly in his hands. "Go on! Open it!"
Tatiana urged.

His knobby fingers tugged timidly at the string knotted across the top. He unwrapped the package with shaking hands and pulled out a green hand-knitted scarf. He
sank his fingers deep into the rich wool, staring at it in
disbelief. Tatiana was surprised to see tears filling his
brown eyes. He snatched Tatiana's hand and pressed his
face against it.

She was startled by his reaction. "You're welcome,
Malchus. Hasn't anyone ever given you a gift before?"

Malchus was shaking his head. He pulled out a slate
and slate pencil and wrote: *No one but Jesus.*

Tatiana was temporarily as speechless as Malchus. He
eagerly wrapped his scarf about his neck. Seeing that he
was about to go out, Tatiana asked: "Will you be back
soon?"

Malchus saw the loneliness in her eyes. He nodded his
affirmation with a warm smile and swung his gangly self
out the door. Tatiana sat down heavily on the bench and
traced the words Malchus had written. "Dear Jesus," she
whispered. "Help me to be content. You spent your first
Christmas in a barn surrounded by a gaggle of dirty shep-
herds! I have no reason to complain."

Tatiana was surprised when Malchus returned in only
half an hour, a perplexed look on his face. Tatiana rose
from playing jacks with Tobias. "What is it, Malchus? Is
something wrong?"

He turned jerkily and motioned behind him. She saw
Samantha Culbertson stepping timidly into the room.

"Samantha!" Tatiana squealed, flying across the room in only a few steps. She gave her friend a suffocating embrace. "Oh, tell me you aren't a vision, Sam! I was dreaming that you might come, but I kept telling myself it wasn't possible! Oh, you are none other than a gift straight from God!"

Samantha was laughing and crying at the same time. "I'm here, Tatty, and I'm real! It was Rose's idea for me to come. She helped me arrange everything. I had a cabby bring me as far as your street, but I wasn't sure which house. Then I stopped and asked that young man for directions and he brought me here! Oh, it's so good to see you!"

Tatiana clutched Samantha even harder. "I can't tell you how homesick I've been. How long can you stay?"

"A week!"

Tatiana squealed with delight. "Oh, Samantha that's so …" her expression suddenly changed, "terrible!"

"Terrible? Why?"

"When Jonny came to visit me, Reverend Wolfe threw him out on his ear! What if he does the same to you? I've got to hide you!"

"Hide me? Is that really necessary, Tatty?"

"I think I would just die if Reverend Wolfe threw you out, Samantha. I've got to! What do you think, Malchus?"

The young man scratched his head and appeared to be pondering the situation.

"Just as I thought," Tatiana interrupted. "Come on!" She grasped Samantha's wrist and poked her head out into the hall. Like two frightened mice, they went scurrying across the foyer. Tatiana dragged her friend up the right wing of the stairs and peeked down the hall to make sure all was clear. Then she rushed Samantha into her bedroom. Leaning against her door to catch her breath,

Tatiana said: "Now, you'll have to stay here, at least until Reverend Wolfe is out of the house. Are you hungry? Do you want me to fix you something?"

"That would be wonderful." Samantha sat down on the bed with a sigh and took out her buttonhook to undo her boots. "My bags are still downstairs."

"Oh, I'll have Malchus bring them up."

Samantha's eyes grew wide. "That young man who showed me in? He frightens me. I think he dislikes me for some reason, because he hasn't spoken a word in my presence."

Tatiana smiled. "He's mute, Samantha. He's really very nice."

"Mute! Oh, yes, you told me about him in a letter." Tatiana headed downstairs to prepare food for Samantha and to make sure Malchus took up her bags.

"Who was that girl?" Tobias asked curiously as she entered the kitchen.

Tobias! She had forgotten about him! His innocent little tongue could so easily give Samantha away! Tatiana quickly knelt in front of the little boy. "Toby, that girl is my friend Samantha. But I need you to do something for me, all right?"

Toby's big eyes looked up at her trustingly and he nodded.

"Don't tell your daddy that Samantha's here. Just don't say anything about her at all."

Tobias scratched his head. "Why not?"

Tatiana bit her lip. "Because your daddy might be mean to Samantha. He might send her away, and that would make me very sad."

Tobias seemed to understand. He put his hands determinedly on his hips. "I won't tell him."

Tatiana smiled and ruffled her charge's hair. "Thank you, Toby. You're a treasure."

"Oh, I think I would give anything to have hair like yours, Samantha," Tatiana mused, twisting the thick, nutty brown locks into a braid. "All those rich waves! You look like a Canaanite princess!"

Samantha studied her warped reflection in Tatiana's cracked bedroom mirror. Tatiana had shown her that by standing at an odd angle, far to the left side of the mirror, she could see her entire face in one piece, without the warping caused by the crack. It was late, but the two girls were enjoying each other's company so much that they hardly noticed the hour, or how far down the candles had burned. "Bah! I'm much too plump!" Samantha retorted. "I look like a stuffed pheasant."

Tatiana snorted. "Pheasants aren't all that big, you know."

"A goose then!"

"Don't jest, Sam! You look like a queen!" Tatiana draped a shimmering veil over Samantha's head. The creamy fabric caressed the smooth line of Samantha's face and fell in gossamer ripples around her shoulders. Her brown eyes looked bigger and darker than ever. "See that?" Tatiana exclaimed. "You could very well be the beautiful Queen Esther!"

Samantha blushed and turned from the mirror. "And who are you?"

"I ..." Tatiana began, wadding her hair up and tying a band around her head, "am the evil Haman!" She twisted her face into a sneering scowl, put her hands on her skinny hips, and strutted about the room like a rooster. In her thin chemise, with bony shoulders protruding, Tatiana was quite a sight to behold. "Bow to me, Jew! If you don't, I'll have you killed!"

Samantha struck a regal pose. "Never! You will not harm my people! I'll tell my husband, the king!"

"Have me hung, will you?" Tatiana shrieked, leaping onto the bed. "Ha! Only if you can catch me first!"

Samantha tossed her hair with a giggle. "I may be Queen, but I can catch villains better than the sheriff!" She lunged for Tatiana, who slipped from her perch and tumbled onto the floor on the other side of the bed.

"Man overboard!" Tatiana howled, cackling giddily. She lay in a jumbled heap on the floor, breathless from laughing. When she could speak, she said, "Ah-hah! You haven't killed me yet!"

A knock on the door shocked both the girls into a fearful silence. "Miss Bergman!" Reverend Wolfe growled from out in the hall. "What is the meaning of this ruckus?"

Tatiana quickly sat up, clutching the headband sliding over one eye. "I was just acting, sir."

"Acting!"

"One of Shakespeare's works, sir. *Othello*, to be exact."

"Acting is a sin, Miss Bergman."

"Then I confess to doing it and beg for forgiveness, Reverend Wolfe."

"May I come in?"

Tatiana jumped to her feet. "I-I'm not dressed, sir."

There was a long pause. "Can I not even trust you to behave with propriety when you are all by yourself, Miss Bergman?"

"I am a sinful creature, sir," Tatiana admitted remorsefully. "I pray that the Lord will have mercy on me."

"You had best pray that I shall have mercy as well!" Reverend Wolfe snarled. "Good night, Miss Bergman!"

"G'night!" Tatiana called. As soon as the man's footsteps faded, the girls burst into hushed laughter.

"Oh, heavens, Tatiana, you're hilarious!" Samantha gasped. The two friends flopped back onto the bed. "I never could have stood up to him like that. He seems like an awful man."

"He does have some unpleasant tendencies," Tatiana acknowledged. "I don't know how I would have survived staying here without Malchus." She propped her head on her hand. "So, what do you think of Malchus?"

Samantha shrugged. "I thanked him for bringing my bags and he just smiled and left."

"He smiled? Well, that's quite something. He didn't smile at me for at least a week after I arrived. He must like you."

"Really, Tatty, you jump to such hasty conclusions!" Samantha declared. "He's much more likely to care for you since you're the one he sees every day."

"Yes, and he's the one I complain to every day! I've probably scared the poor man off." Tatiana played with the end of Samantha's braid. "I can see how a lot of handsome young fellows would like you. You're so pretty and sweet. And I'm just like a skinny little peafowl, always squawking about something. I reckon I'll have to find someone who's deaf."

Samantha chuckled, and then said: "Tatiana, Jonny still cares for you."

Tatiana sucked in a deep breath. "Jonny? How do you know?"

"I can just tell. His eyes light up whenever he hears your name, and he's always asking your sisters if they've heard how you're doing."

Tatiana closed her eyes. "I suppose I'll believe it when I see it."

The girls lay in silence for a while and then Samantha whispered, "Good night, my friend."

Tatiana leaned over to blow out the candle. "Sleep well, dearest."

Dipping the ladle into the kettle that hung over the fire, Tatiana added more hot water to Toby's bath water, pouring it well away from his body. She lathered her hands with soap and worked her fingers through the little boy's wet hair. "Close your eyes, Toby. I'm going to wash the soap out now." The boy squeezed his eyes shut as Tatiana poured warm water over his head.

A giggle from the kitchen table made Tatiana look up. Malchus and Samantha were having a 'slate conversation,' using Malchus's slate and slate pencil. The two of them took turns writing on the slate. They had done this several times over the past few days. At first Tatiana had thought little of it, but now...

She could not help noticing the radiant expression on Samantha's face and the excitement that shone in Malchus's eyes. They had become fast friends, and Tatiana had to wonder if it was becoming something more. She had been jesting when she suggested that Malchus had taken a fancy to Samantha, but it was beginning to look like she had spoken the truth unknowingly. She frowned as the two exchanged a long look before bending back over the slate. *My eye! They're falling in love!* This was one thing for which Tatiana was unprepared. For some reason, she felt as if it were her own fault. *What now, Lord? Is*

*this a mistake? Should I have told Samantha to go home as soon
as she arrived?*

Tatiana put a big towel on her shoulder, lifted Tobias
from the tub, and deftly wrapped him and rubbed him dry
with the towel. Holding the shivering little boy close, she
eyed her two friends again. *What an odd-looking couple
they would make! Should I say something? Should I intervene?
What a mess this is!*

She sighed and rubbed Tobias's back. "Let's get you
dressed, Toby. I laid your clothes by the fire so they would
get nice and toasty warm! See?"

Toby nodded eagerly. "Good! I'm c-c-cold!" His teeth
chattered a little as he struggled to pull his nightshirt over
his head. His arms thrashed in the white garment and he
staggered a few steps backward. Tatiana quickly caught
him. When his damp head finally emerged from the top
of the shirt, she planted a kiss on his forehead.

"All right, sleepy boy! It's time for you to get to bed."

He stretched his arms upward. "Carry me?"

She smiled and scooped him up into her arms. "Well,
I suppose I can. But I won't be able to very much longer
because you are getting **so** big!"

Toby grinned with delight and threw his thin arms
around Tatiana's neck. "And soon I'll be as big as Daddy!"

Tatiana laughed and nuzzled her nose against his soft
cheek, breathing in the smell of clean little boy and lavender soap. "I'm sure you will, Toby. And then you'll be a
man, won't you?"

Toby's liquid brown eyes grew earnest. "And I'll be
very good, like Malchus."

Tatiana opened the door to the boy's bedroom and
squeezed him tightly. "That's right, Toby. Malchus is a
good man, and I'm sure you can grow to be just like him."

"But I can talk," Toby said matter-of-factly. He knelt by the bed and said his prayers, and then Tatiana pulled back the covers and tucked him into bed. "Malchus can't talk at all." Tobias's eyebrows furrowed thoughtfully. "But God still loves him, doesn't he?"

"Yes, Toby," Tatiana answered, tucking his blankets around him. "God loves him very much. And he loves you too." She held Toby's hand for a minute longer and then left him to sleep. What a sweet child he was! Indeed, Tatiana could not help wishing that he were her child.

Tatiana was weary by the end of the day. She was so tired that she nearly fell to her knees halfway up the stairs; but she knew how pathetic she would look if she crawled the rest of the way, so she resisted the urge. She found Samantha sitting at the dressing table in Tatiana's bedroom, reading a book by the light of an oil lamp. Tatiana sagged onto her bed and somnolently kicked off her shoes.

Samantha looked up and asked, "Tatty, did you ever dream of finding your prince?" Samantha gazed down at the cover of her book that portrayed a fetching young knight helping a delicate maiden onto his strong, white charger. "I mean, maybe you didn't dream of an actual prince, but did you dream of the perfect man searching you out? A dashing, charming, confident gentleman who was intent on wooing you in the most romantic way— taking you to rich parties and dancing elegantly with you at the finest balls? Someone who would bring you flowers and jewelry and whisper poetic words into your ear?"

Tatiana smiled. "I suppose every girl dreams of such a man, in some form or another. My imaginary prince was a little more swashbuckling than yours, but it's the same concept. Why do you ask?"

Samantha stared down into her lap. "I always told myself that I wouldn't settle for anyone less than the prince of my dreams, but..." She stared out the window into the darkness for a moment. "He has none of the qualifications I once thought were important. He isn't dashing or charming or rich. He isn't handsome or confident. Tatiana, he can't even talk! All I know is that he's a good man who loves Jesus Christ."

"You really care for him," Tatiana said softly.

"What can I say? He's stolen my heart! Yet I'm afraid that I'll make a commitment to Malchus and then my prince will show up and I'll regret it. I know that sounds selfish, but what if my 'prince' comes searching for me, and I miss him because I'm impatient and I marry the first man who comes along?"

Tatiana pulled the pins from her hair and shook her long, silky locks free. "Have you prayed about it?" She seated herself on the floor by Samantha, who began to massage her shoulders.

"N-no. I didn't think it was something I should ask God about."

Tatiana sighed as her stiff muscles relaxed. "By all means, ask Him, Sam! God is the inventor of romance, is He not? I don't want to speak out of line, but I will say this. Right now, for all we know, the prince of your dreams is living off in some castle in the clouds, but Malchus is right here, right now. Don't go off looking into the clouds for a perfect prince who might not even exist while the man who loves you is standing directly before you."

Samantha nodded and sniffled. "Thank you, Tatty. I'll think about it."

Samantha's week with Tatiana was flying by with startling speed. Tatiana had enjoyed every moment with Samantha, and at times she felt that it was all just a wonderful dream that would disappear when she awoke. She had wished for so long to see her bosom friend that Samantha's visit hardly seemed real.

One afternoon she and Samantha were playing with the children in the parlor. Tatiana helped Toby build a tower of wooden blocks while Samantha held Naomi. The baby was quite occupied with trying to grab the shiny locket dangling from Samantha's neck.

Both girls looked up as Malchus came rushing in with a panicked look on his face. "Malchus, what's wrong?" Tatiana questioned.

The young man pointed urgently toward the door and drew his face into a good imitation of Reverend Wolfe's perpetual scowl.

"Oh, merciful heavens!" Tatiana cried, peering out the window. "He's home early and we haven't a moment to hide you!" Her employer was already at the door: she could hear him stomping the snow from his boots. The only thing Tatiana had time to do was snatch Naomi from Samantha's arms and thrust her friend behind one of the heavy drapes bunched at each side of the front window.

Reverend Wolfe entered briskly and tossed his coat to Malchus. Rubbing his hands together, the minister entered the parlor and scooped Toby into his arms. "It's quite a fine day for December," he commented.

Tatiana was so unaccustomed to any form of pleasant remark from her employer that she simply stared at him.

Reverend Wolfe squinted at the sun that streamed in the window. "The sunshine is lovely, but the curtains should be drawn or else it will fade the furniture."

Tatiana's heart dropped and she stepped forward quickly. "Certainly, sir. I will see to that as soon as I can."

The man raised his eyebrows. "No, it must be done immediately. But don't let it worry you. I can take care of it."

He started for the curtains. In one last bold attempt to avert disaster, Tatiana stepped in his way. "Please allow me, sir! I ... I am very fond of drawing curtains!"

Reverend Wolfe actually chuckled in a low, growly sort of way. "Don't be daft, Miss Bergman! It's something you'll have many an opportunity to enjoy." With this he grasped the pull-ropes and drew the curtains shut. With the fabric stretched to its full width, Samantha's form was quite apparent behind it, but Tatiana remained silent and hoped Reverend Wolfe wouldn't notice.

But, alas, he did! "What is this?" he questioned, pulling the curtain aside. Both of the girls gasped simultaneously and Reverend Wolfe stepped back in alarm at his discovery. "Who in heaven's name are you and what are you doing in my curtains?" he bellowed.

Samantha shrank back in fear. "I'm a friend of Tatiana's, sir," she quavered. "She was afraid you would throw me out if you knew I was here, so she hid me."

"Your name, girl?"

"Samantha Culbertson." She gulped in fear, now that she was meeting the ogre Tatiana had described in letters. "Please, don't be angry with us, sir," she pleaded. "I didn't mean to cause a smidgeon of trouble!"

Something in Reverend Wolfe's face softened at Samantha's contrite apology. "You are forgiven, Miss Culbertson," he said generously. "Now, do take the children out of the room. I must have a short exchange with Miss Bergman."

Samantha took Naomi and grasped Toby's hand, flashing Tatiana a sympathetic glance. As soon as they were gone, Reverend Wolfe turned on the slim young woman before him. "Miss Tatiana Bergman, what sort of charade are you playing at? Do you think, for some perverse reason, that you can entertain guests in my house without my knowledge?"

Tatiana blithely rubbed the back of her neck. "I must admit, sir, that until now I was quite successful."

A sharp intake of breath whistled in Reverend Wolfe's nostrils. "Well, you've been discovered. I must say, I have never before dealt with such flagrant rebellion, and you seem to have an inexhaustible store of it!" He rubbed his chin. "What shall I do with you?"

"I was hoping to receive the same forgiveness that you so freely bestowed upon my friend."

"Forgiveness!" Reverend Wolfe barked. "You are so undeserving of my forgiveness that it is almost laughable! Your friend was truly sorry for what she had done and was willing to beg for mercy. But you ... well, just look at yourself! You haven't the grace to display even a shred of remorse."

"Perhaps it is because I have none," Tatiana snapped. "However, I am quite interested in what my punishment shall be."

"That is yet to be determined, but I am considering your dismissal."

"Could you do without me?" Tatiana questioned. She was worried by the thought of losing her job, but her pride prevented her from showing it. "Surely Malchus cannot do all my work."

"He is likely more capable than you!"

Tatiana drummed her fingers on the side table. "Really? Even though he is unable to speak?"

"Especially so!" Reverend Wolfe exclaimed, taking a threatening step toward Tatiana. "Malchus is the best servant I have ever had, and I doubt I will ever find another so faithful. His disability is of no consequence to me. And, to tell you the truth, I have wished to God time and time again that you were mute as well!"

"I?"

"Yes! If only your poisonous tongue were silenced, I think you would be a very fine young lady. You are hopelessly proud and stubborn!"

"I am proud and stubborn? What of yourself? You care so little for others, I'm surprised you can even remember the names of your own children! I think you like to contradict me for nothing but your own amusement!"

"And you apparently rebel against me for no reason at all! Have you learned no manners? Have you never been taught to show deference to your authorities? I tell you, I am at my wit's end with how to handle your cold indifference!" When Tatiana did not reply, Reverend Wolfe asked her a question in a different tone. "Why do you resist me so?" His strangely earnest voice brought Tatiana to full attention.

Tatiana thought of a hundred small offenses she could hold against him, but at the moment they all seemed petty.

"And what can I do to dissolve your resistance?"

Tatiana raised her eyes to her employer, a vulnerable look on her face. "It will likely happen when you win my respect."

"And how is that to be done?"

Tatiana gazed at the thin strip of light that seeped through a gap in the curtains. "Some respect those who instill fear within them. Others respect anyone who is powerful or prosperous. I give my respect to men who do justly, love mercy, and walk humbly with their God."

"That is a high expectation, Miss Bergman." Reverend Wolfe turned and began to exit the room.

Tatiana was disappointed at ending the conversation without resolution. A Bible verse lay heavily on her heart: '*God resisteth the proud, and giveth grace to the humble.*' She had allowed her terrible pride to rise up within her heart—had actually embraced it! She couldn't bear the thought of God resisting her! God was her Father, and oh, how she needed Him! Her conscience gave her a sudden urging and words leaped from her mouth.

"Reverend Wolfe!" The man turned. His face had hardened once again. He looked at her skeptically. Tatiana shakily stepped forward. "I am sorry." His expression did not change. She closed her eyes for a moment, praying for strength. "I am sorry for all the wrong I have done you. I have usurped the authority the Lord gave you over me as my master. I have deceived you by keeping my friend here, and I treated you disrespectfully. I know you said earlier that you would not forgive me, but I want to ask you again—I plead with you to forgive me of my rebellion!"

The proud, broad shoulders straightened. After so long, he had finally heard the words he had always wished to hear from his obstinate young servant. However, this was too soon. Her insults were still ringing fresh in his ears. He would not grant her so easy a victory. "I will consider it," he said stiffly. "Make sure that your friend gets safely on the train by tomorrow morning."

Then he walked away, leaving Tatiana alone in her turbulent sea of emotions.

CHAPTER THIRTEEN

Robbers!

Tatiana glumly watched a shopkeeper as he took the wreath down from his door. Christmas was well over. Malchus had driven Samantha to the train station that very morning. Tatiana stayed with the children after sending her friend off with a long hug.

Now it seemed that a long, dismal winter stretched out before her. Taking a deep breath of night air, Tatiana continued on down the narrow street. She knew she would have to head back to the Wolfe house soon, yet walking made her feel more peaceful after a harried day with the children.

She prayed as she walked. The night enchanted her, even with the factory smoke that hung like a dirty blanket over the city. Darkness came early at this time of year, and the streets were quiet already. She was nearing a long row of shabby tenement buildings when she heard a scuffle of footsteps and realized how far she had come. Tatiana glanced anxiously about her, but she saw no one. *Perhaps,* she thought, *I should head for home.*

She turned about and was startled to see a ragged young boy standing close to her. He was shivering in the cold—a pitiable, bedraggled little creature. His grimy little fists were rubbing at his eyes, and he sniffled loudly. Tatiana went immediately to his side. "What's wrong, laddie? Why are you crying so? Are you lost?"

The boy hunched his trembling shoulders. "I w-want m-my mama!"

Tatiana reached for the child's hand. "Well, come with me, little sir. Let us see if we can find your mama."

Before she could clasp his blue fingers, a rough hand slammed down over her mouth and she was jerked backwards; her scream was muffled by flesh. Her head banged against a bony sternum. A wiry arm clamped around her waist like a tight latchet and a voice growled in her ear. "Let's have your purse, girl."

Tatiana's frightened eyes flickered over to the little boy who had been crying. His tears had magically vanished and he was now looking on with a cruel smile. By turning her head a little she could see two other rogues. They were young and thin, yet they had grim expressions and an unsettling look of desperation in their eyes.

Tatiana raised her chin, and the man holding her gave her a shake. "Your purse, girl! Empty it!"

She tilted her head, trying to get a look at her captor. "I would gladly, only it already is empty. At the moment I haven't a copper to my name."

"You lie!" the man growled.

Tatiana felt a strange sense of peace filling her. *He has given me a peace that passes all understanding,* she thought to herself. "Try me, sir. If you will free my arms, I can show you."

The man hesitated. His comrades made a tighter circle around their fair captive. When Tatiana's arms were released, she pulled a lambskin drawstring bag from her skirts and turned it inside out for the whole band of robbers to see.

This seemed to irritate the scoundrels; they circled around her like hungry wolves. "Ain't you scared, girl?" one of the thieves hissed, brandishing his knife. "You know we could kill you if we wanted."

"Well, you're dressed fine enough, you little peacock," said the man who had first grabbed her. He was tall and thin and seemed to be the leader. "Give us your coat."

Tatiana smiled as a Scripture came to her mind. Without protest, she drew off her splendid Cheviot wool coat and handed it to one of men. Then she undid the buttons of the short jacket she wore underneath. "And please, give this to the little boy. He looks so very cold, and the jacket should fit him nicely. If you remove the rosette on the front, no one will ever know it was a girl's jacket."

The tall thief stood stiffly, staring hard at Tatiana. Then he motioned to the compatriot who held Tatiana's coat and said in a husky voice, "Give it back."

The young man looked bewildered. "Give it back? But—"

"Give it back," the man repeated menacingly.

Tatiana found her coat once again in her hands. "Thank you, gentlemen," she said softly. Inwardly, she thanked the Lord as well. "But please, do keep my jacket for your little friend. He needs it more than I."

One of the robbers laughed raucously. "You're a stupid girl!"

To Tatiana's surprise, the tall thief refuted this: "She's not stupid, Jim."

Tatiana turned around for the first time. *Why would a thief stand up for me in such a way?* As her eyes searched the haggard face before her, she suddenly gasped in recognition. The face was older, harder, and his jaw was covered in dark bristles, but those glinting green eyes had not changed. "Moses Drake?"

The youth ducked as if she had thrown a punch. "Yes."

Tatiana's chest ached with sorrow for her schoolmate. Moses had been a troublemaker his whole life, but Tatiana had never foreseen such a fall from grace. Moses had pulled pigtails, tweaked noses, and hid behind corners to jump out and frighten people. He wasn't a thief! "Moses, what are you doing here?"

Moses wiped his nose on his patched sleeve, his eyes flicking nervously about. "Listen, I never would have lifted a finger against you if I had recognized you earlier. I'm sorry. And I'd sure be obliged if you didn't tell your sister about this."

"Gretchen? Well, I—"

Moses interrupted her by turning to the other three and saying, "Hey, fellas. Go take a stroll around the block or something." They nodded in understanding and slunk off. Moses stood staring at the ground. He used his tongue to retrieve the wad of tobacco he had been storing in his cheek and began to chew on it sullenly. "I know you probably don't think much of me right now."

Tatiana raised her eyes to his stony face. "Mostly I'm just worried. I don't understand why you would choose to come here and do this when you have a family who loves you back at home."

"I'm helpin' these blokes," Moses said, jerking his head in the direction his friends had gone.

"You aren't helping them by encouraging them to break the law," Tatiana insisted. "You could do so much, Moses. You know these streets by now, and you know the people who live in them. If you truly want to help these people, why not go about it the right way? You could make such a difference in their lives!"

Moses snorted and stared off at the glowing windows of a tavern down the street. "I'm not like you, Tatiana. I'm not good and caring and sweet all the time. I guess I'm just a bad seed. Before long I'll turn out to be a ruined mess like him." Moses pointed with his chin toward a drunken man who came staggering out of the tavern and tripped on the last step. He landed in an undignified heap and sat, muttering confusedly to himself.

Tatiana tore her eyes away from the broken man and folded her arms over her chest. "You can change, if you have a mind to," she said softly. "You can ask Jesus to make you a new man."

Moses shot a stream of brown tobacco juice from between his front teeth into the gutter. "Jesus can't help a wretch like me."

"Moses, that's what He came for."

"Bah! You sound just like Reverend Matthew!" Moses scoffed. He rubbed his chapped hands together. "Religion is for rich folks who don't have nothin' better to do with their money than toss it in the offering plate. Jesus don't care for poor folks who don't have nothin'. He don't understand."

Tatiana arched her eyebrows. "The One who was born in a barn doesn't understand poor folks? I should say he does!" Tatiana looked up as Moses' three companions approached. "He knows your heart, Moses, and He loves you just the same."

Moses briefly raised his eyes to Tatiana and she looked deep into them, seeing the loss, pain, and confusion that dwelt within him. Moses gave her a short nod. "I best be on my way."

He turned to go, but Tatiana caught his clammy hand and squeezed it tightly. "May God have His will in your life."

Moses seemed taken aback by her words. Touching his cap, he slipped away. His thin form had soon disappeared in the shadows. Tatiana wiped a tear from the corner of her eye and pulled her coat tightly around herself. It was time to get home.

Light glowed from the parlor as Tatiana slipped into the house. Softly shutting the door, she crept toward the stairs. Glancing into the parlor she saw that Reverend Wolfe was fast asleep in his chair with his feet propped on the fender. His newspaper, which lay partially over his face, fluttered a bit every time he exhaled. She turned to tiptoe away, but a floorboard creaked like a tattling child.

Her heart sunk as Reverend Wolfe leapt from his chair. He passed a hand over his eyes and then cried: "Thought you could sneak in, did you? What do you mean by gallivanting all over the city in the middle of the night?"

"It is hardly the middle, sir," Tatiana said quietly. "I returned as soon as I could."

"And what, pray tell, delayed you for so terribly long?"

"I was beset by robbers."

"Robbers!" The color drained from Reverend Wolfe's face. He started forward and anxiously clutched Tatiana's hands. "Are you all right? Are you unscathed?"

Tatiana nodded mutely, wondering at his strong reaction. But Reverend Wolfe was not finished. He pulled Tatiana to him, pressing her head to his chest. "Thank the Lord you are unharmed! My own brother was killed by robbers not four years ago in these very streets! God must have put His shield of protection around you, my child, and I praise Him for it!"

Tatiana was feeling very perplexed but she choked, "God is very gracious." Reverend Wolfe released her. Tatiana saw with surprise that tears glittered in his eyes. She respectfully lowered her gaze and spoke slowly, "I am grateful for your concern, Reverend Wolfe."

"And I for your safety! Go on to bed now. A man sleeps well when he has a thankful heart."

Tatiana was truly thankful as she ascended the stairs to her room. She could see the work of the Lord in this evening, and it left her in complete awe. He had softened the hearts of both a band of thieves and her impenetrable employer. "Your ways are both mysterious and wonderful, Father," she told Him as she entered her room. "Thank you for allowing me to see them."

CHAPTER FOURTEEN

Rose's Sickness

"Candies, miss? They're only a nickel."

Tatiana turned from the train window to the lad standing before her. He was eyeing her hopefully and holding out a package of peppermints. She shook her head, "Thank you, but no." She sat up straighter. "Are we almost there?" she asked anxiously.

"In about twenty minutes, miss." The boy continued on his way. Tatiana sat back with a sigh. The candies had looked nice, but at the moment she could think of little else but her older sister's letter. Bits and pieces of Gretchen's message kept floating through Tatiana's mind.

"Rose ... terribly ill ... scarlet fever ... unsure if she will recover ... wishes to see you ... come quickly."

Poor Rose. Tatiana closed her eyes to take a short rest. However, she was so laden with worry for her sister that sleep did not come to her. As the train screeched its way into the station, Tatiana buttoned her coat and reached for her bag, feeling exhausted.

She stepped into the aisle. She smiled to see that she was the only passenger disembarking. How unlike Philadelphia this was, and how Tatiana loved it! Even her worry for Rose couldn't extinguish the happiness she felt at going home, even if it was for just a short time.

When she reached the train door, she was surprised to be lifted in someone's strong arms and swung directly down to the wooden platform. "Goodness, Robert!" she exclaimed, looking up at her old friend. "I didn't think anyone would be here to meet me!"

He touched his cap. His kind eyes were shining. "I wasn't about to leave you to walk all the way home. It might be sunny for the moment, but it's still February." He took Tatiana's bag and loaded it into the back of the stylish buggy he had brought. Then he gave Tatiana a hand up.

"Home," she repeated. "I feel like I haven't been there in ages, even though it's only been about five months that I've been away. "

Robert leapt into the seat beside her and unwound the reins from the brace. "You had a birthday last month, did you not?"

"I did," she answered, pleased that he remembered. "I'm fifteen now. Heavens, doesn't that sound frightfully old?"

Robert smiled. "Not particularly. If you call fifteen 'old,' then I'm—"

"Perfectly ancient!" Tatiana finished, shaking her head remorsefully. "I'm not sure that I care for this whole business of growing up—especially when everyone else seems to be so remarkably better at it than I am." She ran her fingers over the buggy's smooth horsehair seat cover. "This is a fine buggy, Robert. Is it yours?"

As Robert nodded, Tatiana noticed the handsome cleft in his chin. "I've been saving for it for quite some time. Father calls it a courtin' buggy." He smiled mirthfully.

"And have you used it for that?" Tatiana asked nosily.

Robert's face colored and he cleared his throat nervously. "I haven't really had anyone to take courting."

"No one, Robert? Surely there's some fine young lady you've had your eye on."

The young man kept his eyes on the road. "There is one, actually. But she was out of town ... until now."

Tatiana felt the blood rushing to her head. She stole a glance at Robert's stoic profile to make sure he was serious. What was the proper response for something like this? The heroines in novels always knew the perfect thing to say in such a situation, but Tatiana was at a loss. Did she care for Robert? She enjoyed his friendship—no, more than that, she loved him! But it was the love a sister would have for her brother. It was that love that tied Tatiana's tongue into knots; she hated the thought of saying anything that might hurt him.

No reply came to her mind. Disconcerted, she began to hum a church hymn. After a few measures, however, she realized that the song was 'Blest Be the Tie That Binds,' a popular wedding chorus. A fresh wave of blushes rolled over Tatiana's face; she slumped lower on the satiny seat.

When they pulled up at the Bergman household, Robert got down from the buggy and walked around to the other side to help Tatiana down. By the time he got there, however, she was already halfway up the front walk.

Tatiana burst through the front door as she always did and nearly crashed into Gretchen. Gretchen cried out in excitement and threw her hands into the air. She then threw her arms around Tatiana. "Oh, I am so glad you're here! It's been so long." They held each other close for a moment. "I was afraid you might come too late," Gretchen whispered.

"How is she?"

Gretchen raised her eyes toward the top of the stairs. "I'm afraid that she is much altered. Father is distraught. He has been praying and fretting over her almost constantly." Gretchen took Tatiana's chin in her hand and kissed her forehead. "You should go on up. She has been waiting for you."

Tatiana put on a brave smile and went upstairs. She pushed the bedroom door open and sagged at the sight before her. Sweet Rose lay like one dead. She was flat on her back with her hair spread out limply over her pillow. Her white fingers were folded lifelessly over her heart; Tatiana noticed that the skin was peeling. Her face held a ghastly pallor. Her body had wasted away to skin and bones, and her cheeks were sunken. A fine sheen of sweat glistened on her thin face. "Oh, Rose!" Tatiana choked, falling to her knees beside the bed.

Rose drew in a breath that rasped between her lips and rattled in her lungs. Slowly, almost cumbersomely, her eyelids lifted. Her hollow eyes stared blankly at Tatiana for a moment, and then a weak smile tugged at the corners of her mouth. "You came back." Her once melodious voice wavered like an old woman's.

Tatiana smiled through her tears. "Of course I came back! I wanted to see my favorite sister."

Rose's forehead wrinkled. "I'm your favorite?"

Tatiana giggled. "Shhh! Don't tell Gretchen!"

Rose smiled feebly. "I won't."

Tatiana reached for Rose's hand and gasped. "Rose, your hands are like ice!" Taking her sister's hands, she began to rub them between her own warm palms. At least Rose wasn't feverish now; Gretchen had written when Rose had become delirious with fever and unable to keep food down.

"I think—" Rose began and then broke into a fit of violent coughing. When she finished, she paused to catch her breath and said: "I think now that you're here I might have a chance of getting better. You always knew how to cheer me up."

"Well, you had better recover, Miss Rosie-Posie!" Tatiana replied, "Because I need your help."

Rose's eyelids fluttered. "My help? For what?"

Tatiana held Rose's hands to her mouth and blew on them a few times. "See, I need you to distract Robert for me. I think he wants to try out his new 'courtin' buggy' on me."

A husky laugh sputtered from Rose's lungs. "How would I distract him?"

"You could just bat your lovely eyelashes at him and then he would start turning as red as a beet," Tatiana suggested.

"I probably would too," Rose whispered, and Tatiana noticed that her sister's eyelids were drooping from exhaustion.

"Just rest now, Rosie," Tatiana advised. Smoothing Rose's hair back from her face, she took her leave. She walked quietly down the stairs and met her father in the hall. He had more gray hair than when she had last seen him, and he was leaning heavily on a wooden cane. He held out his free arm for her and she ran to him. In his embrace, the tears she had been holding back came bursting forth. The floodgates opened as Tatiana wept into the soft material of his shirt.

"Oh, my brave girl," Hans sighed, clutching her tightly. "You'll be all right."

"But Rose might not!" Tatiana sobbed. "What if she dies? I won't be able to take it!"

A shudder went through Mr. Bergman's frame. "We can only pray for God's healing."

Tatiana raised her tear-streaked face to her father. "Surely He will give it to someone as pure and good as Rose!"

Hans smiled in a bittersweet manner. "We all wish that, Tatiana."

Tatiana thumped her fist down into the warm lump of bread dough. She generously dusted the tabletop with flour and then threw the dough down onto it. "Not a whole lot seems to have happened around here since I've been gone."

Gretchen shook her head as she flicked her paring knife over the potatoes she was peeling. "No, not much has. But don't go thinking that the world stands still without you." She raised her head. "You know Jonny left town?"

"I did not. When was it?"

"About a month ago. He went with Mr. Smith's brother, Isaac Smith, to southern Ohio."

"What are they doing there?"

Gretchen shrugged and rinsed another potato in the water basin. "Isaac Smith is a woodsman and a surveyor. I suppose he is teaching Jonny his trade. No one knows when they'll be back. Mrs. Smith said it could be years."

"Oh," Tatiana said meekly, trying to hide her deep disappointment.

Gretchen held up her finger as she thought of another bit of news. "Ah! Daniel Weston and Arietta Jones are courting now. And as couples go, I think they're the most ill-matched pair I've ever seen."

Tatiana watched a spider dancing on thread from the ceiling. "Hmm, yes. Those two are both so chock full of trouble that I doubt they have any room left for common sense. I can only imagine how they must be together!"

"You'll find out soon enough," Gretchen predicted. "They seem to grace every town gathering with their irksome presence."

The sisters worked in silence for a few moments, and then Tatiana spoke. "Gretchen, I think Robert wants to court me."

Gretchen looked up abruptly. "He asked you?"

"In a ... roundabout sort of way."

"And what did you tell him?"

"Nothing. I just started humming."

Gretchen snorted. "Quite a demonstration of fine social graces that was!"

"Well, I was taken off guard and I didn't know what to say!" Tatiana drew her hand across her forehead, accidentally leaving a streak of flour. "I don't love Robert in that way. At least, I don't think I do. I always cared more for Jonny, but I kept it under wraps because of his unbelief. I don't know which one of them to encourage."

Gretchen clicked her tongue. "Oh, that I could bear such burdens as yours, Tatiana!"

"Oh, that I could share them with you!" Tatiana replied. "I am in such a terrible quandary!"

Both girls heard a scraping noise outside and saw that Robert was shoveling snow from their front walk; it had snowed the night before. Gretchen held the lacy curtain aside for Tatiana to look out. "He has taken good care of us ever since Father was injured. Without request or pay, he works to keep us and our house taken care of." Gretchen glanced at her younger sister who was gazing thoughtfully out the window. "He is a good man, Tatty."

"I know it." Tatiana stepped back to her bread dough. "I know it all too well."

CHAPTER FIFTEEN

Shaky Adulthood

"Jonny's back," Gretchen announced as she strode into the house. "I found this on the fencepost." She handed Tatiana a fat tomato.

Tatiana took the vegetable gleefully. "A tomato! We never discussed this one. I wonder what it means."

"Let's see," Gretchen intoned dryly. "A big, bright red tomato that just happens to be in the shape of a heart. What could it possibly mean?"

Tatiana's cheeks flushed as red as the tomato. "Oh, that rascally boy!"

Nearly three years had passed since Rose's bout with scarlet fever. Just as Gretchen had predicted, Tatiana had grown into a beautiful young woman, while retaining her lively spirit. None of the sisters had married yet. Rose, for the most part, had recovered from her illness, but the fever had weakened her heart: she would never be as robust as she had been before her health crisis.

Tatiana had returned to Philadelphia once Rose began recovering from scarlet fever, much to the relief of Mr. Wolfe's sister, who cared for the children during Tatiana's absence from the city. By then, her father was once again working full-time, and the family's financial crisis was soon over. While she had once thought she would leave the employment of the cranky Mr. Wolfe the first minute that was possible, caring for the children fulfilled her, and she enjoyed earning her own money.

That same spring, Samantha had moved to Philadelphia to live with her cousin Charles and his new wife. Tatiana relished having her friend so near; she and Samantha met often. Only a few months later, Samantha had become engaged to Malchus, and they were married the following spring. By then, Samantha adored the Wolfe children as much as Tatiana did, so when Tatiana began to long for home, Samantha agreed to take over as their caretaker soon after her wedding.

Tatiana returned home with a light heart and a bit of savings that she hoped to spend on her future, but she had no idea what that future might be. Jonny was still surveying in the wilderness as settlers moved ever westward. While she might sometimes dream about him, his lack of faith was still a huge obstacle.

After her return from Philadelphia, Tatiana had busied herself with housework, sewing, and taking care of the Smith boys, James and Peter. One month after she turned seventeen, Robert Matthew formally asked if he might begin seeing her. Tatiana was a bit reluctant, given her feelings for the absent Jonny, but she was also lonely, so she said yes to Robert's request. They had been courting for the last five months. While he was a good man and was kind to her, she felt discontented with their relationship. Something seemed to be missing, which was a good way to sum up her life, she thought.

Now Jonny was back, and Tatiana felt more excited than she had in a long time. She rose from her chair and strolled over to the window with forced carelessness. "I think I might go for a walk since it's such a lovely day."

Gretchen rolled her eyes but said nothing. Rose slipped up behind Tatiana. "Are you hoping to see him?"

Tatiana lowered her eyes. "I suppose I am." Rose was quiet. Tatiana looked inquiringly at her. "Why are you looking at me so? Don't you think I should go?"

Rose raised her slender hand and stroked Tatiana's hair. "Just don't forget who you've given your heart to."

A steely look entered Tatiana's eyes. She shook her sister off and started for the door. "You make it sound as if I'm already married to him! I've made no promises to Robert!"

Rose looked sadly after her younger sister. Tatiana had grown up in the last two years, but she still had a fiery temper and the stubbornness of a mule.

Gretchen and Rose can be such restrictive grouches! Tatiana thought angrily. *That's probably why they're old spinsters now.* Mounting Jack, Tatiana started to ride him north toward the Smith farm. She had gone a little way when she began to feel guilty. *What are you doing, Tatiana? You are courting Robert and going to visit Jonny! That's most improper!*

She thought about turning around, but she wasn't quite ready to face her sisters yet. With a click of her tongue, she directed Jack toward the forest behind Reverend Matthew's house.

She reached the pleasant little spot that was Robert's favorite fishing hole. She tethered Jack in a small, grassy clearing and then sat on a flat rock beside the water. Removing her shoes and tugging off her stockings, Tatiana dangled her feet down into the chilly stream. A warm breeze pulled at her thick black braid as if trying to free her tresses from their binding.

Tatiana's fingers moved over the grainy surface of the rock, remembering the day she had sketched Robert here. So much had changed since then! Her father's accident and Rose's illness had reminded her that a future with those she loved most was not guaranteed. In Philadelphia, she had learned how to work for an unpleasant man and discovered how much she liked caring for children.

Gazing searchingly into the rippling water of the stream, Tatiana could make out the blurred reflection of a slim, dark-haired young woman. She grasped a rock in her right hand. "Oh, Father," she prayed, "More than anything I want to be like You. Yet, it seems like even when I try to be more like your Son, Tatiana keeps taking over. My fleshly will keeps rising up and quenching the godly spirit inside of me." Tears slid down Tatiana's face as she cried out loud: "I don't want to return to the sinful ways that I left at the foot of the cross! I don't want to be the person I once was!" Tatiana hurled the rock toward the reflection in the water.

Reaching into the hidden pocket sewn into her dress, Tatiana pulled out her little red Bible and opened its dog-eared pages. She flipped through it hastily, knowing the verse she was looking for. When she found it, she read it prayerfully: "Search me, O God, and know my heart: try me, and know my thoughts: And see if there be any wicked way in me, and lead me in the way everlasting."

Upon finishing her prayer, Tatiana's heart felt lighter. She sprang to her feet with renewed energy. Wiping away her tears, she splashed across the stream and walked barefoot through the lush forest on the other side. Her eyes flew about, and it seemed that everywhere she looked she could see God's marvelous handiwork.

Suddenly she froze in her tracks like a hound does when he spots his prey. A shiver made its icy way up her spine. Even though she had heard nothing, she sensed that someone was nearby. She turned in a slow circle, her eyes scanning every branch, twig, and leaf that was around her. She saw nothing amiss. She stood there for a moment longer in complete perplexity. She jumped as she felt someone's breath hitting the back of her neck.

She whirled about and gasped to see the man standing directly behind her. "Jonny! What? How?"

Jonny laughed in his usual way, throwing his head back. "I'm sorry if I startled you, Thelma. I was just practicing my tracking skills a bit, and I spotted you. I hadn't really expected to find you cavorting out here like a wild Indian princess."

Tatiana blushed. "And I hadn't really expected to be stalked like a deer!"

Jonny slipped his arm through hers. "Now, now! No complaints! You're very fortunate that I'm not planning to eat you."

"Of that, I am grateful," Tatiana answered wryly. She studied her old friend. Her eyes swept over him, from his bare head down past a fringed buckskin shirt and matching trousers to beaded moccasins. He carried a long flintlock musket over his shoulder with ease. Looking back at his face, she saw that his boyish, freckled features were long gone. They had been replaced by a strong, swarthy countenance. From the chiseled planes of his face to the powerful stance of his legs, Jonny was all man—and a very rugged one, from the looks of him.

"So, how does it feel to be home?"

Jonny's eyes drifted over his surroundings and then returned to Tatiana. "It feels good. I think I almost forgot about all the simple things I loved about this place—like how the air smells."

Tatiana laughed. Jonny noticed how her voice had taken on a deeper, fuller tone. "I missed that when I was away too."

The friends walked slowly, reminiscing about old times and sharing recent news. When they came to the place where Jack was tied, Tatiana turned to face Jonny. "Are you coming to the Weller barn dance tomorrow night?"

Jonny's calloused finger brushed her cheek. "I will if you allow me to be your escort."

The light faded from Tatiana's eyes, and her face became troubled. "I already agreed to go with Robert."

A deep furrow appeared in Jonny's forehead. "Robert? Isn't he supposed to be off at college learning to be a preacher or something?"

Tatiana fiddled anxiously with her braid. "He finished seminary this February. We've been seeing each other for nigh on five months now." She held back from saying that she couldn't have courted Jonny anyway until he accepted Christ in his heart, lest he claim a belief he didn't have.

Jonny reeled as if he had been struck. "Five months?" he choked, with his eyes boring down into Tatiana's. His expression was one of disbelief. He stood in silence for a moment longer before bounding off through the trees like a frightened stag.

Jonny ran until he had to stop to catch his breath. He leaned, panting, against a tree and put his face in his hands. How could Tatiana have done this? Didn't she know that he loved her? Was her impatience so great that she couldn't wait for his return? Didn't she know he had left to earn money for their future?

No, she didn't, because he had never told her, not before he left or when he had sent occasional messages to her. The way she had looked at him told him that she felt the same way he did, and he had assumed she would wait for his return—and yet he had never told her when the wait would end. Jonny felt like weeping, but he had been taught not to cry when he was only a little boy. His grief would be kept inside.

During all the cold, hungry nights in the wilderness, thinking about Tatiana had kept his spirits high. When forging turbulent rapids, the memory of her kind words had given him courage. When he felt lost and alone, recalling her sweet face had given him solace. And now ... now that she was finally within his reach, she had been snatched away by another man.

The young man took a deep breath to calm his jangled nerves. She could yet be his. A grim smile crossed Jonny's stalwart face. Robert didn't know what he was up against.

Tatiana's arms were curved elegantly over her head as she carefully coifed her hair into a stylishly loose knot on top of her head. She heard someone stirring behind her and glanced toward her sister's bed. Removing the hairpins from her mouth, Tatiana called: "Rose, dearest, you should get up if you want to be ready in time."

Rose opened her eyes and stretched languidly. "Ah, such a nice nap that was! I had the loveliest dream!" Tatiana raised her eyebrows expectantly and Rose explained, "I dreamt that Mother was still alive. And we were all having tea and eating raspberry tarts."

Tatiana smiled. Rose was always so sweet and innocent! She wondered occasionally if God might have accidentally placed a little angel child into the Bergman family. "Are you going with us, Rosie?"

Rose sat up slowly and pressed a hand to her temple. "No, I don't suppose I will. I wouldn't do any dancing anyway, though I very much enjoy sitting by and watching everyone else."

Tatiana lowered her arms and studied her reflection critically. "I'm always amazed by how little it takes to content you, Rosie. I swear I would go stark, raving mad if I could only sit and watch!" She reached up and tugged a strand of hair down in front of her ear.

"Did you see Jonny yesterday?" Rose joined Tatiana at the dressing table and sleepily began to run a brush through her wavy locks.

Tatiana rummaged through the drawer for a necklace. "I did. I want you to know I did not seek him out. He found me when I was walking in the woods."

Rose aimed a quick glance at her younger sister. "And how was your reunion?"

Tatiana did not answer immediately. She had found a certain arrowhead necklace in the drawer and was studying it pensively. "I think I wanted to recapture my childhood by talking with him," she said with a sigh. "I spent the best days of my life with him, Rose, and I futilely believed that Jonny had the power to summon them back. He has changed just as much as I have—no, probably more. Those days are over, and I must enjoy the ones I have now. The present is for living, not for looking back."

Rose slipped a warm arm around Tatiana's shoulders. "And you have so much to look forward to, Tatty. You don't have time to be gazing back over your shoulder."

Tatiana sniffled and quickly dabbed her eyes with the back of her wrist. "I ... I just sometimes feel so insecure. Father doesn't understand me like he once did, Samantha has married and lives in Philadelphia, and now Jonny's gone off and gotten all s-strange and ... and ... manly! I feel so lonely and unsure of myself sometimes."

"There, there." Although Tatiana had passed Rose in height, her older sister still possessed a gentle authority over Tatty. "The Lord will not see the righteous forsaken. He will order your steps according to His perfect will."

Tatiana fumbled for her handkerchief and wiped her nose with it. "How are you always so calm and undisturbed by anything, Rosie? Does nothing in this life frighten or upset you?"

"Of course it does!" Rose exclaimed. Tatiana noticed as if for the first time the dark circles under her sister's eyes; Rose's skin had retained its fragility from the fever and her face was so pale that it was nearly translucent. "But I have put my trust in God and I give all my fear to Him. He replaces my vulnerability with His divine strength."

Tatiana threw her arms around her dear sister, pulling the frail body close. Rose's serenity was in such contrast to her fragility. *Such a feeble temple for such a mighty faith!* Rose's confidence in God never seemed to waver, no matter the tribulations that came.

Once released from their embrace, Rose left to go downstairs and Tatiana lifted the arrowhead necklace from the dressing table. With a pensive smile tugging at her lips, she tied it about her neck.

Tatiana glanced at Robert, who was deep in conversation with Mr. Weller about this year's sweet corn. Subtly sliding her arm out from under his, Tatiana walked toward the open barn doors. The sun was making a majestic show of setting, regardless of whether anyone was there to see it or not. A band of bats fluttered from the loft above out into the warm evening air. Tatiana heard giggles and saw two little girls go skipping by hand in hand. The bows on the ends of their braids bobbed gaily.

Oh, Samantha, how I miss you! Tatiana cried inwardly. *I miss having someone who truly understands me—someone who allows me to discard all my stiff manners and be myself. I wish you well, my dear friend.*

"Well, aren't you the social butterfly!" a snide voice exclaimed.

Tatiana turned and saw Arietta posed prettily at her elbow. Tatiana sucked in a deep breath. "Well, if it isn't Mrs. Weston! How have you been, Arietta?"

"I've been quite busy lately, working on the house." Arietta tugged at her elbow-length gloves, an unsuitable accessory for a barn party. She looked over at Tatiana again. "I say, Tatty, I'm quite intrigued by that necklace you have there. Wherever did you get it?"

Tatiana touched the familiar arrowhead with a smile. "It was a gift from a very special friend of mine."

"Well, it looks like some sort of Indian jewelry, if you ask me," Arietta said decisively. "Oh, that reminds me, did you hear that Jonny Creek is back in town?" Tatiana nodded. Arietta continued, "I haven't seen him yet, but I've heard from others that he's wilder than ever! I never quite trusted that boy. I always half feared he might scalp me in my bed if I so much as looked at him cross-eyed. But he is so very dashing!"

Tatiana bit back a reply and forced her lips into a smile. Neither time nor marriage had succeeded in taming Arietta's irrepressible tongue.

Mr. Weller took his instrument and hoisted himself into a wagon bed that served as stage. The fiddle music began with a bouncy lilt. Arietta and Tatiana drifted back inside as people quickly found their dancing partners. Robert caught Tatiana's hand with a smile and swung her easily onto the dance floor. Boots stamped and skirts swirled as the barn came alive with happy dancers. A big, gray mule watched the festivities from its stall and twitched its long ears comically, as if annoyed by the intrusion.

Just as the first dance was ending, Tatiana spotted Jonny coming into the barn. She hadn't expected to see him tonight, and she was even more shocked to see Johanna Easley draping herself from his arm! Tatiana's face suddenly grew hot. Her hand flew to the necklace she was wearing.

"Are you all right, Tatiana?" Robert asked, hovering over her with a worried expression on his kind face. "You look flushed."

"A little warm from dancing, that's all," she answered briskly, fanning herself with her hand. "If you will excuse me for a moment." Mr. Weller began coaxing the notes of "The Arkansas Traveler" from his fiddle. Seeking privacy, Tatiana skirted a towering stack of hay bales that defined the dance floor. Muttering angrily to herself, she worked to undo the knot that held the arrowhead necklace around her neck.

"What a fool you are, Tatiana!" she hissed at herself. "It was utterly stupid of you to flaunt this necklace as if it grants you some claim to Jonny, because you have none! You gave him up, remember?" She dropped the necklace into a pocket and breathed a sigh of relief. Several cows watched her lazily from their pen in the corner. Their quiet eyes followed her movements and their jaws moved rhythmically. Tatiana pressed her hand to her forehead. "I'll have to face Johanna for sure and she'll be as happy as a cat that's gotten into the cream jar. Lord, put a harness on my tongue and post a sentry at the door of my mouth!"

She breathed deeply and plunged back toward the dancing. As she rounded the haystack, she nearly ran into the very cause of her upset. Jonny caught her arm to keep her from falling. "Well, hello there, Miss Bergman! And just what were you doing in the dark recesses of the barn?"

Tatiana wrenched her arm from his grasp and refused to make eye contact. "I was having a lovely conversation with the cows."

Incorrigible Jonny took her elbow again. "Well, this we must fix! We must find you pleasanter company than those cud-chewing beasts back there."

Tatiana briefly raised her eyes to give him a questioning look. My, he was looking handsome tonight! His buckskins had been replaced with black trousers, a white shirt, and a stylish vest. His hair had been trimmed and combed, and he looked fresh-faced and clean.

"Now, don't give me that look!" He glanced over his shoulder and smiled. "Here comes someone now! Isn't this providential?"

Jonny stepped aside with a flourish. Tatiana found herself face to face with Johanna, who was nearly bubbling over with excitement. She clasped Tatiana's hands eagerly. "Good evening, Tatiana! Isn't this so fine? Did you know Jonny was back in town?" She babbled on without waiting for an answer. "I hadn't a clue until he came knocking on my door. I was so surprised, and then of course I had to make sure that Father and Mother didn't see him, because that would have been a first-rate disaster! Anyhow, I always knew we'd make a splendid couple." She gazed admiringly toward Jonny where he stood talking to Daniel Weston. "You have Robert Matthew, and now I have Jonny Creek! I'm glad everything has worked out so nicely."

Tatiana raised her eyebrows. "Indeed."

Johanna slid her arm companionably around Tatiana's waist. "I daresay, now that this whole affair is settled, I believe we shall be great friends!" A girlish giggle bubbled up from Johanna's throat. "I do believe I'm the happiest woman here tonight! And Jonny is the handsomest man of all, isn't he? Not to cast a shadow on your Robert, of course, but Jonny is much more striking."

"So it would seem," Tatiana replied levelly.

"Well, I had best go rejoin my toothsome beau!" Johanna chirped, licking her lips delicately. "I'm sure he's anxious for a dance."

Tatiana's arm fell back to her side as Johanna flittered away. She suddenly felt as if she had been drained of all her energy. Thank the Lord she had said nothing rash! Holding her wayward tongue always proved to be a terrible strain.

She felt a tap on her shoulder and saw Daniel Weston standing behind her, grinning in his usual fox-like fashion. "May I have this next dance?" he wanted to know.

Looking around, Tatiana saw that Johanna had waylaid Arietta. She managed a tired smile and took Daniel's hand. "I don't see why not."

As Daniel spun her onto the floor, his green eyes sparkled with the ever-present mischief that always lurked beneath his sandy shock of hair. "We had better make this dance a good one, since this is making up for the time you refused me at the barn raising."

"Oh, heavens, Dan! That was ages ago!"

"I haven't forgotten it." Daniel dipped Tatiana far back on his arm.

When he raised her again, Tatiana shot him a fiery glance. "Don't forget that your wife and Robert are watching."

Daniel winked buoyantly. "I'll do my best to remember, but no promises."

The evening passed quickly for Tatiana. She danced several times with Robert and stayed quite occupied avoiding a certain someone else. The hard thing was that she could not seem to get that 'someone' and Johanna out of her sight. Every time the two of them went swooping by on the dance floor, Tatiana turned nearly green with jealousy. Johanna was smiling up at Jonny, and her eyes were glowing. He was resting his hand gently on her lissome waist. Tatiana ground her teeth.

Late in the evening, Katarina Siegfried arrived with no escort. She sat down against the wall by herself. Out of politeness, Jonny headed over to invite her to dance. He was rising from a polite bow when she shrieked, "Get away from me, you heathen!"

Jonny concealed his hurt as he rose to his full height. He gave Kitty a curt nod and returned to his place beside Johanna.

Tatiana was taking a cooling swallow of lemonade at the refreshment table when the last dance was announced. Before she could spot Robert, a low voice asked, "May I have the pleasure of this next dance with you?"

Tatiana choked on her lemonade. Holding her handkerchief over her nose and mouth, she turned red with embarrassment at her graceless behavior. She stared up at Jonny with wide eyes. Regaining her breath, she said, "Jonny, it's the last dance! You know it belongs to the person you came with, same as the first dance."

Jonny winked shamelessly. "I suppose I know that." He held out his hand.

Tatiana stared down at Jonny's scarred hand. The little and ring fingers were nothing but knobby stubs, and his middle finger was cut off at the second knuckle. Not knowing what reckless notion had possessed her, she reached out and clutched that brown, disfigured hand and allowed herself to be pulled out on the dance floor.

Tatiana did not even see the rest of the dancers. She was too busy staring into those alluring golden eyes. In a low voice, she demanded, "What did you mean by bringing Johanna with you tonight?"

"Ah, so you noticed."

"Of course I noticed! And I think it's despicable!"

A sly smirk crept over Jonny's lips. "I think I see your sapphire eyes turning green, Miss Bergman."

"If you don't honestly care for her, how could you use her in such a shameful way?" Tatiana continued. "She thinks you really love her and you're bound to hurt her terribly."

"You hurt <u>me</u>," Jonny pointed out.

"It's not the same," Tatiana insisted, twirling under Jonny's arm and returning to his side. "I didn't do anything to deceive you."

"Didn't you?" Jonny asked bitterly. "When everything you said and did declared that you loved me, what else was I to believe?"

Tatiana's eyes widened. Was that really how it had seemed to him? She had always thought that she had masked her feelings.

"You are speechless, Miss Bergman."

Tatiana licked her lips. "I don't know what to say."

Jonny released her right hand to step around her and take her other hand. "Let me help you. You can say that you don't want Robert and you really love me."

Tatiana set her teeth. "Jonny, I do not care for you!"

"Oh, come now, Thelma. You'll have to pray long and hard for forgiveness for that hulking great lie. You're trembling even now."

Tatiana jerked her hand free. "I should be going. Good evening, Mr. Creek."

The dance was not yet over, but Jonny did not attempt to stop her. "Likewise," he said, giving her a gracious bow and a thunderous look.

Tatiana beat a hasty retreat to Robert's side. He took her hand and walked her out. "What did Jonny say to you?"

Blushing, Tatiana shook her head. "Nothing."

"I know you to be a sensible girl, Tatiana," Robert asserted, helping her into his buggy. "You don't get upset at 'nothing.' If he insulted you—"

"No, no, he didn't. We simply disagreed on something."

Robert clucked to the horse and shot her one more worried look. "Well, let me know if you ever need me to fend him off."

Tatiana stared down at her hands clasped in her lap. "Thank you, Robert. You are too kind."

"I need your advice, Gretchen!" Tatiana cried as she strode unannounced into the kitchen and closed the door behind her with a resounding slam.

"Good heavens, Tat!" Gretchen exclaimed. "Am I granted no privacy at all in this house?" Gretchen was slumped low in the big wooden bathtub that she has positioned near the fire. Her head rested on one edge, and her legs dangled out the other side. She was wreathed in steam, and her hair hung in long, wet ropes.

"If it is any consolation to you, Gretchie, I wasn't looking for you," Tatiana replied, boosting herself to sit on the table.

Gretchen twisted her neck to look back at her sister. "Yes, you are, Tat. Otherwise you wouldn't have said you need my advice."

"You heard that?" Tatiana smoothed her nightgown over her knees. "I didn't plan to disturb you, really, but I couldn't sleep. I'm not sure what to say to Robert."

Gretchen sighed and leisurely crossed her ankles. "I'm afraid I don't see your dilemma. Just tell him the truth!"

Tatiana slid down from her perch and began to restlessly pace the room. Her high-necked nightgown brushed the tops of her bare feet. "But I want to avoid hurting him as much as I can. He has been so good to me, Gretchen! I haven't a single complaint of ill treatment from him. He has the kindest, most loyal heart I've ever seen in a man."

This statement confounded Gretchen. She had never had the opportunity to be pursued by such a man, but she had often dreamed of it. How could Tatiana refuse someone so eligible? Bringing her hand down onto the water with a splash, Gretchen cried: "Then why, in mercy's name, do you wish to terminate your courtship?"

Tatiana thumped herself down on the hearth. "Because I can't love him with my whole heart! I have tried; I really have tried, Gretchen. I enjoy being in his company, but that's about all I can say. He is a wonderful man and a good Christian, and I know that he cares for me with a pure, unconditional love. But I don't deserve it! I will never be able to love him with the undying devotion that he deserves; to consent to marry him when he could have another who would truly love him would be robbery. I couldn't do such a thing!"

Understanding shone in Gretchen's eyes as she reached out and clasped Tatiana's hand with her own damp fingers. "Then you are doing the right thing, Sister."

Tatiana ran her fingers through her loose hair. "But I still don't know what to say to him!"

"Tell him what you just said to me. It's simple, it's clear, and, above all, it's honest."

"Thank you, Gretchen. Pray that the Lord will give me courage for tomorrow evening!"

"I will. And now, if it's not too much to ask, I would like a little peace and tranquility!" Gretchen declared.

Tatiana giggled and lowered her face to a few inches above her older sister's. "With me in the house? Never!"

Gretchen pretended to be cross and flicked a bit of water into Tatiana's face. With a squeal, Tatiana fled from the room and Gretchen sank back with a sigh. Annoying though Tatiana was, Gretchen loved her little sister dearly. "Guide her steps, Lord," she prayed softly.

The next night, Tatiana met with Robert and explained why she could not continue their courtship. The young man took it hard, but it did not take him long at all to recover from the blow. He soon returned to his normal work of tending the Bergman garden and bringing in wood. A few weeks later, Robert asked Rose out for a buggy ride, and within a short time, he proposed.

Tatiana stood at the door to see off the newly married couple. She was happy for the ecstatic Rose and felt that Rose and Robert made a perfect couple. "I don't know that I've ever seen Rose look so happy before," she remarked to Gretchen, as they waved the couple goodbye.

"She does look elated," Gretchen admitted. "I find the whole matter quite amazing, but I wish them the best."

CHAPTER SIXTEEN

A Maiden Pursued

Robert strode along the outer aisles of the church, opening the windows to let some fresh air into the stuffy sanctuary. Sunlight streamed across the room in long, slanting beams and settled its golden warmth over a few select members of the congregation who happened to be sitting in its path. Tatiana turned her head just enough to watch Robert taking his seat beside Rose on his family's pew. Once that had been Tatiana's place, but she had relinquished it gladly.

The song leader called out a song. Tatiana flicked through her hymnbook to "My Faith Looks Up to Thee." The parishioners were halfway through the first verse when someone slipped through the door. It had been several years since he had set foot within these doors. He sauntered nonchalantly toward the front and took his seat next to Tatiana.

Tatiana, engrossed in singing, hadn't heard the latecomer. She looked up in surprise when someone slid into the pew beside her. It was Jonny Creek! *What was he thinking? Whatever gave him the audacity to plant himself here beside me?* It didn't occur to her that she had done the same thing to him, the first day she saw him. She shot him a bewildered look, but the young man was too engrossed in singing to notice; his voice rang out with a sincere fervor, and his eyes were fixed on the page that Tatiana was holding open.

Tatiana doggedly faced forward and launched into the second verse at the top of her lungs. "May Thy rich grace impart strength to my fainting heart, my zeal inspire; as Thou hast died for me, O may my love to thee, pure, warm, and changeless be, a living fire."

All during the service, Tatiana sat rather tensely. Reverend Matthew was preaching a convicting salvation message. Tatiana had to resist the urge to glance at Jonny for clues about what he was thinking. While she perched there on pins and needles, Jonny seemed to be quite comfortable. He sat back lazily with his arms folded easily over his chest and listened quietly.

Tatiana was inwardly curling up into a ball. She wished she could be far away from the spirited young man sitting beside her. *What kind of statement is he trying to make? What of Johanna?* As she mused over her questions, Jonny casually stretched his arm out to rest along the back of the pew so that it was touching Tatiana's shoulders.

Flushing from embarrassment and anger, Tatiana reached delicately up to where his injured hand rested against her shoulder and pinched his index finger.

Jonny got the message and dropped his arm, his eyes remaining focused on Reverend Matthew. "To those of you who are married," the Reverend was saying, "your marriage will never succeed in the way God intends it to unless you can hold up Jesus the Christ as your first love. That means you must put him before your husband or before your wife, and give your heart fully to Him. Only after you have done this, can God truly bless your marriage and make it prosper."

Tatiana realized what a good reminder this was for her. She stole another glance toward Jonny. Rather, her eyes went to where his calloused hands, void of a Bible, were clasped together on his knee. *What if he wants to talk to me after the service? I won't know what to say!*

The Reverend seemed to preach for an inordinate amount of time. As the congregation was singing the last hymn, Tatiana rose and politely slipped out. As her skirt brushed across Jonny's knees she forced herself to look away from his searching eyes.

She hurried across the commons toward the willows along the creek, praying as she walked. The sunbaked grasses rustled under her feet and grasshoppers went bounding erratically in all directions as she disturbed their hiding places. "Oh, Lord, I have given my heart to You, and I won't let him steal it. You are my first love, Jesus, and I pray that I will never try to put you in second place." Tatiana seated herself on the grassy bank beside the creek and swept her straw bonnet from her head. "Jonny doesn't know you, Father, and until he gives his heart over to you, I won't let him have a bit of mine!"

With these words, Tatiana buried her head in her hands and wept. Why was she struggling so? Tatiana's real trouble was that her mind was telling her that she was in love with Jonny, while her spirit was screaming in protest. "Please, Lord," she whispered, "keep me from temptation. Help me, Jesus." As she said this she heard footfalls and she folded herself up even tighter until she looked like a babe in the womb.

Jonny ducked through the willow branches as he neared the place where Tatiana was sitting. The leafy branches moved in the wind and seemed to passionately reach out toward anyone who came near them. "Ah, I thought I might find you here," Jonny said. "This reminds me of when we first met, and you chased me all the way out here in a raging fit of anger."

When he received no response, he seated himself beside Tatiana, picking up a willow branch and peeling the thin bark away from the green wood. "So why did you flee before church was over?"

Tatiana kept staring at the rippling water in the creek, hardly trusting herself to look at him. "I didn't want to talk to you." Her short reply made her sound like a sulky child.

"I have something important I want to tell you," Jonny said, using a leafy branch to tickle the inside of Tatiana's ear in an effort to gain her attention. "I made a big decision the other night."

Finally Tatiana turned to look at him with wide eyes and a heart full of hope. Could it be? Had he finally accepted Jesus into his heart?

Pleased that he finally had convinced her to listen, Jonny leaned back on his elbows. "I am going to run for mayor!"

Tatiana's heart sank. She managed a wintry smile. "That's very ambitious of you, Mr. Creek. I hope it goes well for you."

Jonny surveyed her thoughtfully. He could tell that she was withholding something from him. "Why so solemn, Tatiana?" Reaching out, he cradled her chin in his hand. "I remember when those blue eyes of yours used to dance all the time—always full of mischief. Why can't you be jolly again?"

Tears glistened in Tatiana's eyes. She relished the touch of Jonny's hand, but she forced herself to raise her chin from his palm. "I'm afraid I cannot. I have too much of a burden in my heart."

Jonny's golden eyes bore down on Tatiana's liquid blue ones. He was looking at her probingly, as if trying to comprehend what she was saying. "I do hope I'm not causing it ..." Jonny said slowly. Tatiana only looked at him in reply. Jonny shifted uncomfortably. "I don't understand, Thelma." With these words, he rose and walked away across the field.

Tatiana raised her head to watch his retreating figure. She would never have him— never would she have the chance to express her great love for him. Plucking a handful of grass, she flung it toward the water. "Why did you have to fall in love with such a man, Tatiana?" she asked bitterly. "This is nothing but madness." She thought of Robert and tears again filled her eyes. "It's likely that I have carelessly thrown away my only chance to get married!" Getting to her feet, she stretched out her hand to part the thick willow branches. "Tatiana, you are a terrible fool."

Tatiana tied off a bundle of rosemary and climbed onto the chair to hang it from a rafter in the Smith cabin. Hopping down, she surveyed her work with pride. The air was heady with the scent of rosemary, thyme, sage, dill, and lavender, and the rafters were full of neat little bundles of fresh herbs as she worked to help the Smiths store their harvest for winter. Today, she was alone with the boys while the Smiths and Jonny were running errands in town.

"Tatty, you forgot this one!" four-year-old Peter Smith piped up, extending a long stalk of dill toward Tatiana.

Tatiana smiled and took the stalk, tucking it into one of the other bundles. "Thank you, little man! Now, we'd better see where your brother went." Affectionately rubbing her fingers through Peter's silky blonde hair, she went to the window.

The sight that met her eyes was enough to make her heart nearly stop. "Oh, Lord, have mercy on him!" she cried. Wrenching the door open, she leapt across the porch and dashed across the yard, her eyes never leaving the disaster that was playing out before her eyes.

Seven-year-old James was clinging desperately to Beauty's back. His thin legs struggled to grip her slippery sides and his hands grasped frantically at her whipping black mane. The spirited filly was leaping and bucking, trying to dislodge her inexperienced rider.

Tatiana watched in horror as boy and beast rose high into the air. Never had she seen Beauty rear so far! She feared that the horse might topple over backwards. James went sailing through the air with a terrified scream, and the horse dropped back down to all fours with an obstinate shake of her head.

A small cloud of dust rose up as James's body hit the ground. Clutching her skirts, Tatiana ran to him. She scrambled over the fence and was at the boy's side in an instant. "James!" She pushed the lanky golden hair back from his forehead. Oh, he looked so pale! He wasn't moving either, but Tatiana could see his chest rising and falling as he breathed.

Running her shaking hands down his arms and legs, Tatiana prayed that James would be all right. "Please, God, let this dear child be uninjured!" Pulling him into her arms, she held the boy close, pressing her cheek against his smooth hair.

She heard soft hoofbeats and felt a warm current of breath on the top of her head. Clutching James tighter, she glared up at the horse. "Go away, you hideous animal! Look what you did to this poor boy!"

Beauty stared at Tatiana with big, shimmering eyes. Her wide nostrils were still flared and her mane hung messily down over her nose. Her burnished coat was shining in the late afternoon sun. Lowering her head, the horse sniffed curiously at James's body. She gently lipped his sandy hair and then gave a low whicker.

"If that's your apology, it's hardly suitable," Tatiana told her, gathering James up and carrying the limp boy toward the house.

She was nearing the porch when the boy's blue eyes opened. He stared up at Tatiana in confusion for a moment. "What happened?"

Sitting down on the highest step, Tatiana used her free hand to wipe some of the dust from the boy's face. "Beauty threw you off, James."

James coughed and wiped his mouth. "Did you see me ridin' her though, Tatty?"

"Yes, and you looked just like an Indian on a wild mustang."

A smile spread over James's dirt-streaked face. "Really? A wild mustang?"

"Yes, and you had better not do that again unless Jonny is here to help you. You could have been killed!" She clasped him tighter at the dreadful thought.

"I reckon I won't ever learn to ride as well as Jonny if I'm dead," James reasoned.

"I reckon so," Tatiana agreed. "Now let's get you washed up."

Not long after that Mr. and Mrs. Smith arrived with Jonny. James was only too eager to tell them about his wild ride. Mrs. Smith clutched him to her chest, and Mr. Smith turned pale before gathering himself to lecture the boy.

Tatiana was washing the supper dishes when Jonny joined her at the dry sink. Taking a dish she had rinsed, he cheerfully set to drying it, whistling as he worked. "The town meeting is tonight," he reminded her.

Tatiana nodded, "I'll go if I can get there in time."

"Don't worry about that. I can drive you in," Jonny offered. "I picked you up so I'll take you. I sure hope I get voted in as mayor tonight."

Tatiana scrubbed at some burnt remnants in the bottom of a cast iron frying pan. "Do you think you'll get the position?" Shortly before Jonny returned from the wilderness, the boundaries of the township had been expanded to add the farms closest to town, including the Smith property.

"Well, I didn't attend all those boring town council meetings for nothing!" he said, rinsing the pan and briskly toweling it off. "I figure it's me, grouchy old Grable, or else snooty Mr. Easley who's too big for his britches already."

"It should be an interesting evening," Tatiana allowed, and Jonny agreed with a throaty groan. They finished the dishes. Jonny went to change his clothes while Tatiana emptied the dishwater outside. Coming back in, she was greeted by a small red tomato that was balanced on the edge of the table.

With a rueful smile, Tatiana dropped it into her apron pocket. That boy and his tomatoes! Thankfully there wouldn't be many more growing this year.

Jonny swung up into the wagon beside Tatiana and grasped the reins. "Well, let us be off, my lady!"

Tatiana didn't reply until after he had slapped the reins across the horses' backs. "You know, Jonny, you don't always have to try to be charming. Just be yourself."

Jonny had not been expecting this unprovoked verbal attack. "I ... wasn't trying to be charming."

Tatiana primly tucked her shawl around her body. "I prefer how you used to be—when you weren't trying to make any great impression on me. You spoke your mind and you held no pretenses."

Jonny chewed the inside of his cheek. "So let me get this straight: you'll like me if I stop being charming?" Tatiana moaned and put her face in her hands. Jonny rested his elbow on his knee in irritation. "Tell me something, Thelma. What am I doing wrong? I have made it clear to you that I care for you, but you keep holding back. Is there something I do that bothers you? Do I have some great flaw that prevents you from returning my affections?"

The wagon hit a pothole and Tatiana fell briefly against Jonny's strong shoulder. She quickly righted herself. "Yes, there is something."

"Well, for pity's sake, what is it?"

Tatiana wrung her fingers nervously. "I ... can't tell you."

Jonny took a deep breath and gazed off toward the forest for a moment. "Tatiana, if you don't tell me what I'm doing wrong, how am I possibly supposed to fix my mistake?"

"It's something I hope you will discover on your own." Tatiana toyed with one of the tassels on her shawl. "However, it should have been made crystal clear to you if you had listened at all to Reverend Matthew's sermon on that first Sunday you came back to church."

Jonny lifted his hat to tug at his hair in vexation. "Well, that's been awhile. I guess I've forgotten it."

Hopeless! This is hopeless! Tatiana thought sadly. *If I tell him that it's because he's not a Christian, he will falsely claim that he has accepted Jesus in order to have my hand in marriage.* "I care deeply for you, Jonny. But all I can say is that there is a major, life-altering difference between us that holds us apart."

Jonny's heart felt as if someone had just poured molten lead into it. *So that's it. This 'difference'—this chasm that she speaks of, could be nothing other than my Indian blood. Even with all she ever told me about considering me as an equal, she is no different from the rest. Tatiana is just another proud white person who thinks she's better than the likes of me. I sure don't remember any sermon about that, but what else could it be?*

Clenching his jaw, Jonny drove the rest of the way in silence. They were nearing town and Tatiana said, "Please, Jonny, drop me off here. I need to stop at my house before continuing to the meeting."

She doesn't even want to be seen in the same wagon with me! She's ashamed to be in my company. Well, I'll show her!

With a slap of the reins he urged his horses on. When Tatiana saw that they were not stopping, she spun to look at Jonny in surprise. "Jonny, what are you doing?"

He did not answer as he navigated the wagon through the center of town. He smiled grimly. Everyone going to the town meeting would be sure to see them now. He glanced over at Tatiana and was chagrined to see that she did not seem to be distressed. Her expression would be better explained as mildly confused.

They reached the schoolhouse where the meeting was to take place, and Jonny helped Tatiana down with a triumphant grin. "Thank you for the ride, Jonny," she said politely. "I need to run home now, but I'll try to be back in time for the voting."

Jonny noticed Tatiana's ragged work dress as if for the first time. His eyes trailed down over her stained apron, the dirt under her fingernails, and her stringy hair that was slipping from the knot on the back of her head. Of course! She wanted to go home to freshen up before the meeting! "I'm sorry, Tatiana. Let me drive you home." He turned to the wagon but she raised her small hand.

"No, don't bother. You can't miss any of the business tonight. I'll be fine."

Hot shame flooded over Jonny as he got one last glimpse of her tired eyes before she trotted off toward home. Some gentleman he was! And some mayor he would make. He rubbed his eyes as he turned toward the schoolhouse. Sometimes he felt like he had the brains of a sheep.

"Have all the ballots been collected?" Reverend Matthew's voice rang out over the cramped schoolroom. "If anyone has been missed, please raise your hand." His eyes scanned the room, but he saw no raised hands. "All right. Mr. Bergman and Mr. Weller, you may proceed to count the ballots."

Mr. Weller strode to the front of the room. There was a short pause, then everyone craned heads to look for Mr. Bergman to see him entering with Tatiana. Tatiana swiftly helped her father out of his coat and hat. He briskly hobbled to the front of the schoolroom.

There was a pause as Hans quickly cast his vote. Then a hush fell over the room as the men counted the ballots. There was only the light sound of rustling papers and muffled whispering. Finally Mr. Weller stood and made one last mark on the slate he was holding. "We have our results."

"Go ahead and read them for the whole assembly to hear," Reverend Matthew instructed.

Mr. Weller cleared his throat. "Mr. Conrad Easley has a total of twenty-three votes. Mr. Hedrick Grable has a total of seventeen. And Mr. Jonathan Creek has two."

Reverend Matthew had been scribbling the information down in his notebook and he looked up abruptly. "Before you sit down, Mr. Weller, could you repeat that last result?"

Mr. Weller glanced at his slate again. "Mr. Jonathan Creek has a total of two votes, sir."

The Reverend made note of it. "Very well, folks. It has been decided by majority vote that Mr. Conrad Easley will serve as our new town mayor."

Jonny hardly heard the final minutes of the meeting. He felt a strange buzzing in his ears as the meeting was adjourned. Mr. Weller's words kept replaying in his head. *Two votes. I got two votes. For all my work and effort, I got one other vote.*

He felt dazed as he joined the departing townspeople. He nearly stumbled as he reached the door and didn't notice Tatiana standing in front of him until he bumped into her outstretched hand. He shook it numbly and heard her softly say:

"I'm sorry you didn't get the position, Jonny."

Sure she's sorry, he thought bitterly. "I got two votes," he repeated with a miserable croak in his voice. "Nobody wanted me to be mayor except for that one poor sap who voted with me." With this he ran to his wagon.

Tatiana watched soberly as Jonny drove away. Hans had been standing nearby and he gently took his daughter's arm. His gray eyes twinkled as he watched Jonny's retreating wagon. "Well, I must admit: I'm the 'poor sap' who voted for him."

Tatiana looked up at her father in surprise. "Truly, Father?"

Hans nodded in confirmation. "And I'd do it again."

CHAPTER SEVENTEEN

A Broken and Contrite Heart

And I pray, Lord, for little James. He's been so sickly lately. I ask that you relieve his illness and bring strength to his lungs, if it is Your will. This I ask in Jesus' precious name. Amen." Tatiana opened her eyes and rested her cheek against the soft quilting of her bedspread.

Little James had been diagnosed with tuberculosis several years back, but he had worsened lately. Tatiana had been at the Smith cabin several days this week to help tend to him. He rested often because he was too weak to do much else. It pained Tatiana to see the lively little boy confined to his bed.

A year had passed since Mr. Easley was elected mayor, and Tatiana assumed that the chip firmly lodged on Jonny's shoulder was because he had found the loss in that race humiliating. He was haughtier than ever, looking down his nose at just about anyone who tried to approach him. When Tatiana had met him in Weller's store only yesterday, his eyes had been cold and distant, and he answered her curtly when she asked how he was. How hardened he had become! She felt that she hardly knew him anymore.

With a sigh, Tatiana took her little red Bible from her bed and cradled it in her hands. She turned the worn pages reverently, reading over the verses as if they were her old friends. She came to Psalm 51 and paused on verse 17. She read aloud:

The sacrifices of God are a broken spirit: a broken and a contrite heart, O God, thou wilt not despise,

"If only Jonny's heart could be broken and humbled before you, God!" Tatiana cried. "I have prayed for him for so long, and he seems to be farther from you than ever."

With these words in her mind, Tatiana blew out her lamp and climbed into bed. She had only slept a little while when she heard someone pounding on the door downstairs.

"Is someone at the door?" Gretchen moaned.

Tatiana was wriggling into her housecoat. "I'll go, Gretchen." Tatiana shivered as her bare toes met the cold wooden floor as she hurried downstairs. Opening the door, she was greeted by a rush of cold wind and rain. She saw Jonny standing stolidly waiting. "Jonny?"

"It's James," came the husky reply. "He's dying, Tatty, and he's asking to see you."

Tatiana wasted no time. "Come in. I'll only be a moment." She motioned for Jonny to step inside and then she turned and rushed back upstairs.

"Who was it?" Gretchen wanted to know.

Tatiana yanked off her housecoat, tugged a dress over her nightclothes, and slid her bare feet into boots. "Jonny. I'm going with him now. James is dying. Explain where I am to Father if I'm not back by morning."

"Wait, Tatiana!"

But the young woman was already tearing down the stairs. She yanked on a coat and turned to Jonny's shadowy figure. "I'm ready."

Stepping outside, Tatiana saw that Jonny had tied Beauty to the fence post. Jonny swung her up onto the horse and scrambled up in front of her. Wordlessly, he kicked Beauty into a gallop. Tatiana clung tightly to Jonny's lean waist as they traveled speedily through the freezing torrents of rain.

Don't take him, Lord. Don't take sweet little James away from us so soon! She prayed: *Please, God. We all love him so much!*

Upon reaching the cabin, Jonny sprang to the ground and hauled Tatiana down off the horse like a sack of potatoes. Snatching her hand, he rushed her toward the house. A dim light glowed from one of the windows, and Tatiana felt pulled toward that light as she splashed up onto the porch.

Bursting through the door, Jonny yanked his cap from his head. "She's here!" he called, clumping toward the bedroom in his muddy boots.

Mrs. Smith came to the bedroom doorway and looked at them both. She was holding her hand over her mouth, and Tatiana could see that her eyes were red with tears. "He's gone, Jonny." Her voice quavered with raw grief. "He just left us."

Every muscle in Jonny's body seemed to lock up. "No," he whispered hoarsely.

Tatiana slipped into the sick room. An oil lamp cast a warm, flickering light on the pale face of the eight-year-old boy. Falling to her knees beside the bed, she reached out to touch James's sweet, gentle face. He was still warm! Tears slid down her cheeks as she clasped the child's hand.

Such a young, innocent life—so tragically stolen away! In her mind she could see James smiling up at her as she held him. She could hear his lilting little voice saying: "*I reckon I won't ever learn to ride as well as Jonny if I'm dead!*"

Fresh sobs burst from Tatiana's bosom. "Oh, James!" she wept, pressing her face to his nightshirt and breathing in the little-boy essence captured there. The lively little imp was now lying still and lifeless. She heard Jonny coming into the room. She laid a soft kiss on James's unresponsive lips and stepped aside to make room for her old friend.

Jonny looked down at James for a moment. His knees seemed to buckle and he slid to the floor. He buried his face in the bedsheets. His strong shoulders began to shake. As she heard him cry for the first time, she knew it was the sound of a heart breaking.

Tatiana left the bedroom and sat in a rocking chair by the cold fireplace. She wasn't sure if the Smiths wanted her to stay, or how she was to get home, but she figured she could make herself useful by lifting them up in prayer.

Peter was curled on the rug like a forlorn little puppy. He stirred in his sleep. Tatiana scooped the five-year-old into her lap. She rested her cheek on the little head that lolled against her shoulder. "It'll be all right, Peter. Everything with be all right," she whispered, more for her own sake than his. A salty tear landed in Peter's fair hair.

After quite some time, Jonny came out and stood over her. "Come. I'll take you home."

Tatiana rose wordlessly, laid Peter back on the rug, and followed Jonny onto the porch. The rain was still falling. He paused under the porch roof, gazing out. "You know I named him," he said suddenly.

Tatiana looked up at him so he would know she was listening.

"I asked if we could name him James so we could be 'James and John,' just like the brothers in the Bible. We weren't really brothers, but ..." Jonny began to weep again. "Tatty, that little fellow meant everything to me! And now he's gone."

Tatiana reached out to touch Jonny's arm and he shook her off, suddenly becoming furious.

"Now, I want you to answer me this, Miss Tatiana Bergman! Why would your good, loving, merciful God make James die? If anyone should be dying it's me! I'm the sinful heathen around here, not James. He didn't do anything wrong. All he wanted was to be a horseman like me when he grew up. And now he's dead.

"Does God hate me for some reason? He let my blood family die, He let me be maimed for life, He didn't help me become the mayor, and now this! Now He takes away the person I care for the very most in this life. Why doesn't He help me?"

Tatiana raised her eyes to Jonny. His hair was still wet from his mad dash to get Tatiana. It clung to his face in muddy strands. His dark eyes were wild and his shoulders shook with grief. Slowly, Tatiana opened her mouth to speak. "First, Jonny, I want you to ask yourself this: How can God have any influence in your life when you have completely shut Him out?"

"But He's God, isn't He? I've heard about Him performing miracles and raising the dead back to life. He didn't have to let James die!" Jonny slid down into a crumpled heap. "What does God want from me?"

"I think He wants your heart," Tatiana said simply.

"My heart?" Jonny's face clouded. "This isn't about me! I'm not the one who's dead."

Tatiana took a deep breath. "You're dead inside, Jonny. James is in Heaven right now. He's resting in the arms of the God you've just been screaming at."

Jonny glared up at her. "You know what? You are a miserable comforter!"

Tatiana sat down quietly beside him. "And you are very difficult to comfort." She sat still for a moment, and then rested her head lightly on his shoulder. "I love James too, Jonny."

Jonny sighed and kissed her damp hair. The two of them remained there for a bit, watching the rain. After a while, Jonny sprang to his feet, nearly dumping Tatiana on the floor. "I need to take you home," he muttered. He gave her a boost onto Beauty, jumped on, and rode off like a madman, with Tatiana clinging on for dear life.

It was several days before Tatiana saw Jonny again except at James's funeral, but she hadn't had a chance to speak to him there. She was just coming out of Weller's store with a heavy basket of groceries when she saw him approaching on foot.

"May I carry that for you?"

"Yes. Thank you," Tatiana handed him the basket and eyed him curiously. "I was worried about you after you dropped me off the other night. You were so desperate looking, I was afraid you might do something daft."

"Such as take my own life?" Jonny asked.

Tatiana nodded. "I stayed up for the rest of the night, praying for you."

"Well, your prayers were effective, because it was that very night that my life was saved."

"Saved?"

"I couldn't get your question out of my head. You asked me: *How can God have any influence on your life when you have completely shut Him out?* That night, as I rode Beauty home, I felt that I had nothing. I felt that I had been stripped of everything, and I suddenly felt naked and sinful before God. I was a broken man, Tatty. Just like you said, I was dead inside. It was then that I asked Jesus into my heart."

Tatiana had been gawping at him as he spoke, and now she threw her arms around him and hugged him tightly. He eased the basket to the ground before she could tumble the contents. "Oh, praise God!" Tatiana exclaimed. "You finally did it, Jonny! Do you know how long I've been praying for this day?"

"I'm guessing it's been a long time."

Tatiana shook her head emphatically. "Years. But, as a good friend of mine once said, 'Some things are so important, you could spend years waiting for them, and it would still be worth it.'"

"I'm that important, am I?" Jonny asked kiddingly. In a moment his face sobered and Tatiana knew he was thinking of James.

"Someday we'll both be able to see James again in Heaven," she whispered.

Jonny sighed wistfully. "I wish I could skip my time on Earth and go there now!"

"Oh, but you would miss the joy of walking with the Lord here!" Tatiana pointed out. "That time will come soon enough."

Jonny took Tatiana's hand and picked up the basket with his other hand. Tatiana's slim fingers relaxed in his warm, reassuring grip. Jonny slowed his stride to match Tatiana's and they walked in silence for a while. In silence, they could communicate all the mixed feelings of sorrow and joy much better than with words. It felt good to simply walk together and breathe the same air.

When they reached Tatiana's house, she paused, not wanting to release Jonny's hand. She looked up at him as he stood there, holding her basket, and something leapt in her heart. She wanted to throw her arms around him again and hold him tight. She longed to stroke his sweet face and kiss all his heartache away.

Startled by her own thoughts, she quickly pulled her hand away from his. *I still love him, God. I love him even more, now that he belongs to You.*

In the weeks that followed, Tatiana felt that her heart couldn't get much fuller. Her only disappointment was that Jonny had not mentioned the prospect of marriage. As the days passed, they spent time discussing God's Word and the beauty of salvation, but Jonny never brought up the subject that lay in the forefront of Tatiana's mind.

I turned him away so many times, she told herself. *I can see why he wants nothing to do with me.* Still, she had hoped … She often found herself studying Gretchen. Gretchen was cheerful and content, as always. Her youthful beauty was still fresh, and her figure was unmarred by childbirth. She wondered: *Could I ever be fully happy as a spinster?* She remembered her long-ago wish to be a nun before Jonny had won her heart—before the Creator had begun to shape Jonny's character into that of the Godly man of her dreams.

"Wait patiently, Tatiana," Gretchen advised her. "Our heavenly Father has perfect timing."

But Tatiana sometimes felt such yearning in her heart that she went to sleep crying in her lonesomeness. "Consume my heart, Jesus," she often whispered. "Help me to be satisfied with Your love."

Jonny also was puzzled by Tatiana's behavior. He cherished the time they spent together. He yearned for a future with Tatiana, but he kept recalling her cold words on the wagon into town that fateful day. She could never love him because he was an Indian. Still, her sweet smile never failed to tug at his heart. Often he would notice her looking at him with some strange sort of expectation in her eyes. He had no clue what it meant, but it tore at his insides.

"I'm still in love with her, Lord," he admitted one day as he mucked out horse stalls. Beauty whickered at him and tossed her mane. Jonny snorted back at her. "I'm sorry, but I'm not talking to you, old girl." He raised his eyes again, gazing up into the loft. "What do I do, God? Should I ask her one more time?"

She had rejected him so many times. Jonny wasn't sure if he could handle being turned away again. *I know what she told me, but I keep getting this feeling that I should talk to her again.* Jonny sighed. Grabbing an armful of hay, he tossed it into Beauty's stall and then swung the door shut. Leaning his rake against the wall, he dusted his hands on his trousers. "I'll do it, Father. Please, give me the courage."

Hans had given Jonny permission to ask for Tatiana's hand in marriage months earlier, but Jonny hadn't found his faith then, so he wanted to ask again. Now, Hans happily sent him out to talk to his daughter. He found her trying to dig up a trench of potatoes.

Her small, gloved hands clutched the bulky spade handle, and she bounced on the top of the blade, trying to drive it into the hard ground. Jonny stood watching her in amusement for a moment before holding out his hand. "May I?"

Tatiana looked up at him, and her face flushed. "Certainly–I don't have the most effective method."

With one thrust of his foot, Jonny had pushed the spade deep into the soil. He quickly turned the dirt over, revealing a mass of spuds. Tatiana brought a basket. They worked together until the basket was half full. By this time Jonny's nerves were terribly on edge. "Tatiana?" he panted. "Could I ... ask you something?"

Tatiana straightened her back and tugged off her mittens. "Of course! I could use a short break anyway."

Jonny plunged his hands deep into his pockets and took a few long breaths to steady his thundering heart. "I know we've been through this before, Tatty, and I know very well where you stand on the matter, but ..." he swallowed hard. His mouth became as dry as the dirt. "I still have this undeniable conviction that you and I were meant to be together. You are in no way required to accept my proposal; I only ask that you might reconsider it. I know I'm only a half-breed Indian, but I feel that with God's blessing, our marriage could still prosper."

Tatiana wanted to shriek out her eager assent, but something he had said baffled her. "What do you mean 'only a half-breed Indian'? You know your race doesn't matter to me."

Jonny shrugged. "Well, that's why you wouldn't marry me before ..."

Tatiana gasped. "Jonny, your breeding had nothing to do with it! I couldn't marry you because we would be unequally yoked. You hadn't given your life to Christ when you first asked me. But now ... well, now we are standing on even ground under the shadow of the Cross." She smiled joyously.

Jonny could hardly believe his ears. "You mean there's nothing ... there's no difference between us?"

"Nothing, besides the fact that you are a man and I am a very embarrassed woman!" Tatiana cried.

With trembling hands, Jonny reached into his pocket and pulled out a ring. He dropped on one knee in the dirt and asked the question Tatiana had been waiting to hear for so long. "Miss Tatiana Bergman, will you marry me?"

Tatiana said, "Yes!" as happy tears slid down her cheeks. Onto her finger he slipped the most unusual ring she had ever seen.

Jonny was pleased that his creation of dyed porcupine quills strung with tiny blue beads fit her ring finger perfectly; he had used his pinky finger as a measure.

Tatiana suddenly wished that she had something to give Jonny in return. She had nothing, but her heart was overflowing with gratitude. Reaching out, she grasped his left hand and ran her fingers over the hard, bony ends of his stubby fingers. Then she raised his hand to her lips. "I would be honored to become your wife, Jonny Creek."

"I can hardly believe the wedding is only two days away!" Rose sighed, her fingers splayed dramatically over her heart. "You will make a good wife for Jonny."

Tatiana looked up from the hunk of beef that she was sawing. "Yes, though I certainly do not portray a very elegant picture of a romantic bride at the moment!" she declared, indicating her blood-spattered apron and messy hair. "But Rose, I am convinced that every marriage that takes place between two followers of Christ is nothing short of a miracle. I'm still so pleased that you and Robert could get together. 'Twas truly the hand of God!"

Rose smiled wanly. Tatiana suddenly noticed her sister's pale face. Rose's skin was the color of porcelain; she looked as fragile as a china doll. "I confess that I still feel undeserving of his love. I am so frail, Tatiana. I might not live to be thirty, and unless there is some great miracle, I will never bear him children. I am nothing but a shell of a woman, Tatty! Of what worth can I possibly be to him?"

Tatiana, immersed deeply in her own romance and on the brink of marriage, felt for her sister. Tatiana hugged Rose clumsily as she tried not to get blood on Rose's pale dress. "Your worth, Rose, is far above rubies, and I'm sure Robert knows that."

"He would not be one to tell me with words," Rose said quietly. "But he proclaims his love for me in his dutiful service and his faithful devotion. Robert is an unshakable, calm man."

Tatiana's butcher knife flashed as she made another attack on the chunk of meat. "And I have a feeling that I will hardly have a calm moment when I am married to Jonny!"

As if she had conjured him with her words, Jonny came bursting into the kitchen after a cursory knock at the door from the garden. He spun gaily on his heel and planted a kiss on Rose's cheek. "Good morning, sister!" Then he rounded the table and buried his nose in Tatiana's nest of hair. "Mmm, you smell like potato and onion soup!"

"Such a compliment!" Tatiana laughed.

Jonny leaned against the table and fished in his pocket. "Look what I found!"

"A tomato! Wherever did you find this poor little fellow? His season is far past!"

"Out in your potato trenches, actually," Jonny informed her. He poured clean water over his prize.

Tatiana rinsed her hands and her knife and began to slice the tomato.

"Good heavens!" Jonny cried theatrically. "What does this mean for our relationship?"

"It means that I like tomatoes," Tatiana replied, beaming. "Here, have some."

Jonny bit into a slice of the juicy vegetable. "This is a good one, despite how late he is. I must say though, I still feel somewhat cannibalistic eating the very symbol of our love."

Rose got up from her chair. "I just saw Robert's buggy pull up."

Tatiana briskly washed her hands again and embraced her sister. "Goodbye, dear! I'll see you tomorrow."

"And here, have some tomato," Jonny added. "It will put some color in your face."

After Rose had left, Jonny stood for a moment watching his beautiful young bride-to-be. Honestly, he was more than watching her. He was feasting his eyes on her and loving every visible detail—her silky wild hair, her cute little nose, her delicate hands now boldly wielding the butcher knife. "Thelma," he said abruptly, "what would you think of moving west?"

"West?" Tatiana's busy hands stopped working. "When were you thinking?"

This was the hard part. Jonny scratched his chin. "I was thinking about two days from now."

"Two days! But our wedding ..."

"Will go as planned and we'll leave directly afterward on a little trip like we planned—but we just won't come back for awhile ... a very long while," Jonny explained. His eyes searched hers, attempting to read her emotions.

"Where will we go?"

Jonny took Tatiana's hand, greasy as it was from working with the meat. "I figure we'll start heading west and I can map out the land as we go. When we find a spot we like, we can settle down and build our home there. What do you say, Miss?"

Tatiana looked up almost shyly at Jonny. "Can we settle down somewhere near other people?"

Jonny grinned. "Do Indians count? Because I figure, if we're fast enough, we can reach them with the Gospel message before they scalp us."

Tatiana laughed and tossed her hair. "Oh, don't worry, Mr. Creek. I know how to handle Indians."

Jonny held up his hand. "My only request, Mrs. Soon-to-be-Creek, is that you use a different technique on them than what you used on me."

"Don't worry," Tatiana giggled. "I will."

"So, westward ho?"

Tatiana's laugh dissolved and her eyes suddenly looked hollow and frightened. She had pined for her family when she moved to Philadelphia, but at least she had been in the same state, only a train ride away. Her light-hearted teasing could no longer cover her trepidation. "I've always longed for adventure, but now, in the very face of it, I feel so afraid," she admitted. "I'm not sure I have the mettle to go striking out into the wilderness, Jonny."

Jonny slid his strong arm around her waist and quoted: "Be not afraid, neither be thou dismayed: for the Lord thy God is with thee whithersoever thou goest."

They stood together for some time, strengthening each other. The two young people did not know what adversities would test them as they journeyed into the wild lands to the west; all they knew was that they would stand together against whatever trial should come, with their feet braced by Jesus Christ, their Solid Rock.

Tatiana closed her eyes as she felt a heavenly courage filling her heart. God would be with them, for His Spirit dwelt in their hearts.

ABOUT THE AUTHOR

Born and raised in northwest Ohio, Madeline Brock is the oldest of five children. She grew up running around barefoot, chasing down barn cats, and making up adventures for her younger siblings. After graduating from high school, she moved to a Native American reservation in New Mexico where she currently works with the Navajo people.

For Madeline, writing stories grew naturally out of an early love of reading. The precocious author finished writing her first chapter book when she was nine and has been writing ever since. She is passionate about mission work, her family, and the Lord.